"Aren't you the least bit curious to know what kissing each other would be like?"

Samantha nodded. "It's only natural. We've known each other a long time."

Leaning over, Jack drew Samantha into his arms and kissed her. The kiss was brief, nice...and not at all what she had expected. She felt nothing extraordinary and was almost relieved.

"Your turn," he said.

Nervously she leaned toward him, and their lips touched again. But this time he clasped her head between his hands and kissed her as if he really meant it. His lips moved over hers softly yet firmly, then his tongue slid between her lips and she could hear him moan. Or was that her? Somewhere in Samantha's mind lurked the thought that she should stop kissing Jack before things got out of control. Finally, and with a great deal of effort, she pulled back.

"Well, well," he said, his smile disgustingly erotic. "You are full of surprises. Must be my lucky day."

Millie Criswell

No Strings Attached

HQN™

ISBN 0-373-77064-2

NO STRINGS ATTACHED

www.HQNBooks.com

Printed in U.S.A.

To my son and daughter-in-law,
Matt and Staci Criswell—
brilliant attorneys, wonderful parents
and the best son and daughter-in-law
a mother could ask for. I love you both!

CHAPTER ONE

IN THE LIVING ROOM of Samantha Brady's Upper East Side apartment, right next to her aging laptop, sat a small, green ceramic frog.

The frog would have been considered ugly by most standards, with its bulging dark eyes and a semblance of a mysterious smile, as if it knew something she didn't. But Samantha loved it. Her best friend, Jack, had won it for her years ago at the Dutchess County Fair, and it had come to symbolize all the unsuccessful relationships with men she had experienced over the years.

Samantha had kissed a lot of frogs while looking for her Prince Charming, but all she'd gotten for her trouble was chapped lips.

The Big Romance that everyone wrote and sang about continued to elude her. The closest she'd come was The Bastard, which was how she always thought of Tony Shapiro, the man she had given her heart to shortly after her arrival in the city, and the man who had caused the naive little farm girl from upstate New York to smarten up and quick.

The Bastard had been married with three children. She'd been humiliated and decimated by the experience. But it had served to teach her a good lesson: Men were pigs, not frogs!

The exception to that was Jack Turner. She and Jack had grown up together in the quaint upstate community of Rhinebeck. He was exasperating and bullheaded, but also kind and caring.

She'd had a secret crush on him in high school and entertained wildly romantic ideas about him during her senior year. But he'd begun dating the very popular Suzy Stedman exclusively, and Samantha knew she was no match for a gorgeous cheerleader with boobs the size of bowling balls; hers were more in the golf ball category. At any rate, she'd put aside her foolish notions and settled for being best friends.

To the left of Samantha's computer sat another ceramic figurine—a shiny red apple that her mother had given her before she'd left home to pursue a writing career. An inscription in gold leaf read: *Take a bite out of the Big Apple. Love, Mom.* She'd taken many bites of that apple since arriving to pursue her career as a freelance writer and novelist. But so far Samantha had come up with a lot more seeds than pulp.

And quite frankly, it was the pits.

Writing a book, especially finishing it, was a lot harder than Samantha had originally thought, owing to the fact that she was something of a perfectionist and agonized over every word. There was also the minor problem that none of the publishers she'd queried were interested in a humorous pseudo-mystery/romance novel about two old ladies and their niece, who ran an inn and were suspected of murder because of some buried bones found in their basement.

Apparently, those uninformed editors hadn't seen *Arsenic and Old Lace,* or they'd have jumped at the chance to buy her book.

"Are you going to sit there and stare out the window all day, or are you actually going to write something? I thought you had a deadline."

The front door closed and Samantha turned to face her roommate. Arms crossed over his chest, six-foot-one Jack Turner was disgustingly handsome, every woman's idea of Prince Charming. He was frowning at her in that no-nonsense way he always did, but she could see the twinkle in his dark eyes and knew he was only teasing.

He'd been her knight in shining armor when she'd finally gotten the courage to move to the city despite her overprotective father's vehement protests, and then hadn't been able to find a decent apartment, if there was such a creature to be had.

It had been Jack who'd insisted she move in with him, taking most of the financial burden from her shoulders. That had been almost six years ago, and she hadn't regretted a single day.

Well, except for maybe today.

"I thought you were going to eat breakfast with the adorable Bunny this morning," she retorted, referring to Jack's latest bimbo—*uh, girlfriend*—who resembled a Siberian husky with her long, dyed platinum hair and ice-blue eyes.

Jack was into bimbos: women with large breasts, small brains and the inability to converse on any subject not having to do with fashion. He was also into noncommitment, so his bimbos—*uh, girlfriends*—fit the bill perfectly.

"Why are you home so early? Was the sex that lousy?"

His eyes filled with amusement, but he didn't respond. Instead, he ruffled his dark brown hair and grinned.

"It's Sunday, in case you've forgotten," she went on. "I don't have to work if I don't want to. This article isn't due till next week, so leave me alone."

Pulling a bag of bagels from behind his back, he dangled it in front of her, like the devil tempting Eve with that damn apple. The aroma of freshly baked goods surrounded Samantha, making her stomach grumble and Jack grin.

She was a sucker for bagels, donuts, pies, cakes and most unhealthy foods, despite her claim of eating only organic products. Sugar was her downfall. Chocolate was…well, chocolate was chocolate.

In addition to her freelance writing jobs, she'd been working part-time at the Starbucks around the corner, sucking down mocha lattes by the gallon and literally devouring the store's profits.

"You still have a deadline to meet. But I'm going to be magnanimous and let you take a break to eat your breakfast first."

Making a face, Samantha headed for the kitchen, Jack following right behind. "Are these bagels organic? You know I only eat organically grown food."

Disbelief edged his laughter. "That's a crock and you know it. I know for a fact that you ate four Snickers bars yesterday. I found the wrappers in the garbage. How you stay so slim is a mystery."

Suffering from a serious chocolate addiction for which there was no cure—at least none Samantha wanted to try—and hating being called on it, she felt heat rise to her cheeks. "I have a very high metabolism. And why were you looking through the garbage? What kind of sicko rifles through the trash?" She'd purposely hidden the wrappers at the bottom, hoping he wouldn't find them.

"The kind who's looking for a receipt. And to answer your other question, sex with Bunny was great. It's her constant talking I can't take."

"You can't have everything, Jack," Samantha said, slapping cream cheese on an onion bagel and handing it to him. "No wonder you aren't married. You're too damn picky."

"Like you should talk? Christ! You find fault with every guy you date. Chuck Simmons was a nice guy, very down-to-earth, and he was crazy about you. And you still dumped him."

"Chuck had body odor. Maybe you didn't notice it, but in the heat of passion it became unbearable." Samantha could stomach many things, but B.O. wasn't one of them. Having her head cradled in Chuck Simmons's armpit had been the equivalent of having a skunk go off in her face.

Jack laughed again. "Maybe you should have worn a surgical mask, or you could have asked poor Chuck to take a shower."

"Quit being stupid! Chuck did shower. It's just that he has some kind of glandular problem, and— why the hell am I telling you this? It's none of your business."

"Because I'm your best friend and you tell me everything."

It was true. Samantha knew about the women he slept with; Jack knew when her period was due. Living together was rather like being married, only without all the emotional upheavals that accompanied a marriage certificate.

The perks without the pukes, as Jack so eloquently put it.

"Sometimes it's embarrassing to discuss my personal relationships with you, especially when you don't share all the nitty-gritty about your love life." Not that she'd had that many. Meeting good men in New York City was like waiting for your ship to come in. Unfortunately, hers was in dry dock at the moment.

Biting into his bagel, Jack replied around a mouthful of cream cheese, "I don't have a love life. I have a *sex* life." He gulped his coffee before continuing. "There's a huge difference. And I like it that way. Most women bore me—they talk a lot and say nothing."

"That's because you have the attention span of Morris here." With a lift of her head, she indicated the ceramic frog. "Maybe someday when you grow up, you'll learn to appreciate the intricacies of the female mind and date someone who has a brain bigger than her boobs."

Jack threw back his head and laughed, and the booming sound reverberated off the walls of Samantha's heart. There was something about Jack's laughter that made her feel all warm and cozy inside, not to mention that his dimples were adorable.

"Christ! No wonder you scare off all the men you date."

"I do not!" But Samantha knew that was a lie. She tended to speak before thinking, to share her opinion about every little thing, and most of the men she dated hated that, especially if her opinions were of the negative variety, which they usually were.

Was it her fault she was picky and sought perfection? If she settled, she'd end up with someone like...well, Chuck. And she had no intention of settling.

Honesty, Samantha had found out the hard way, was not an admirable trait in a woman, since men's egos tended to be bigger than their...

Brains!

Well, except for Jack's. She'd seen his *brain* by accident once when he was coming out of the bathroom and she was going in. They had collided, causing him to drop his towel, and she'd gotten a good glimpse of a very impressive—

No wonder he was so smart.

"If you didn't have to have everything so perfect, you'd be a lot happier. And by the way, I didn't appreciate your lining my underwear drawer with lilac-scented paper," he said, wrinkling his nose in disgust. "I smell like a hooker!"

"You're just ungrateful. A man secure in his masculinity wouldn't be bothered by a womanly fragrance. And besides, I thought the scent was nice. I'm sure Bunny loved it."

Jack sighed and shook his head. "You make things too complicated. Just go with the flow, like I do."

Samantha rolled her eyes, her mouth dropping open in disbelief. "Now who's lying? You hate your job, even though you make gobs of money, and you date women who are dumber than rocks. What's that say about you?"

She waved him off with a flick of her wrist. "Go away and leave me alone. I have work to do."

"Aha! So you finally admit it."

Samantha's eyes narrowed. "I'm not sure why we're friends, Jack Turner. We have nothing in common. And you are extremely annoying."

Grinning widely, Jack tweaked her nose. "If I thought you meant that I'd pack up and leave. Oh wait! I own this apartment, so I guess I can't. Now then, your nasty mood means you're either PMSing or your book got rejected again. Which one is it?"

It was very disconcerting living with someone who knew you better than you knew yourself, Samantha thought. She hated to admit to Jack that she had failed again in her attempt to get published.

She wanted to pull her weight financially and contribute more to their living arrangement. Although she did most of the cooking, cleaning and errand running, Jack paid the majority of the bills. It was the way he wanted it, and she couldn't afford to change things too drastically, at the moment. But some day she'd be making lots of money—at least, that was the goal.

"Why do all those stupid publishing people hate my book? It's better than a lot of stuff out there. You liked it. Why don't they?" Dropping onto the sofa, she heaved a dispirited sigh.

Samantha had aspirations of becoming the next Nora Roberts or Nora Ephron. But instead she was Nora Nobody, unpublished novelist at large. Maybe she needed a new pen name.

"Maybe I'm just not good enough. I should have stayed in Rhinebeck and worked on the family farm like my dad wanted me to." Her parents would have loved nothing better than to keep her close at hand. Though Sam had appreciated their well-meaning advice, it had eventually become smothering and she'd needed to escape to live life on her own terms.

Taking a seat beside Samantha, Jack took her hand. "You know you are. Hell, you were always the smartest kid in class, acing all the tests, showing up the rest of us."

Like that mattered, when my boobs were smaller than Suzy's!

"I liked what I read, but the book's not finished," he continued. "You might have a better shot at selling it if you'd finish the damn thing. You've been working on it for years. You could have written the friggin' history of the world by now."

Samantha finally smiled. "*The World According to Samantha.* I like that."

He patted her knee. "Don't give up. There are still plenty of publishers out there you haven't tried yet."

"I'm on a first-name basis with many of their assistants. How pathetic is that?"

"Very, but only because you've been hounding them."

"So I'm anal. Sue me. There are worse things to be. At least I follow up on things."

He rose to his feet. "Great! Now just apply that tenacity to finishing your book. But in the meantime, I suggest you complete the magazine article you're supposed to be sending off."

"For someone who hates his boss, you're very bossy, do you know that?"

"Yeah. But at least I'm not a prick like O'Leary. The selfish bastard is greedy and self-serving."

Samantha knew Jack was unhappy with his job. She'd heard the frustration in his voice many times over when he talked about his new boss. "You should be working for yourself, Jack. You're very talented. There are very few real estate agents in the business as good as you are. Must be your facility for bull-shit." She smiled, and so did he.

"Thanks. But that's the problem. O'Leary feels threatened. He's been forcing me to work shitty hours on the floor. And on those rare occasions when he does give up a lead, either it's lousy or he hands it off to someone else."

"So quit! There's nothing keeping you there. You've got your broker's license."

"That's easier said than done when you have financial obligations."

"Jack, you own several apartment buildings, including this one. You could probably support yourself on what you earn from those."

"It's not enough. I need more money in the bank before I can go out on my own. New York is an expensive city. Just the office space alone will cost me a fortune, not to mention the licenses, office furniture and personnel. Shall I go on?"

"You encouraged me when I was unsure about moving here and wanting to write. So now I'm saying the same to you—if you don't try, you'll never know if you can do it."

"But what if I fail? I can't allow myself to do that."

"Why? Because of your father?" She shook her head. "How long are you going to let him run, or should I say *ruin*, your life?

"You're nothing like Martin Turner. Your dad's an alcoholic who never kept a steady job in his life.

You're already a much better man than he could ever hope to be."

His eyes filled with pain despite her assurances. "Tell that to my mother. She never says a bad word about my dad. You'd think he was a saint instead of a lush."

"Your mother is clinging to the memories of your father the way he was before he started drinking. But he wasn't always that way, was he?"

"No," he replied, bitterness edging his words. "He started after I was born. What does that tell you?"

Jack's relationship with his family, especially his father, was a painful one. As a child, he'd been neglected and shoved aside, while his dad devoted his time to the bottle and Charlotte Turner devoted hers to an alcoholic husband who didn't love her, and to trying to keep her miserable marriage intact.

He'd spent much of his childhood at the Brady home. Samantha's parents had tried to provide Jack with a stable environment and the normalcy that was missing from his. And though Samantha understood and sympathized with his bitterness, she still wanted him to reconcile with his parents so he could put the past behind him and get on with his life. Until that happened he'd always be second-guessing everything he did.

"Have you called your mom lately? You know how much she misses you."

He laughed, but there was no humor in it. "Charlotte doesn't miss me—she has dear old Dad to keep her company."

"Don't be cynical. It doesn't suit you. And she *is* your mother, whether you like it or not."

"You women always stick together."

"I'm right and you know it, Jack. You just don't want to admit it."

"At least Ross takes my side. He knows the kind of shit I've put up with from my parents."

"My brother has a big mouth and should mind his own business."

"Yeah, Ross gossips like an old woman. But he's been a good friend."

"Speaking of Ross, has he mentioned his plans for marrying Ellen? They've been dating off and on for years, but they still don't seem very well suited."

"Sometimes opposites attract."

"True. But I don't sense any sexual energy between them, do you?" They gazed at each other for several moments, and Samantha's heartbeat quickened. Then Jack cleared his throat and the spell was broken.

"You've been watching your *Sex and the City* DVDs again, haven't you?"

In fact, she had, but she wasn't about to admit it. "This is serious. Do you know anything or not?"

"I wouldn't break Ross's confidence even if I did.

But I assume he loves Ellen or he wouldn't have stuck it out for so long. Two years is a long time to date someone."

"Not necessarily. I detest you and I'm still here."

He tweaked her nose. "You'd be lost without me, and you know it. Besides, we're not dating."

"Someday you're going to meet a woman who'll knock you off your feet. Then you'll leave and get married." Samantha knew it was bound to happen sooner or later, and when it did it would break her heart. She never allowed herself to question why.

Jack was too good a man not to be part of a wonderful relationship. She just hoped he found someone deserving of him—and that wouldn't be any of the Bunny, Kitty or Fawns that currently traipsed through his bedroom.

He shook his head. "Don't bet on it, sweetheart. I'm not interested in tying myself down. I'd rather serve time in prison. Same thing, if you ask me."

Samantha knew exactly where her friend was coming from. After growing up in a houseful of domineering males, she had no desire to live under any man's thumb. Men were too opinionated, too direct and some of the stuff that poured out of their collective mouths was pure idiocy, yet they considered it to be manna from heaven.

Just like you, Samantha.

Oh, all right! So maybe I'm a tad opinionated, but I'm nowhere near as bad as a man, thank God!

Marriage just wasn't in the cards for her. Not now, not ever, as far as she was concerned. Sure, Samantha had once bought into the dream every young woman had about meeting Mr. Right, falling madly in love and living happily ever after. But at thirty-one, she had finally come to the conclusion that marriage was not her destiny.

Perhaps her unfortunate affair with Tony had soured her on love, or maybe it was just the fact the man she had secretly desired all those years ago— the one whose name she'd written over and over again on her notebooks...*Mrs. Jack Turner, Samantha Turner, Samantha and Jack Turner,* would never be hers.

And since she and Jack were just good friends, and since she didn't settle, there was really no point in marrying anyone else.

CHAPTER TWO

"THANKS SO MUCH for offering to babysit," Samantha's next-door neighbor said. "I really need to get out of this apartment for a little while. I never realized how all-consuming a new baby is."

"No problem, Mary. We all need a little time to ourselves once in a while." Samantha peered into the crib at the infant sleeping soundly and felt her heart squeeze. She was pink, perfect and oh so precious. "Melissa's beautiful. You're lucky to have her."

"Jim and I feel blessed. We've been trying for years to have a baby, and then when we were just about to give up, I found out I was pregnant."

The Walkers were a lovely young couple who had moved into the building a year ago, and Samantha was thrilled for them. "Well, don't worry about a thing. Just take your time and enjoy the afternoon. I'll take good care of Melissa."

"I should be back before she wakes up, but in case I'm not, there are bottles of formula right next to the crib. No need to heat them up—she takes her bottle at room temperature. Just pop the nipple and you're good to go."

"Sounds easy enough," Samantha said with a lot more confidence than she felt. She hadn't spent a lot of time around babies. Most of the kids she'd previously babysat had been a lot older and didn't poop their pants.

"I'm using Pampers on Melissa," Mary said, as if reading Samantha's mind.

"We'll be fine. Now go and enjoy the fresh air, window shop, have an ice-cream sundae. Relax."

Mary exited the room with a huge smile on her face, and Samantha tiptoed out of the nursery and headed for the living room, where she'd left her work in progress. Settling onto the sofa, she had just picked up her pen when she heard the first wail through the baby monitor.

Fear and uncertainty filled her momentarily, but she figured she was a lot bigger and smarter than a one-month-old baby. How hard could it be to comfort a screaming infant, anyway?

Turns out, very.

Upon entering the nursery, she made a face at the unpleasant odor that assailed her and knew immediately that Melissa had made a doodle in her diaper. Samantha could have called it shit, but doodle sounded much nicer for an infant.

Picking the baby up, she set out to change the offending diaper while trying to hold her nose closed. But that was easier said than done. Melissa's tiny legs were flailing as she removed the Pamper. Shit flew everywhere, including in Samantha's hair.

"Quit being gross, Melissa. I'm new at this so give me a break, okay?" The baby stared back at her intently for a moment, giving the illusion that she had actually listened, but then began squirming again. So much for reason.

Grabbing a handful of baby wipes, Samantha cleaned the mess out of her hair, and then went to work on Melissa. After changing her diaper, she put the baby into an adorable pink stretchy thing called a onesie, and then carried her to the rocking chair situated beneath the window.

Nestling her nose in the baby's downy hair, Samantha inhaled. Melissa smelled wonderful, like spring blossoms and sweet chocolate cake, all rolled into one. For some reason, babies always smelled good…well, when they were doodle-free, that is. Like new cars, the smell only lasted for a brief time, but it was so distinctive that you never really forgot it.

The baby stared wide-eyed at Samantha, taking her measure, she supposed. Samantha smiled and cooed, and as she held the baby in her arms the strangest thing happened—her heart actually felt so full she thought it might burst.

Samantha had always been so dead-set against marriage that she hadn't given a great deal of thought to what not getting married would mean. She'd never have a child. She'd never change a poopy diaper or hug a sweet-smelling baby to her breast, and she would never know the joy and pain of childbirth, of experiencing one of God's greatest gifts.

Then again, she didn't have to be married to have a baby. She wasn't saying she would, but if she really wanted a baby, she *could* have one on her own.

It was an intriguing possibility.

AN HOUR LATER, the baby was finally asleep. But no sooner had Samantha sat down with her work again than a soft knock sounded on the door.

It couldn't be Mary; the woman had a key. She peered through the peephole to find Jack staring back at her.

"Hi!" he said when she opened the door. "I found your note." He held it up.

"*Ssh!* I just got Melissa to sleep."

He arched a brow. "I'm impressed. I didn't think you knew much about babies."

"It's instinctive for a woman," she told him loftily, though she had no idea if that were really true. It sounded good though. "Would you like to see her? She's quite adorable."

He shrugged, not looking at all comfortable with

the idea. "I really just came by to see if you'd picked up the cleaning. I can't find my new blue shirt."

"It's hanging in my closet. I didn't have time to sort everything out before Mary called. Come on," she urged. "Come see Melissa."

"Oh. Well, I guess I can take a quick peek at her."

They stood side by side in the darkened room, gazing into the crib. Jack had an expression of awe on his face.

"Melissa's perfect, isn't she?" Samantha asked.

"She's so small," he whispered.

"I know."

Their hands met on the crib rail, and Jack looked over at her with an expression she'd never seen before. Her palms started to sweat and she pulled her hands to her sides. "Makes you wonder, doesn't it?" he asked.

"Wonder?"

"What we might be missing by—"

"Oh there you are!" Mary said, entering the nursery and cutting off whatever else Jack was about to say, much to Samantha's dismay.

But she'd heard enough to start her wondering.

SAMANTHA COULDN'T STOP thinking about babies. Everywhere she went, it seemed parents were hauling their young children around or nannies were pushing baby carriages in the park.

And the more she saw, the more she thought, and the more she thought, the more she yearned.

She wanted a baby. She wanted to have a child of her own. She supposed deep down she always had.

From childhood, girls were raised to be mothers. It was the expected course to take. But that course typically included marriage, and so she'd decided to detour and take a different route.

But suddenly her biological clock was ticking like a time bomb. Samantha wanted to have a baby before she got too old to conceive, with or without the benefit of marriage.

In this advanced day and age a woman didn't need to rely on a man to conceive—only his sperm. It would have been nice to get pregnant the old-fashioned way, to experience the event with someone she cared about, not some stranger who'd made a donation to a sperm bank, but beggars couldn't be choosers and she had no daddy candidates on the horizon.

Women of today enhanced their breasts through implants, held back the clock with plastic surgery and achieved orgasms through battery-operated devices, so it wasn't unnatural or unacceptable to conceive a baby by artificial means. Millions of women had done so successfully, and so could she. Besides, lots of good things came frozen: ice cream, waffles, diet dinners. So why not sperm?

"I'M GOING TO HAVE A BABY!"

Patty Bradshaw's jaw dropped so low it almost landed in her Cobb salad. "You're not serious! Who's the father? I didn't know you were seeing anyone. And why the hell weren't you using protection? Do you have a death wish? Did you skip Sex 101 in high school?" She stared at Samantha as if she'd lost her mind.

As Patty fired questions at her with the rapidity of a Gatling gun, Samantha just smiled. Patty was a lawyer, a borderline feminist and a damn good friend.

The two had met shortly after Samantha's arrival in New York City. She'd been coming out of Bloomingdale's after an interview that had gone nowhere, while Patty had been on her way in, to buy fabulous clothing, no doubt.

Colliding in one of those purses-flying incidents that had them howling in laughter, they had hit it off immediately and been best girlfriends ever since— probably because Patty had as many opinions as Samantha did, and never hesitated to voice them. But she was a whole lot tougher than Samantha, owing to the fact that she had to compete in the legal profession with ego-driven males, who viewed the attractive woman as little more than a sex object. But then, men often thought with their dicks, not their brains.

With deep auburn hair, pretty green eyes and a killer body, Counselor Patricia Bradshaw was hot and knew it. In fact, Patty played on that image. She hadn't met too many men in her thirty-four years that she didn't want to try on for size, and fortunately for her, most of them fit. But Patty was also a damn good attorney who'd won the majority of her cases and was considered an ace in her field of employment law.

"Okay, I didn't say that right. What I meant to say is, I *want* to have a baby. It's all I've been thinking about lately." *Obsessing* would probably have been a more accurate term.

Patty gulped her wine, poured herself another glass and then looked Samantha straight in the eye. "Are you crazy? Have you lost whatever sense you were born with? A child will tie you down, destroy your life as you know it, not to mention that you're not married. Not that that's a requirement these days, but it sure as hell makes things easier."

"Well, I can't help that. I want to have a baby, and I'm not going to change my mind. I'm thirty-one. My time is running out. If I don't do this now, it'll be too late."

"But you're not even dating seriously at the moment. How are you planning to get pregnant?"

Samantha shrugged, forking a cucumber into her mouth while she continued talking—something her mother always chided her about. "Of course, I'd love to get pregnant the old-fashioned way, with someone I love, or at least care about. But I have to be realistic. I've dated most of the men in this city, or at least it seems that way, and I haven't met my Prince Charming yet. At this point, it's doubtful I'm going to." A fair assessment, based on the last two dates she'd had, which had been nothing short of disastrous.

Lyle Prentice had stared at her chest all through dinner, which normally would have been flattering, since Samantha wasn't that well endowed, until one considered the fact that Lyle was a plastic surgeon who had offered to provide her with a pair of breast implants at cost.

And then there'd been Bob Bartlett, a fastidious accountant who kept excusing himself to floss his teeth after every kiss they'd shared, as if her mouth was loaded with gingivitis.

The frogs definitely outnumbered the princes.

"There *is* no Prince Charming. That's a fairy tale for little girls and dreamers, which is why I just go for the sex. Marriage is for wimps, and 'love' is a far dirtier four-letter word than 'fuck,' if you ask me."

It was obvious that someone in Patty's past had hurt her very deeply. But she'd never confided in Samantha about it, and Samantha wasn't about to ask. "I don't want to get married either, Patty, which complicates matters a wee bit."

The woman's big green eyes got even bigger. "No kidding, it complicates matters!"

"I know you think I'm stupid for wanting to do this, but I'm determined."

"Determined to do what, ruin your life?" Patty shook her head, her tone softening somewhat. "I don't think you're stupid, Samantha. I think you're insane. There's a difference. But if you're positive that having a baby is really what you want, then there's always in vitro fertilization. You could use a sperm donor."

Samantha smiled gratefully, knowing her friend's effort to be conciliatory didn't come easy. "That's what I've been thinking, too. But I intend to explore all my options first." She heaved a sigh. "Maybe I'll get lucky and someone will happen along and—"

"That would require you to have unprotected sex, and that's a one-way ticket to the morgue. Better to be safe than sorry. Don't do anything stupid. Promise me, Samantha."

Samantha's brows rose. "Are you saying you use a condom every time you have sex? Hell, that must cost you a fortune."

Patty threw back her head and laughed, a throaty, sensual sound, and it wasn't surprising that men found the woman irresistible. Well, except for Jack, who found Patty too in-your-face and, well, too masculine to suit him.

Samantha shook her head. "Just think about it. In our mothers' day, all women had to worry about with regard to having sex was getting pregnant. Now we have to consider all kinds of diseases, including *MASH*."

"*MASH?* That's a new one on me," Patty said, her brows drawing together in confusion.

She grinned. "Men Actually Staying Hard."

Her friend laughed again. "Honey, no worries about that. We have Viagra now. It's the best invention since air-conditioning."

"Yeah, only Viagra makes you hot, not cold."

"Amen to that!"

THAT SAME AFTERNOON across town, Jack and his co-worker, Tom Adler, were knee-deep in discussion about their favorite topic: Acme Realty's new sales manager.

"I'm sick and tired of that asshole," Jack said. "O'Leary pulled three more leads from me today and gave them to Susan. And that woman couldn't sell her way out of a paper bag if her life depended on it."

Leaning back in his swivel chair, which squeaked like nails raking a blackboard, Tom replied, "Susan's got some attributes you don't possess, my friend."

At Jack's confused look, he smiled. "Her rack is a lot bigger than yours. The scuttlebutt around the office is that O'Leary's trying to get in her pants, but my bet is he already has. Mike's been looking pretty smug lately."

Grimacing in disgust, Jack shut the door to Tom's office behind him, taking the chair in front of the metal desk. As Acme's two top agents, they were the only salespeople to rate private offices. The other agents worked on the main floor in cubicles.

Of course, Mike O'Leary had already threatened to change that policy. He'd come in four months ago to replace the retiring Will Price, and things at Acme had immediately begun going downhill.

First the lunchroom had been turned into a copy center. There were no more office parties to celebrate birthdays or big sales. Then O'Leary had replaced the contract forms with more confusing ones that took ten times longer to fill out, all in the name of progress.

Mike reminded Jack of his dad——self-important, domineering and ego-driven——which was one of the reasons he disliked the man so much, and didn't speak well of Jack's relationship with his father.

"I'll be honest with you, Tom, unless things improve around here…" He shook his head. "I can't work under these conditions much longer. Life's too short, and I'm not getting any younger." Samantha's advice kept running through his mind.

Tom leaned forward across his desk. "What are you saying, you'll quit?"

Jack sighed, tunneling impatient fingers through dark hair. "I don't know. Maybe. O'Leary's high-handed actions are starting to affect how I earn a living, and I won't allow that to happen. I've worked too hard to get where I am."

"Trust me, I hear ya. I really miss old Will. He was a good guy, a great manager and he was fair. He really cared about the people who worked under his regime, not just the bottom line."

"My roommate thinks I should quit and start my own real estate business. The more I think about it, the more tempting the idea is."

Tom's eyes widened. "Sam said that? He must really respect your abilities."

Jack had never corrected his friend's assumption that his roommate "Sam" was a man, believing that if Tom knew Samantha was actually an attractive, single woman he'd be on her like white on rice. And Jack wasn't about to let that happen, for reasons he dared not question.

Not only was Tom not Samantha's type, he had a history of using women and then dumping them. Jack had to protect Samantha from the Tom Adlers of the world. After all, that's what friends were for. And though he and Tom might share similar dating philosophies, the difference was that Jack wasn't interested in his roommate as a sexual partner—not that he wasn't attracted to Samantha's pretty corn-flower-blue eyes, million-dollar smile and great sense of humor. Even as a young girl, she'd had the ability to make him laugh. Samantha had a sort of topsy-turvy, upside-down way of looking at life. It was one of the things he adored about her.

He cherished their friendship far more than he needed another notch on his bedpost, so Jack had decided a long time ago that he and Samantha would just remain good friends. Though he had to admit, if only to himself, that when he'd watched her gaze down at the Walkers' baby with warmth and affection, crazy thoughts had started going through his head.

What if he and Samantha had a different kind of relationship? What if they'd gotten married? What if...?

"I might be interested in getting in on the ground floor if you decide to go your own way, Jack," Tom said, interrupting his disquieting thoughts. "Hell, this place would be like a tomb if you left. Not sure I could work here by myself."

"My plans are still in the formative stage at this point, Tom, but it's good to know you're interested. It would be a lot easier having a partner, someone I could trust with the day-to-day operation of the business, if that's what you're offering."

His friend nodded. "Adler/Turner Properties. I like the sound of that."

"I was thinking more of Turner/Adler Properties," Jack retorted with a smile. "But we can iron all that out, if and when this idea comes to fruition. I think we're getting ahead of ourselves."

The blond man stuck out his hand. "I hope it does. I'm in, if you decide to take the step."

"Then obviously you're just as insane as I am for even thinking about doing something like this. We're both making good money right now. We could starve on our own. I hope you realize that."

"But we won't. We're too damn good at what we do."

"I wish I shared your self-confidence. There are a lot of good real estate agencies in the city. We'd really have to scrounge for clients. It would be like starting all over again." Something Jack dreaded. Referrals were the bread and butter of the real estate business. Without them, a realty firm was doomed before it ever got off the ground.

"Nah. We'll just steal them from here. We've earned every single one of them. And wouldn't it be nice to put the screws to O'Leary?"

"And here I thought you only liked screwing women. It's refreshing to know you're an equal opportunity fornicator, Adler."

Tom grinned and wiggled his brows. "Speaking

of fornicating, I'm going out with the delectable Cindy from accounting tonight. I hear she's hot in bed. Care to double? She's got a horny friend."

Shaking his head, Jack was even more grateful that Samantha remained a secret. "Thanks, but I think I'll stay home tonight and crunch some numbers, see if this idea of mine is feasible. There are a lot of things to consider before taking such a big step."

"I've got thirty thousand I can invest straight off. I can probably get another ten from one of my investment accounts, if we need it. I had a good year."

Jack was impressed and pleased by the offer. "That's very generous. I'll keep that in mind and let you know what I come up with."

"If you change your mind about tonight, give me a call. You know the number."

Suddenly filled with an optimism he hadn't felt in a very long time, Jack exited Tom's office with a much lighter step than when he'd entered it. And the one person he wanted to share his excitement with was Samantha. She would be happy for him; she'd understand what a huge step he was contemplating.

He owed Samantha for suggesting the idea to him in the first place, and he was going to thank her by taking her out to dinner tonight.

CHAPTER THREE

TO SAMANTHA, Italian food was what water was to plants—she had to have it at least once a week. So when Jack offered dinner at El Toula's, a new Italian eatery in their neighborhood, she jumped at the chance.

"This calamari *fritti* is absolutely delicious, Jack. Thanks for bringing me here tonight. It's such a nice surprise, and it's not even my birthday." She dipped a piece of the fried squid into the marinara sauce on her plate.

"I thought we deserved a break, and I confess to having an ulterior motive. There's something I want to discuss with you."

"I'm all ears, but I hope nothing's wrong. I thought you seemed a little preoccupied tonight."

He shook his head. "Quite the contrary. Remember when you suggested that I start my own business? Well, I've been giving that idea of yours some more thought."

Her eyes widened. "You mean—? Oh, Jack, that'd be great! What made you change your mind?"

"I spoke to Tom Adler today about the possibility of starting my own real estate company and he wants to buy in. He was very enthusiastic and made me feel that we could actually make it work."

She clapped her hands together. "That's wonderful! Are you going to do it?"

"I'm not sure. I still haven't made up my mind. I want to do a bit more research, find out what's involved. This would be a big undertaking, and I don't want to screw it up."

"I can help. You know I'm a whiz at Internet research. Just let me know what you need."

He nodded. "I'd pay you for your time."

Samantha, who always felt uncomfortable about accepting Jack's money, shrugged. "I'm happy to help whether or not you pay me, you know that. That's what friends do. And God knows I could never repay you for everything you've done for me."

"I won't allow you to work for free. Your time is valuable, what little you have of it. You've got your job at the coffee shop, your freelance articles, babysitting and you need to finish your novel."

"Tell me what you need in the way of research and I'll get started on it first thing in the morning," she said, ignoring his objections.

His right brow shot up. "Should I assume that your magazine article has already been submitted?"

"Yes," she replied, making a face. "But they'll

probably blue-pencil it to death. And I'm not sure there'll be much of an audience for what I wrote. After all, who wants to read about the trials and tribulations of an unpublished writer?"

"A lot of people. Me, for instance."

"You're just saying that because we're friends and you feel sorry for me."

Jack sighed. "You always sell yourself short, Samantha. You need to have more confidence in your abilities. You're good at what you do. And I'm not just saying that because we're friends. I really think you have talent as a writer."

"Thank you," she said quietly, pushing the calamari around her plate and silently debating whether or not to tell Jack about her plan to get pregnant. Samantha rarely kept secrets from him, but she wasn't sure how he would react. Jack had been overly protective since grade school after all—this would probably freak him out completely.

"I had lunch with Patty today," she began.

Jack's face filled with distaste. He was not a Patty fan. "That woman is a piranha. Who's she crucifying this week?"

"It's Patty's job to take bad employers to task," she rebutted. "Just because she goes for the throats of those corporate execs is—"

"Throats? Ha! She goes straight for their balls and doesn't let go until they've been castrated."

"Well, someone has to stand up for what's right. And if Patty were a man, we wouldn't be having this conversation. She takes her job seriously, and I don't see anything wrong with that."

Jack set down his wineglass after taking a generous gulp of Chianti. "I know you like Patty, so I'll try to temper my comments. But I admit, I'm glad you two are nothing alike. She's too hard, too jaded, while you're soft and kindhearted."

"Maybe if I had Patty's backbone, her chutzpah, I'd be more successful. You can't say she hasn't done well for herself. She lives near the park, makes gobs of money, shops at all the really expensive stores." Samantha sighed. "I'm still a regular Macy's customer."

"I know she does well. But that doesn't make her any more likeable."

Sipping her wine, Samantha said, "Anyway, I discussed an idea with Patty, something I'm planning to do."

"Is it something we've talked about?"

"No, not yet." She swallowed nervously. "I wasn't quite sure how you'd take the news, so I tried it out on Patty first." She feared Jack's reaction would be pretty similar to her friend's—he'd hate it. And Jack's opinion was very important to her.

"There's not much you can say that will surprise me at this point. I think you know that."

She took a few moments, sipped more Chianti to bolster her courage and blurted, "I've decided to have a baby."

Eyes widening, Jack nearly choked on his veal parmesan and reached for his water glass. After a moment, he said, "I take it back. I'm surprised." His brows drew together in confusion. "What am I missing here? Have you been dating someone that I don't know about? Are you getting married?" He paled at the thought.

"I don't have a husband waiting in the wings. I'm doing this all on my own."

His right brow cocked. "Really? Now that would be interesting. As far as I know, there's only been one immaculate conception."

"Ha! Ha! Ha! Very funny. Obviously I can't impregnate myself. I'm going to need help with that. Care to volunteer?"

He ignored her. "I assume since you're not as ballsy as Patty that you're talking about artificial insemination?"

"It's not my method of choice, but under the circumstances I don't see another way."

"You could wait for the right man to come along, fall in love, get married. You know, the usual road to conception."

"I've been that route with no luck. You of all people should know that. We have that flaw in common."

"I don't consider it a flaw. I consider it a lifestyle choice," he retorted, adding, "Look, Samantha, I think you'd be making a big mistake if you go through with this crazy scheme of yours. You might think you want a child, but this isn't the way to go about it."

"Why not? Plenty of single women have babies. Jodi Foster did it, and Diane Keaton, not to mention Rosie O'Donnell, who adopted her kids."

He rolled his eyes. "Come on. Be sensible. Having a kid on your own isn't a good idea. Those celebrities you've mentioned have money—you don't."

Hurt filled her voice. "I was hoping you'd be more supportive. This is important to me."

"I wouldn't be a very good friend if I didn't give you my honest opinion, now would I? I've never lied to you, Samantha, not in all the years we've known each other."

"I guess you're entitled to your opinion, but just don't go giving it out to anyone else. We'll be going to my parents' house soon for the annual apple harvest celebration, and I expect you to keep my confidence and not blab my plans to anyone—including Ross."

"You know you can trust me. I'd never betray your confidence."

"No, just my friendship."

His lips thinned. "That's not fair. I'm just trying to save you from yourself. Sometimes you act without thinking."

"Is that what you think this is? Just because you don't want to settle down and have a family? Well, that's not me. Maybe I don't want to get married and have a husband, but I do want to have a child."

"That's because you've never had one or been around kids for any length of time. This is just some fantasy you cooked up after babysitting the Walker baby."

"It is not! I've given it a lot of thought. In fact, I've thought of little else. And you said yourself that we might be missing out."

He shook his head. "Tell me how you plan to support yourself and a baby. How will you work and take care of a child? A baby is a huge responsibility, not to mention expensive. There'll be hospital and doctor fees, baby furniture to buy, clothing, diapers, food. You can't afford a child."

She stiffened. "I'm quite capable of taking care of myself, Jack. Just because we live together doesn't mean I can't manage without you. I've already lined up several freelance jobs. And I intend to ask Gary to increase my hours at Starbucks. With the holidays coming, they'll need more help. And I can always babysit to supplement my income, if I need to. There are a lot of jobs I'm capable of doing, and that includes working for you.

"And you don't have to worry about me infringing on our friendship because I don't intend to."

Jack heaved a deep sigh and looked as if he was about to say something else, but Samantha cut him off.

"And don't forget, there's always a chance that my book will sell for gobs of money."

And maybe pigs would fly.

CHAPTER FOUR

"YOU APPEAR TO BE in excellent health, Ms. Brady,"
Doctor Phillips told Samantha a few days later.
The gray-haired gynecologist, who resembled
George Hamilton without the tan, had been recommended by a friend of a friend of Patty's and was
touted to be one of the best in his field. Patty had
pulled a few strings to get Samantha an appointment. And knowing how many patients were waiting to see the sought-after specialist, she owed her
friend big-time.

"I'll still need to wait for the results of today's
tests before I can determine the best way to proceed
with the insemination process, Ms. Brady. And I
want to make certain that your left ovary isn't going
to be problematic."

Samantha filled with alarm. "Do you think it will
be?" She got her period every month, so she'd assumed her ovaries were working just fine.

"I'll have my nurse schedule a sonogram so we
can take a peek at what's going on with it, okay? It

could very well be nothing, but I want to make sure that it isn't a cyst or a tumor."

Samantha had the strongest urge to borrow that Schwarzenegger line—"It's not a tumor!"—but refrained. Instead, she folded her sweaty hands primly in her lap and nodded. "Whatever you think is best. You're the expert. But I do have a few questions, if you don't mind."

"Fire away. I want you to feel completely comfortable about everything we're going to do. This is a big step you're taking."

"From what I've read, it's my understanding that I have to be ovulating before you can perform the procedure. Is that correct?"

"Precisely. With both artificial and intrauterine insemination, ovulation has to occur in order for the donated sperm to fertilize your eggs."

"What's the difference between the two? And what's my best bet for conceiving?"

"Depends on what we discover from your tests. With intrauterine insemination, we flush the sperm directly into the uterus by means of a catheter. Artificial insemination puts the sperm into the vagina or on the cervix. But sometimes the woman's cervical mucus is such that it won't allow the sperm to travel through it, thus blocking fertilization."

Samantha's face fell and a stab of disappointment knifed through her. "Oh. I hadn't read that." It would be just her luck to have body fluids that hated sperm. First her ovary might be a dud, and now this.

"Once I see the results of your tests I'll be able to determine the best way to proceed. You should know that in either case the percentage for successfully producing a fertilized egg is low."

"Really? How low?" She thought this plan of hers was foolproof. It seemed every girl she'd known in high school who'd had sex before marriage had gotten pregnant.

"It can be as low as eight percent, so you need to be prepared for failure. Of course, I've had patients who have gotten lucky on the first try, but that's rare. It's a crapshoot, if you want to know the truth. It either takes or it doesn't. There's really no way to predict the outcome."

Their discussion was getting more depressing by the minute, and Samantha wondered if she was wasting her time. "I see." But she didn't, not really.

Why did everything have to be so damn complicated? She just wanted to have a baby—something women had been doing for eons.

"My nurse, Mrs. Wilson, said she's already explained to you about making a BBT chart and tracking your temperature. This is how we'll determine whether or not you're ovulating." His brows rose in anticipation. "I assume you're doing that already?"

She nodded. "I started as soon as she told me. I've

been religious about filling out the temperature chart every day. And as close as I can figure based on my last period, I should be ovulating by next week."

He smiled kindly. "Excellent. I'll have my nurse set up an appointment. We'll shoot for the end of next week, providing your tests and sonogram prove okay. How does that sound?"

"Fine." She tried to sound nonchalant, but her heart was racing with excitement.

The doctor hesitated a moment, his face filling with concern. "I should tell you, Ms. Brady, that artificial insemination in any form is not an inexpensive proposition. Have you considered the cost? We sometimes have to do this procedure over and over again to achieve the results we want. And most insurance companies don't cover it, as it's considered an elective course of action."

Samantha swallowed. She had no health insurance, but she had cashed in several of the savings bonds her grandparents had given her at birth. If there were no further complications, she'd have enough money for maybe two attempts.

"I understand. And I'm prepared to move forward."

Go directly to debtor's prison. Do not pass *GO*. Do not collect two hundred dollars.

"All right then. We'll give it a try. Do you have someone you can bring with you to your appointment, to take you home after the procedure? You may experience some discomfort, a bit of cramping, and I'd feel better if you had someone to accompany you home."

"Umm, yes. I'm certain one of my friends will come with me." But that was a crock and she knew it. Jack would rather have his eyelashes plucked out, one by one, than accompany her to the doctor's office. And though Patty had been supportive, she wasn't sure how much her friend wanted to participate in something she felt was idiotic.

Samantha was in this alone, and alone was how she was going to do it.

THE FOLLOWING WEEK, Jack entered the apartment to find Samantha seated at the kitchen table eating a large bowl of ice cream. She was looking rather glum, despite the chocolate flavor, which usually had the power to put a smile on her face. "What's wrong? Did you get bad news from the doctor?"

She looked up, smiled halfheartedly in greeting, and then shrugged. "Not really bad news, but not good news either. The results of my tests were inconclusive, and my sonogram shows that one of my ovaries has a small cyst and is not functioning properly. It's *sluggish,* whatever that means."

"So you're not getting it done?" He looked relieved. "I'm glad. Like I said, it would be a mistake."

"Doctor Phillips postponed the insemination procedure. He said based on what he's seen so far I might have difficulty conceiving."

Crossing the room in three long strides, Jack took her hands, his eyes filled with concern. "I'm sorry, Samantha. I know how important this is to you. But maybe God is trying to tell you something, like you should wait for the right man to come along."

She gazed into his eyes and said, "The right man isn't going to come along, Jack." *He already had and he'd kept right on walking.* "And I'm not down for the count yet. The doctor said to come back on Tuesday afternoon."

"I want to go with you, make sure everything goes okay. You might not be feeling well afterward, and I don't want you going home by yourself. You could faint on the subway, or something."

Smiling softly, she patted his cheek and recalled why Jack was such an important part of her life. "That's nice of you. I wasn't sure you'd want to come, knowing how you feel about doctors and hospitals." But she should have guessed. Jack had always been there for her; he was the one person she could count on, no matter what problems she faced. And she liked to think she'd always be there for him, too.

But she also knew that Jack hated anything having to do with illness. His father had spent a lot of time in hospitals and treatment facilities, trying to dry out. The Turners had been frequent visitors to the hospital during those times, and the memories of those visits remained unpleasant for him.

"I'll survive," he said.

"I know, but—"

Suddenly Jack wrapped his arms about Samantha, unable to contain his grin. "I've got good news."

Her eyes widened with delight. "I thought you were looking rather pleased with yourself this evening. Did you finally sell that monstrosity on West 103rd?"

Shaking his head, his grin widened. "No. This isn't about a sale. I quit my job today, Samantha. I'm free of that bastard O'Leary. Told him to shove it where the sun don't shine."

Laughing, she threw her arms about his waist and hugged him hard. "That's wonderful! I'm so proud of you, Jack. This calls for a major celebration."

He shook his head, his expression suddenly somber. "We'll celebrate *after* I work out all the details. For now, we need to conserve money, just in case this new venture of mine doesn't work out. It's a big risk, and I'm worried about it."

"But I thought Tom Adler was investing."

"He is. But the overhead is going to be big. And until we start making sales, I want to pull back on the spending."

"I understand."

"That doesn't mean that I won't lend you money, if you need it for the insemination procedures. I intend to be here for you, even if I don't agree with what you're doing."

She shook her head. "I appreciate the offer but that won't be necessary." Samantha explained about the savings bonds, and his face suddenly reddened in anger.

"Why didn't you come to me first? I don't want you spending your life savings. What if something unforeseen happens? You won't have anything to fall back on."

"Stop treating me like a child, Jack. I haven't cashed in all of my bonds, only a few. And though I appreciate your advice and concern, I have to do what I think's best. I'm a grown woman, after all. And I do have a job, you know; in fact, I have several."

"I know." He took a deep breath. "But I'm worried about you. You might be biting off more than you can chew."

"Well don't. There's no need. I'm going to get pregnant, and then my life will be complete and wonderful. You'll see."

BUT TWO MONTHS LATER, Samantha still wasn't pregnant, couldn't afford any more visits to Dr. Phillips and had pretty much concluded that a baby wasn't going to be part of her future.

Her mother always said that God had a plan for everyone, but Samantha didn't like this one. She didn't like it at all.

"Thanks for meeting me here on such short notice, Patty. I know how busy you are, but I needed to talk to you. I asked Gary for an extended break." She waved at the smiling Starbucks manager, who had a slight crush on her. And though she hated taking advantage of his interest, sometimes it was necessary.

"Not a problem. You know Starbucks is my one true passion," her friend said, stirring sweetener into her coffee. "But where's your roommate? I thought he wasn't working."

"Jack and his partner are getting their new real estate office set up. They found a really nice place in Midtown, in one of those high-rise buildings. It's very posh and should attract some well-heeled clientele. At least I hope so. Jack's been working really hard."

"I may be able to throw some clients their way. I'll see what I can do and give Jack a call."

Samantha's face brightened. "That'd be great! I'm sure Jack would appreciate it very much."

Patty arched a perfectly formed brow. "Maybe he'll reciprocate by taking me out for a drink. Your roommate is pretty hot. I can't believe you two have never taken your relationship any further than friendship."

"Because we're friends, nothing more." And that's all they ever would be. Samantha had given up her romantic notions long ago. Of course, that didn't mean she wanted to encourage Patty where Jack was concerned. She wasn't his type, not at all.

"Well, if that's the case and you don't mind—"

"Uh, I'm not sure, Patty. Jack's seeing someone at the moment," she lied, hoping to spare her friend any embarrassment.

Jack would not want to date Patty; of that, Samantha was certain and rather relieved, to be perfectly honest. The idea of Patty and Jack sleeping together did not set well with her for reasons she dared not question.

Samantha had thought more times than she cared to admit about what it would be like to be with Jack in a sexual way. And unfortunately, she had a *very* good imagination.

"Too bad. He's cute. What's his partner look like?"

"Tom Adler? I don't know. I've never met him. But Jack says he's nice."

Patty, who almost never ate sweets, took a bite out of Samantha's blueberry muffin. "So tell me what's wrong. You look like hell, and it's only ten o'clock in the morning."

"I just got my period. I'm not pregnant, and I'm never going to be." She fought back the tears threatening to spill, knowing her friend wouldn't appreciate them. Patty was not what one would call sentimental about such things.

"I'm sorry, Samantha. Truly. I know how disappointed you must be."

She sighed. "I never thought it would be this difficult to get pregnant. Seems ironic that I worried all through college about getting knocked up, and now I can't conceive. I feel like such a failure of a woman. I mean, most women get pregnant at the drop of a hat."

"Stop it! I won't let you talk about yourself that way. The timing just wasn't right, that's all. Maybe when you've had time to think this through, you'll find it's a blessing in disguise."

"I don't want to be blessed. I want to be pregnant."

"Have you spoken to Jack about any of this?"

Samantha shook her head. "No. Jack hates it when I'm negative. But I feel like such a loser. I can't sell my book. I can't get pregnant. Hell, I can't even get a date."

"Because you're not putting yourself out there, honey. Why don't we go out tonight, just the two of us? It'll be my treat. We'll find us some men and have mindless sex. Whaddaya say?"

"I appreciate the offer, Patty, but I just don't feel up to it. Plus, I've got my period. There'll be no sex for me." Not that she was into casual sex anyway. She and Patty might be friends, but they were fundamentally different when it came to some things, like having sex just for the hell of it.

Samantha might not be interested in marriage per se, but she wanted to have meaningful relationships. She wanted to care about someone and have him care about her.

Her friend's eyes widened. "You mean, you've never—?"

Samantha screwed up her face in disgust. "No way. The very idea makes me want to puke." In high school the guys used to refer to having period sex as "the red badge of courage." She thought it was totally gross then, and still did.

"God, you're such an infant. Don't knock it if you haven't tried it."

"I haven't tried suicide, but I know I won't like that, either."

Patty laughed. "One thing I'll say about you, Samantha, you keep me grounded. You're the most normal person I know."

Samantha sighed, knowing she wasn't normal at all.

Normal women got pregnant.

Normal women achieved their goals.

Normal women wallowed in self-pity on occasion.

Well, one out of three wasn't bad.

JACK RUSHED into the apartment two hours later, slamming the door behind him, and was relieved to find Samantha reclining on the sofa. He'd been worried as hell since receiving Patty Bradshaw's phone call.

Tears streaked her cheeks and her eyes were red-rimmed from crying. Jack could be macho about a lot of things, but Samantha's tears wasn't one of them. He moved forward to comfort her.

"Thank God you're all right! I've been a mess since I got Patty's phone call."

Samantha righted herself, eyes widening. "Patty called you? I'm sorry, Jack. I told her you didn't want to date her, but—"

"Patty wasn't calling for a date, Samantha. She was worried, said you seemed very depressed because you'd gotten your period. I thought maybe…hell, I didn't know what to think."

"As you can see, I'm fine. I just needed to unload this morning, and I chose Patty to bear the brunt of it. I figure you have a lot on your plate right now. And sometimes it's easier to talk to a woman."

"I'm never too busy for you, you know that." He

seated himself next to her on the sofa, noting how wan she appeared.

She squeezed his hand. "It was sweet of you to come rushing home. I'm sorry you were worried. Patty should never have called. I hope your business plans weren't ruined because of me."

"No. In fact, we got two new clients thanks to Patty. I'll have to send her flowers or something."

"That was quick. She just mentioned giving you the referrals this morning."

Jack smiled knowingly. "I have a feeling Patty Bradshaw doesn't waste time procrastinating. Hell, she practically ordered me to call the referrals right then and there."

"Are you going to date her?"

"Hell no! Whatever gave you that idea? Life's too short to deal with a ball-buster like your attorney friend." Jack's stomach rumbled just then. "I'm starving. I missed lunch today. When are we eating? Soon, I hope."

Rising to her feet, Samantha made her way to the kitchen, Jack following close on her heels. "In just a few minutes," she informed him, lifting the lid on the pot and inhaling deeply. "I made chicken soup. Doesn't it smell great?"

"Soup?" His face fell. "You're kidding. It's got to be eighty degrees outside. Why are we eating soup?"

Indian summer had attacked New York with the

vengeance of marauding Apaches on the warpath. Heat and humidity smothered the city like an unwelcome blanket.

"Because it's comforting and I needed to be comforted. I didn't think you'd want puree of chocolate, which was the other choice."

He reached for her hand. "Listen, Samantha, I know I haven't been very supportive of your decision to get pregnant, but since you're so bent on having a baby, why don't you consider adopting one? It seems the perfect solution to your infertility problem."

She stiffened and pulled back. "I'm not infertile! I'm just too poor to get any more treatments. And no, I'm not borrowing any money from you, so don't offer again."

"Christ! I was just trying to help. There's no need to bite my head off."

Samantha's sigh was desolate. "I know. It's just… Although adoption seems like a good idea, it doesn't allow me to experience childbirth. I want to push my own baby out of my body and see something I created. Being a man, it's probably difficult for you to understand how important that is to a woman."

"But with adoption, you'd have the same result—you'd have the baby you've always wanted."

"Even though I'm working and earning a living, I don't think I'll be considered a very good candidate for adoption. I'm not married, which will go against me. And I doubt I'd pass the scrutiny they put potential parents through. I've heard they're very picky."

"It was just a thought. Maybe you can look into it, see what's involved."

"I guess I could. I don't have the kind of money or connections Rosie O'Donnell does, but if love counts for anything, my child will never go wanting."

Seeing how unhappy she was, Jack changed the subject. "Are we still going to the farm this weekend?" he asked, and Samantha finally smiled.

"Yes, and I'm really looking forward to seeing my family. You and I could both use a little R & R. In fact, why don't we leave on Friday, if you can get away early?"

He was pleased to see her anticipating something fun for a change. "Now that I'm the boss I can do whatever I damn well please. I'll rent the car for Friday, and we'll leave first thing that morning."

"I'll let Mom know. I'm sure she'll want to create some high-calorie meals for her favorite houseguest."

Jack rubbed his stomach. "Man, I love your mom's cooking. She hardly ever makes chicken soup."

Samantha stuck out her tongue at him, and he

laughed, hoping the trip to Rhinebeck would be just what she needed to make her forget about babies, publishers and anything else that made her unhappy.

CHAPTER FIVE

THE TWO-HOUR DRIVE to Rhinebeck seemed longer than usual to Samantha, owing to the traffic heading north out of the city—caused by fall foliage fans, she assumed—and her eagerness to see her family again. So when the weathered gray-and-white clapboard farmhouse finally came into view, she could barely contain her excitement.

"Look, Jack, it's still standing! I always hold my breath until I see it again."

The two-story house had been in the Brady family for generations. Samantha's great-great-grandfather, Benjamin Brady, had built it with his own two hands, though it wasn't nearly as grand back then as it was now. Her mother, Lilly, had insisted on adding a big gourmet kitchen and dining room large enough to accommodate a table where the extended family, including nieces, nephews and cousins could sit together.

Two massive oak trees graced the front yard, providing shade and entertainment for the younger children, who loved to climb them. Surrounding the house beyond the lawns and garden were acres of apple orchards, lovingly tended by her dad and older brother. Ross helped them out on occasion, but his heart wasn't in the land, not like Lucas's.

Fred Brady was fond of saying that your heart had to be engaged when tending apples because they needed as much loving attention as a woman. And if you loved your orchard as much as you did your wife, it would reward you with thousands of healthy offspring every year.

Samantha's dad tended to wax poetic when it came to his apples.

"There's Mom." She pointed toward the wrap-around porch where Lilly Brady was standing. "She must have heard the car." There wasn't much that got by her mother, which had made growing up in the Brady household tough.

"Remember the time my mom caught us smoking behind the barn? As I recall, you got spanked much harder than I did."

Jack made a face at the memory. "And it was your dumb idea that we smoke those stupid cigarettes in the first place. But since I was a bit older, and a boy, I guess your mother figured I deserved the worst of the beating."

Samantha grinned. "Well, at least it taught you never to smoke again."

"I hope your parents don't mind that I'm staying here. I've been worrying about it."

Her brows drew together in confusion. "But why, for heaven's sake? You don't need an engraved invitation to visit my family. My mother thinks the sun rises and sets on you. She also knows how things are with your parents and doesn't mind at all that you stay here."

Despite her reassurance Jack didn't look convinced. "Maybe I should get a motel," he offered, but only halfheartedly.

"Are you serious? What's brought this on all of a sudden?" Jack had stayed with her family many times over the years and had never voiced any concern.

"I don't know. I guess I feel kinda funny coming here and acting like I'm one of the kids. I'm a grown man now, Samantha. Your parents shouldn't be putting me up anymore."

"Mom dotes on you, you know that. She'd be disappointed if you didn't stay, Dad too. And we have plenty of room, so your argument doesn't hold much water."

"Yeah, but I get the feeling that's because your parents think we'll end up together some day."

Knowing the truth of his words, Samantha flushed, but did her best to ignore it. "My mother's an incorrigible matchmaker, you know that. She's wanted you for a son-in-law since we were children making mud pies. I'm sure she's disappointed that she has no other daughters to offer you."

Jack grinned. "Thank God for that! I'm not sure my heart could take another Brady female."

"Oh?"

"You've already shortened my lifespan by at least twenty years."

At his words, Samantha tried hard not to feel insulted, though she did feel a twinge of disappointment. She had a lot to offer a man. Just not Jack, apparently.

Well, that was his loss, though it sure felt like hers, for some reason. She didn't have time to dwell on it, because as soon as he set the car's parking brake her mother came flying off the porch, arms waving and apron flying in the warm September breeze.

"About time you two got here! I expected you an hour ago."

"Your daughter has a small bladder," Jack informed the older woman, who smiled knowingly, brushing tendrils of faded blond hair out of her face.

"It's the curse of the Brady women," she acknowledged. "Fred hates taking car trips with me."

"We hit traffic, if you want to know the real reason we're late," Samantha said, casting her companion an annoyed look. "Too many leaf peepers, not enough road." She exited the car and threw her arms about her mom's ample waist. "I've missed you, Mom. You look great!"

"I've gotten as fat as one of Lucas's pigs, and you know it." She turned to Jack. "But I still want a hug from you, Jack Turner. Now get yourself over here and give me one."

Happy to comply, Jack kissed Samantha's mother on both cheeks and a warm feeling rushed through him. "You're not fat, Lilly. And you smell just like I remembered—apples, cinnamon and nutmeg." They were comforting smells to a child who grew up with the odor of alcohol permeating his house and mind.

She laughed. "Because I've been baking apple pies for you. Look at you both—skinny as rails. Come on in. I've got lunch on the table. Your father and brother will be here shortly. They're spraying the back orchard today. This warm weather has brought the bugs out in full force. Your dad's going nuts."

"And Ross?" Jack asked, unable to hide the eagerness he felt at the prospect of seeing his childhood friend.

"Gone to Ellen's house to fetch her. He should be back soon. Ross is anxious to see you, too, dear."

"Are Ross and Ellen still going strong, Mom? I'm surprised to hear they're still together," Samantha admitted as they made their way into the house. "They don't seem very well suited to me."

"We're all surprised by that. But I'm happy for Ross. Ellen's a good woman, and she really does love your brother. Don't know if the feeling's mutual, though. Ross never says much about her."

Since Lilly was a woman who always cut to the heart of the matter, Samantha decided to do the same. "Are they having sex?"

Her mother pulled up short, and Samantha nearly fell over her and would have if Jack hadn't been there to steady her. "Samantha Brady! Good Lord! What kind of a question is that? How should I know? I don't ask personal questions. But now that you mention it, they never seem very touchy-feely around each other. Of course, Ellen is rather reserved."

Reserved? Ellen Drury made the queen of England look like a harlot.

Samantha's gaze locked with Jack's. "See, I told you! There's no spark between them. Ellen is Ross's security blanket. He's used to her, likes her, but marriage?" She shook her head. "That's a whole different ball of wax. I just don't see it happening."

"There's too much emphasis on sex these days, if you ask me," Lilly said. "There's something to be said for a circumspect woman. Too much flash, not enough substance is what some women are about. Men are fools to be taken in by that."

"You're absolutely right, Lilly," Jack said, as Samantha rolled her eyes and made gagging sounds.

"*Puleeze.* You date the flashiest, dumbest women on the planet. Most of them have no real parts—they're all plastic."

He opened his mouth to object, but Lilly's laughter silenced him. "It's so good to have you two home again. I've missed your squabbling."

"Then you should come visit more often, Lilly," he said.

"Yeah, there's no lack of squabbling at our place, is there, Jack?" Samantha grinned.

The older woman shook her head. "I can't abide the city. Men relieving themselves against buildings, taxi drivers cursing at everyone—" She shuddered. "Too many people and none of them nice."

"That's not true, Mom. You shouldn't make such broad generalizations. Things are different now than they used to be. I've found New Yorkers to be quite friendly and helpful."

Lilly looked skeptical. "Well, that's good to hear, but I still think you two should come back here to live, so we can all be together again. I miss you."

Flashing Samantha a deer-in-the-headlights look, Jack said in a panic-tinged voice, "Ah, am I in the same bedroom as last time, Lilly? I think I'll carry up the bags and get settled in. I'll take yours, too, Samantha."

"Yes, the same one. Go ahead and unpack, but don't be long. We'll be eating in about fifteen minutes," Lilly advised.

Samantha waited until Jack reached the top of the stairs and disappeared, then she pulled her mother into the kitchen, closing the swinging door behind them.

"Mom, you shouldn't be talking to Jack about moving back here. You know how things are with his parents. This place is nothing but one big bad memory for him." Samantha wasn't even sure if Jack was planning to visit the Turners this visit; she rather doubted it.

Sighing, Lilly shook her head. "He needs to make peace with them, Samantha. They're his parents, despite everything they've done. I know his mother misses him. I see Charlotte at church every Sunday, and she always asks if I've heard from you or Jack."

"I've spoken to Jack about it, but he has to do things in his own time. And even if he does reconcile with his family, he won't be moving back home. He's just opened up his own real estate firm in the city."

Her mom's blue eyes, a shade deeper than Samantha's, lit with curiosity and excitement. "Tell me everything! I knew he was unhappy at work, but to quit, just like that?" She snapped her fingers. "I admit I'm surprised."

"It's for Jack to tell. And don't let on that you know, because I'm sure he wants to surprise you and Dad with the news."

"I just love that boy. When are you two going to get married and give me some grandchildren? I'm not getting any younger, you know. And I certainly can't count on Ross or Lucas. I worry that those two are never going to settle down."

"Ha, ha, ha. That's very funny. You know we're just good friends."

"Well, why ever not? You've known each other your whole life, are best friends and like each other. Seems to me that's an excellent beginning for a life-long relationship. I know married couples who aren't as lucky."

"Jack and I would never suit as a married couple—surely you realize that. We argue over the most trivial things, have different views on everything, from politics to movies, and—" And Samantha wanted a child, whereas Jack would rather have a dog. "It just wouldn't work. Plus, I'm not attracted to Jack."

Liar! Okay, so she was attracted. A woman would have to be dead not to be. But she had no intention of acting upon those momentary twinges of horniness. Besides, it was quite clear that the attraction was only one-sided, and she couldn't take rejection, not from Jack.

"Are you crazy? The man is gorgeous. I'm old and even I know that. What makes you think you'll find someone better than Jack?"

I don't. And therein lies the problem.

"I'm going to quit coming home if you persist in hounding me about marrying Jack. It's never going to happen."

Lilly smiled knowingly. "Never say never. And I doubt you'll quit coming home. You love it when your father and I spoil you."

It was terrible being such an open book. And it was true: she loved being spoiled. As the youngest child and only girl, her doting parents had coddled her outrageously, especially her father, who called her his perfect princess and acted as if she could do no wrong.

So far she hadn't disappointed him, but Samantha worried about the day she would. After all, she wasn't perfect. She made mistakes. What would happen when she finally fell off the pedestal her dad had placed her on? The thought was too awful to contemplate.

"How many apple pies did you make? I intend to take at least two home with me."

"Don't worry. There's enough to feed even your bottomless pit. Mercy! I don't know how you stay so skinny. I just look at food and gain weight. It's not fair."

"Whoever said life was fair?" Samantha replied, thinking about not being able to get pregnant, not being able to sell her book, not being able to...

Don't go there, Samantha.

"Sometimes life really sucks."

"Well, then, it's good that I made a lot of pies, isn't it?"

Wrapping her arms about her mom's waist, Samantha hugged her. "Yes, it is. And I'll need about a ton of ice cream to go along with them."

DINNER THAT NIGHT was a loud, boisterous affair. Ross had brought Ellen, who sat quietly listening to the exchanges going on around her. Lucas was there, as was Samantha's father, who at that very moment was grilling Jack about his new venture.

"Do you really think it was wise to leave the security of your job and start over from scratch, Jack? The economy being what it is, it could be risky."

Fred Brady was in no way, shape or form a risk taker. He kept his money in low interest-bearing savings accounts and refused to invest any of it in the stock market or real estate, believing it was too speculative. He always crossed the street at the crosswalk, and he never missed attending church on Sunday, for fear of pissing off God and receiving retribution. Farmers were notoriously superstitious, but Samantha thought her dad's overly cautious ways were a direct result of his own father's financial reverses when he was growing up.

But Samantha's father always said exactly what

he thought, and she was a lot like him in that regard. "Jack's new real estate firm is going to be a huge success," she said confidently. "He's worked very hard to make sure that he has all of his bases covered."

Jack smiled gratefully. "I don't intend to fail, Fred. I've done my homework, I'm good at what I do and I've got a partner to share some of the financial burden, which will make things a lot easier."

"Quit being so negative, Fred," Lilly admonished. "It's the worst part of your personality."

"Hey, maybe I should go to New York and help you out," Ross offered. "I'm sure I'd be good at sales."

Noting Ellen's shocked expression, Samantha felt sorry for the young woman. Her brother's comment did not sound like a man who was madly in love or ready to settle down.

"How are things at the elementary school, Ellen?" she asked. "Has nasty old Mr. Ferguson retired yet?"

Ellen smiled through her obvious distress. "We all thought he would at the end of last semester, but Mr. Ferguson is still going strong. I doubt he'll ever die. He's much too ornery."

"Yeah, well only the good die young," Samantha said.

Roger Ferguson was the principal of Dutchess Elementary. Samantha and Jack had spent many an afternoon warming the seats in his office, listening to lectures on proper classroom and playground etiquette. Not that those lectures had done a bit of good to curb their atrocious behavior.

Jack laughed. "You'll probably find old Fergie dead under his desk one of these days."

"Oh, I hope not," she said, genuinely concerned by the possibility. "That would upset me terribly."

"What doesn't?" Ross interjected with a frown.

"I think Jack was only teasing," Samantha told the young woman, whose face suddenly flamed in embarrassment. She then flashed Ross a warning look, wishing she could kick her insensitive brother's ass up one side and down the other.

Ellen might be a bit too sweet and syrupy for her own good, but she had a generous spirit and a loving heart, and didn't deserve to be ridiculed for it, especially in front of family.

"What have you been doing with your free time, Ross?" Jack asked. "Taken any trips lately?"

"Yes, Ross, tell us what you've been doing to occupy yourself all day long," Samantha added, but not out of curiosity. She knew her brother did very little to keep himself busy.

Ross spent most of his time wallowing in the unfair hand he'd been dealt by the football gods. Once an NFL pro, he'd fractured his right leg in several places during a championship game. He'd been released from his contract when it became apparent that his leg would never heal enough to allow him the speed necessary for a running back.

"Ross is helping coach the high school football team," Ellen informed everyone proudly. "I think the Ravens are going to have a winning season this year thanks to him."

"Why that's wonderful, Ross! Why didn't you tell me and your father about this?" Lilly's proud gaze fell on her son, who looked uncomfortable, not to mention extremely annoyed with his girlfriend.

"I've helped out with a few practices. That doesn't make me a coach," he insisted.

"With your football background you'd be very good at it, son," Fred said. "Perhaps you should think more about it. It'd be a good way to occupy your time. You know what they say about idle hands and all."

"Yeah, Ross, you'd be great. And you'd be able to put your football skills to use." Jack reached for his iced tea and sipped the cold liquid.

"Ross would rather sit on his butt and collect his disability checks than work for a living. Right, bro?"

"That's not fair, Lucas," Ellen said, coming immediately to Ross's defense. "Ross was injured. It's not his fault that—"

Ross shoved his chair back and stood, cutting off whatever else the well-meaning woman was about to say. "I don't need a champion, Ellen—I can speak for myself. What I need right now is some fresh air. I'm going outside." He stormed out of the house, banging the screen door behind him.

All eyes turned to Ellen, whose face filled with apology. "You'll have to forgive Ross's rude behavior. I think he's upset about something, but I don't know what it is." And if she did know, loyal Ellen wasn't saying.

Fred's face reddened in anger. "Ross was downright rude to you, Ellen. You shouldn't have to put up with that. I raised him better than to be disrespectful to women." Samantha's father didn't get mad often, but when his children disappointed him, he could go from zero to ballistic in three-point-two seconds.

"He's not himself, Fred," Lilly said, playing the role of peacemaker and overlooking her son's obvious flaws as she so often did.

"Horseshit! That boy needs a good swift kick in the behind. Quit coddling him, Lilly. He's not a boy anymore."

"Maybe I should go talk to him," Jack suggested, and Samantha's mother breathed a sigh of relief.

"Would you, Jack? Ross has always listened to you."

Samantha shook her head, doubting Jack would have much luck with the pigheaded man.

JACK FOUND ROSS down by the pond, seated on a bench he'd built years ago in high school wood shop.

"For chrissake, Ross! What the hell's the matter with you? In all the years I've known you I've never seen you behave like such an asshole. I feel sorry for Ellen. You seemed to really enjoy running her down. What gives?"

Ross tossed pebbles into the water, one at a time, making concentric circles on the surface. After a moment, he looked up. "I don't know what I'm going to do. Since I lost my football contract, I'm at loose ends. I'm dying here, Jack."

"But that was over two years ago, man. Surely you've adjusted by now? Life goes on. You need to get over this pity party of yours and get back into it."

Ross shrugged his wide shoulders. "It's not easy going from the limelight to spreading lime on a field. I'm not cut out for this kind of life. I'm bored...with everything."

"So move. Do something different. No one's making you stay here."

"That's just it. I don't know what I want to do. Ellen wants me to take the coaching job that's been offered and settle down to the quiet life here, raise a bunch of babies and watch the grass grow. But I'm not sure I can do that."

"Do you love Ellen?"

The question hung in the air for what seemed like an eternity before Ross replied, "To be honest, I'm not sure. Ellen's a great girl, and I like her a lot. But I'm not sure if what I'm feeling is love or just comfort at being with her."

Samantha's words rang in Jack's ears: *Ellen is Ross's security blanket.*

"You've been dating this woman off and on for two years. Talk about stringing someone along. If you're not serious about her—"

"I don't know if I'm serious. If you haven't noticed, Ellen's not the most exciting woman in the world. She's so structured and naive. I'm just not sure I could stand that for all eternity. Hell, I'm already bored. What would another twenty or thirty years bring?"

"Have you spoken to her about it?"

"That would be like kicking a puppy. I don't want to hurt her."

Jack rubbed the back of his neck. "You and Samantha are a lot alike. You never make things easy on yourselves."

"Is Samantha still trying to sell her book?"

Jack decided to not tell Ross about his sister's plans to get pregnant. No sense borrowing trouble when there wasn't any...yet. "Yes, she's very determined to be published."

"At least Samantha knows what she wants. I wish I were that lucky."

"Maybe you should explore your options. Try coaching for a while, do a few other things and see if you like any of them. You're not going to get any answers sitting on your ass being rude to those who love you and are only trying to help."

The tall man sighed. "I guess I owe everyone an apology for the way I behaved at dinner."

"You sure as hell do."

Ross appeared genuinely contrite. "I hate that."

Jack laughed. "Yeah, men never like saying they're sorry. We think it's too wimp-ass."

"Lucas shouldn't have baited me."

"Lucas has been baiting you since the day you were born. That's what brothers do. But he loves you and I'm sure he's concerned. You don't hide your feelings very well."

"He's a good guy, even if he is my brother."

"Look," Jack began, "if things don't work out for you here or you need a place to work things out, come to New York for a visit. There's always something happening there."

"Thanks. I'll think about it. I guess I've got a lot to think about."

Jack sighed. "Don't we all?"

CHAPTER SIX

BY THE TIME Jack turned off the interstate on their way back to the city the following Sunday, rain was coming down in torrents, making visibility poor and road surfaces slick.

Samantha worried that their return trip was an accident waiting to happen and judging by Jack's exaggerated breathing, he did, too. "Maybe we should turn around and go back to my parents' house," she suggested. "It's not safe driving in this weather. I can hardly see a foot in front of the car. And if I'm having trouble, then others are, too." She swiped at the condensation forming on the windshield with the palm of her hand, and then turned up the defroster to clear it.

"It's too late to turn back. We're more than halfway and the weather isn't going to be any better in the other direction. I think it's best if we keep going."

Unease skittered down Samantha's spine. "I hate thunderstorms. They creep me out." She'd no sooner said that when lightning cracked loudly overhead and a boom of thunder bellowed, making her jump in her seat and causing the seat belt to nearly choke her.

"Don't think the guy upstairs liked your thunderstorm comment."

"Yeah, I'm getting that impression. I just wish this stupid rain would stop. I don't want to die in some horrible car crash. If I have to go, I want it to be in my sleep."

Jack smiled at her dramatics. "The storm's caused from the unusually warm weather we've been having. All that humidity builds up. Sort of like an orgasm." He grinned when Samantha's cheeks flushed red.

"Ha! We're going to die and you're making jokes." Now was not the time to think about orgasms, especially when Jack was sitting next to her in a humid car. Her nerves were too frayed to concentrate on orgasms and dying at the same time.

Samantha rocked back and forth to the constant swishing of the windshield wipers, too nervous to think about anything except the horrible storm. Suddenly realizing what she was doing, she forced herself to stop and focus on something besides the weather and Jack's provocative comment.

"Did you enjoy visiting your family?" he asked, and she was grateful for the opportunity to get her mind off org—uh, the storm for a moment. "I had a great time."

She nodded, but didn't take her eyes off the road for an instant. "Yes, but I'm always homesick after I leave them. Guess I should visit more often."

"You have a great family. You're very lucky. But I guess you already know that."

"You should have visited your folks while you had the chance. Mom said your mother's been asking about you."

"I might have, if my dad hadn't been there. I really don't want to see him. I'm afraid we'll get into it, and there's really no point in rehashing all that old crap. I'm done with that."

Samantha silently debated whether or not to tell him what she knew about his father; she didn't want to distract him from his driving. Finally deciding she should, she said, "Mom said your dad's been going to AA for the past six months. Maybe a visit from you would have been therapeutic for him. It wouldn't hurt to support his efforts."

Jack seemed surprised by the news. "I spoke to my mother just the other day. She didn't mention anything about him going. I wonder why? She usually confides in me about stuff like that."

"Because your dad told her not to. He's afraid he'll fail again and you'll be even more disappointed in him than you are already. Your opinion means a lot to him."

Jack's fingers tightened on the steering wheel, his knuckles turning white. "How do you know all this?"

"My mother told me. She wanted to tell you, too, but I told her it would be better if it came from me. I wasn't sure how you'd react to the news, and I didn't want you to take offense and think my mom was interfering in your business."

"I would never think that about Lilly, you know that. And this treatment program is nothing new. Dad's been to AA many times before."

"I know. But your mother seems to think that this time is different. Charlotte told Mom your dad is really making an effort. Apparently he hasn't touched a drop of liquor in six months."

Jack released a sigh. "My mother always thinks that, which is why she's still with him. And she always ends up disappointed. I've spent my whole life waiting for Martin Turner to change. He never does. I'm not putting myself through that again. It's just not worth it."

Hearing the hurt in Jack's voice, Samantha decided to change the subject. Besides, driving in this miserable weather was bad enough; he didn't need any more stress to deal with, at the moment. "Did you find out what's bothering Ross? He seemed in better spirits after talking with you."

"Ross is confused about what he wants out of life.

I think he feels totally lost and useless without football."

"Football was a sport he played. It didn't define who he was or is. My brother needs to figure that out. And what about Ellen? Did he mention her?"

Jack paused a moment, as if weighing whether or not to say anything. Finally, he replied, "He's not sure about her. Ross has feelings for Ellen, but he doesn't know what they are."

"Ellen's a nice woman. But as I said, I'm not—"

Suddenly the car began making clunking sounds.

"Uh-oh. That doesn't sound good."

"It sure as hell doesn't."

"Why's the car making that awful noise?"

"Beats me," Jack replied with a lift of his shoulders. "This is a rental, remember? But it doesn't bode well for continuing our trip."

The clunking grew louder, then steam began rising from the hood. Samantha's eyes widened, her voice filling with alarm. "Is the car on fire? It looks like it's on fire. Do you think we should get out? I don't want to burn alive, Jack. Cremation has never been my thing."

"I don't think so. My guess is the water pump might be going. We'll get off the road at the next exit."

"But it's Sunday afternoon. There won't be any mechanics open."

"Which means we're going to have to find a motel and have the car fixed in the morning, if we can find someone who works on cars. From the looks of our surroundings, the residents here might still be driving horse-drawn buggies."

Ever so slowly, they clunked and clanged their way to the next exit and found a seedy motel that sat back amidst a thick cluster of pine trees.

At the sight of it, Samantha made a face of disgust. "This place is right out of *Psycho*. I don't want to stay here. It gives me the creeps."

"We don't have much choice. It's the Bates Motel—well, Pine Hollow Lodge—or the car. I'm opting for a bed, no matter what the room looks like. At least we'll be inside where it's dry."

Heaving a deep sigh, she said, "Okay. But if the proprietor looks anything like Norman Bates, I'm not taking a shower."

SAMANTHA WAITED in the car while Jack braved the elements to rent them a room for the night. When he returned a few minutes later, he was frowning, and she figured the news wasn't good.

"They've only got one room left. Apparently the storm has stranded a bunch of tourists heading north, and they're full." Just then, the pink neon Vacancy sign added a big red *NO*.

"Oh well. At least we've *got* a room. After sitting

in this car, contemplating the size of the backseat, I've decided to be grateful for that."

"That's my girl. I'll grab the bags. Here's the key. It's number eight. Go ahead and unlock the door, I'll be right in."

SAMANTHA WANTED TO CRY when she stepped into the motel room, which smelled like stale cigarette smoke.

Hell had better furnishings!

The green shag carpeting covering the floor was threadbare and didn't look too clean. A brown, stained and torn chenille bedspread did nothing to disguise the lumpy mattress on the one double bed. She stared at the bed for several moments, unable to keep her heart from racing. She and Jack had never slept in the same bed together.

Don't be stupid! You're perfectly safe with Jack.

Yeah, but is Jack perfectly safe from me?

Why on earth was she suddenly fixating on Jack? Samantha had never done that before. Well, not for a long time, anyway.

It was Patty's fault, she decided. And even her mother had mentioned how hot Jack was. Mothers weren't supposed to notice things like that!

Just then, the door opened to reveal the object of her wayward thoughts, his cotton shirt plastered to his well-muscled chest, his pants wet and taut over his—

"You're back!" she screeched in a voice she didn't recognize as her own. Apparently neither did Jack, because he stared at her strangely.

"Is everything okay? You look flushed."

She nodded, wide-eyed and innocent. "Of course. I'm just fine. Why do you ask?"

He shook his head, and then held up a wicker basket. "I've brought in the pies and the hamper your mom packed for us. Mr. Jenkins said they don't have a restaurant here, and there's none close by."

Surprise, surprise.

"You must be freezing. Why don't you change out of your wet clothes and take a hot shower?" Samantha suggested. "You're dripping water onto this lovely vintage carpeting. I'm sure Mr. Jenkins won't be pleased if we ruin his sumptuous decor."

Jack finally took a moment to peruse his surroundings. "Man, what a dump! But at least we're inside and out of the rain. Jenkins said the worst is yet to come. The weatherman is predicting heavier downfalls for later this evening."

"Mr. Jenkins is just a font of useful information. First he tells us we can starve, and now we've got Noah's Ark to build. Did he happen to mention where we can get the car fixed?"

Jack nodded. "His son owns a towing business, but doesn't work on Sundays. He'll come over first thing in the morning and tow the car to the nearest Ford dealership, have it repaired, then tow it back."

"But how far is that? I can't believe Ford would have a dealership around here. It's nothing but farms and cows."

"They don't. It's an hour's drive from here."

"I take it Mr. Jenkins's son is not doing this out of the goodness of his heart. How much is this going to cost?"

"Two hundred."

She swallowed, picturing the zero balance in her checkbook. "Are you a member of an auto club? They tow for free."

Jack pushed wet hair away from his face. "We live in New York City. Why would I need an auto club? I don't even own a car. Besides, the rental agency will reimburse me."

"That's a relief. Well, go ahead and change. I'll unpack the hamper and we can have an indoor picnic. Don't know about you, but I'm starving."

"Sounds good. Be back in a sec."

After Jack disappeared into the bathroom, Samantha found an extra blanket in the closet, sniffed to make sure it wasn't too gross, and then spread it on the floor in the middle of the room. Placing the picnic hamper on top of it, she opened the lid and her stomach immediately responded to the glorious smells emanating from within.

"Bless you, Mom!" She would have kissed the woman, had she been there, for inside rested Lilly's famous fried chicken, flaky biscuits and cut up carrots and celery. It was a feast. Searching further, she discovered two bottles of whiskey, with a note that read, *Thanks for listening, buddy—Ross.*

A few minutes later, Jack emerged from the bathroom smelling of soap and musky aftershave. His jeans were slung low on his hips, revealing a tuft of dark hair right below his belly button. His shirt was open and the hairs on his chest glimmered in the lamplight. Samantha swallowed, issuing a cease and desist order to her racing heart.

She held up a bottle of the Jack Daniel's. "This is from Ross. There's a note for you. And we've got chicken and biscuits."

"And pie. Don't forget the pie."

Her stomach grumbled. "As if I could." Though she was suddenly hungry for a lot more than pie.

AN HOUR LATER the storm still raged, but inside the drab motel room it was warm and humid. Each time lightning cracked or thunder boomed in anger Samantha swallowed a generous portion of whiskey, which warmed her insides and seemed to lessen her fears. Whoever said courage didn't come from the inside of a bottle was dead wrong. At the moment she felt positively bold.

"I can't eat another bite," she admitted, rubbing her stomach. "I'm stuffed to the gills."

Jack shook his head. "Christ, you can pack it away. You eat like a football lineman. It always amazes me that you can stuff so much food into such a small body."

She grinned. "The result of growing up with two strapping boys, I guess. You had to fight for leftovers in our family. Actually, come to think of it, there were never any leftovers. We ate every morsel every night. Not once did my mother have to lecture us about the starving children in China."

Swallowing the remainder of the whiskey in his glass, Jack poured himself another, filled Samantha's glass to the brim, and asked, "Of all the men you've slept with, who was the best lover you've ever had?"

Her eyes widened and she nearly spewed mid-swallow. "That's rather personal, don't you think? And I haven't slept with that many men."

"I'll tell you mine, if you tell me yours," he taunted.

Jack's mischievous smile was her undoing. The liquor—or at least she hoped it was the liquor—warmed her all the way down to her bare toes. Leaning against the bed frame, she considered the question for a moment.

"I guess Steve Jarvis, the guy I dated in college. He was sweet and very considerate."

Snorting, he made a face. "College doesn't count. Jarvis was your first. The first one is always special. But I'm talking good—the one who made your toes curl and your belly ache with—"

She swallowed, saying quickly, "I get the picture," then sighed. "As much as I hate to admit it, that would be Tony Shapiro. He was incredible, absolutely fantastic in bed. Why, I've never had so many multiple—"

He looked annoyed by her answer. "Yeah, I get it."

"And yours? I hope you're not going to tell me it was the adorable Bunny—rabid rabbit at large?"

Jack laughed. "No way. Mine would have to be Sarah Lassiter."

"Sarah Lassiter! The prim and proper woman who worked at the bookstore? The one who wore really drab clothes and no makeup?" Samantha had always wondered why Jack had been attracted to the colorless woman, who was as dull as dishwater and looked like a librarian.

"The very same. Apparently Sarah had read the *Kama Sutra* from cover to cover and committed it to memory. There were times things got so intense between us, I thought my eyes would cross."

Ignoring the kernel of jealousy that started to sprout, Samantha heaved a dispirited sigh. "I can assure you that none of the men I've slept with suffer from poor vision as a result of our liaisons."

Note to self: Buy Kama Sutra.

He laughed, shaking his head. "You shouldn't underestimate yourself. You're a warm and loving individual."

"You make me sound like a dog." So much for coming across as sexy and alluring, she thought.

"Well, you're as cute as a puppy, that's for sure. And you like having your belly scratched."

"I do not!"

"Do too." Suddenly he lunged for her, flipped Samantha on her back and began tickling her mercilessly.

She screamed, trying to break free. "Stop it, Jack! Stop tickling me or I'll scream even louder." Jack's hands roaming all over her, even in jest, was pure torture.

He let her up. "Spoilsport. Well, since you don't like wrestling, what do you want to play? Truth or Dare? Spin the Bottle? There's no TV, so we need to do something to occupy our time."

"Good grief! I haven't played Spin the Bottle since high school." Samantha made a face. "I had to kiss Walter Clements. Remember Walter? He had those mossy teeth." She shuddered at the memory.

Jack bared his own pearly whites. "I just brushed mine a little while ago. See? Clean as a whistle."

Taking another sip of whiskey, Samantha could feel her reservations slip away. "Why would you want to play Spin the Bottle? You don't even think I'm sexy. Why, you just referred to me as a dog. I'm rather insulted." Only it came out "inshulted."

"Are you kidding? I think you're hot. You've got a great body, beautiful blond curly hair and you make me laugh. That's the one thing I love about you."

Love? Did he just say what I thought he said? Even in her befuddled state, the L-word rang loud.

"It's so comfortable between us, Samantha. None of those stupid games couples always play. You and I are friends, good friends. Remember when you talked about Ellen being Ross's security blanket?"

She nodded.

"Well, you're mine. I take great comfort in the fact that I can come home every night and know exactly what to expect. No pressure. No whining—well, most of the time. You're a good fit for me."

"Thanks." She was starting to feel like a used pair of slippers—comfy, warm and worn-out.

"Is it hot in here, or is it just me?" Jack asked, shrugging out of his shirt. "I hate humidity," he said, and began belting out an off-key—and off-kilter—version of the old Beatles tune: "Humidity… What's that dampness coming over me? Makes me feel just like a wilted tree… I really hate… humidity."

Samantha laughed, then her gaze zeroed in on Jack's bare chest again—a chest she'd seen a thousand times before and never thought a thing about. But now it looked as yummy as a hot-fudge sundae. Seductive, luscious and—

Oh boy, did she like ice cream!

"Don't you want to take your shirt off, too?" he asked, a challenging glint in his eye. "I've got a pack of cards in my duffel bag. We could play strip poker. But I should warn you, I'm pretty good."

Samantha never could resist a challenge—she began to unbutton her cotton blouse. "Don't bother with the cards. I don't have that much to hide." And she still wore a bra, so it wasn't like she was naked. Jack had seen her in a bathing suit; this was no different.

It seemed different.

The bra she wore wasn't one of those pretty, sexy Victoria's Secret bras, but a plain, white cotton number she'd purchased at Macy's. Boring and sexless.

"More than a mouthful's a waste, love, so don't sweat the small stuff."

So Jack had noticed she wasn't that well endowed. *Well, that sucked!*

Cheeks warming, Samantha felt she had something to prove. "Where's that empty bottle? I've never played Spin the Bottle with only two people before, but I'm game if you are."

"Eager to kiss me, huh?"

"Oh, yes. I'm dying to know if those rumors I heard were true."

His brow arched, and he looked totally full of himself. "That I'm a great kisser?"

"No. That your lips are soft and flabby, like a fish's."

"We'll just see about that. I intend to make you eat your words."

Heat suffused every inch of Samantha's body, and she had the sudden urge to shed her pants as well. But she didn't. With the peculiar way she was feeling at the moment, things could get out of hand very easily.

"You go first. But if the bottle doesn't point directly at me, then you have to put a dollar bill in the kitty. Whoever gets the most hits wins the pot."

His brow rose. "And what are you going to do for your wager? I thought you were short of cash till payday."

"I'll make out IOUs and pay you later."

Jack made the first spin and the bottle eventually came to a stop pointing directly at Samantha. She immediately started laughing, a high-pitched, nervous laugh that resembled a hyena on crack.

"What the hell are you laughing at? Most women don't laugh when they kiss me."

She giggled. "I'm not most women, and this seems too weird."

"Aren't you the least bit curious to know what kissing each other would be like? I admit, I've wondered. Does that surprise you?"

She shook her head. "Not really. I've had the same curiosity about you. Guess that's only natural. We've known each other a long time."

Leaning across the small space that separated them, Jack drew Samantha into his arms and kissed her. The kiss was brief, nice and not at all what she had expected. She felt nothing extraordinary and was almost relieved.

"Your turn to spin," he said.

Samantha took hold of the bottle and gave it a good twist. When it stopped, it pointed at Jack, who seemed inordinately pleased, judging by the size of his…*smile.*

Nervously she leaned toward him and their lips touched again. But this time he clasped her head between his hands and kissed her like he really meant it. His lips moved over hers softly yet firmly, then his tongue slid between her lips and she could hear him moan. Or was that her? She wasn't sure. Somewhere in Samantha's mind the thought surfaced that danger lurked just around the corner, that she should stop kissing Jack before things got out of control.

But she liked kissing Jack!

She liked the feel of his mouth on hers, the way his lips moved persuasively, teasing and tantalizing, the way heat emanated from him and flowed into her. Finally, and with a great deal of effort, she pulled back.

"Well, well," he said, his smile disgustingly erotic. "You are full of surprises."

Her cheeks glowed red. "I'm not sure what you mean by that."

"I mean, still waters run deep, sweetheart. You're a damn good kisser."

"We should stop playing this stupid game," she suggested, feeling slightly panicked.

He shook his head. "Not a chance. It's my turn to spin."

Swallowing hard, Samantha grew almost dizzy as she watched the bottle spin around and around. It took forever to stop, but it finally did…right in front of her.

"Must be my lucky day." Jack drew her into his arms once again, wrapping himself around her, and then kissing her with a passion she had only read about in romance novels.

The Bastard might have been good in bed, but he'd never kissed like this!

The kiss continued on for what seemed like forever. Samantha couldn't breathe, couldn't think. The room was spinning as fast as the bottle had.

"I think we should stop, Jack. I'm starting to feel dizzy." *And frightened. And turned on.*

Jack ran his thumb over her lower lip, and she had the strangest urge to suck it. His touch was gentle, his lips soft when they nuzzled her ear. "Your kisses are sweet and very addictive. How can I stop?" His tongue plunged into her mouth then, and Samantha felt a warm stirring low in her belly. Tentatively, she touched her tongue to his, and in that age-old mating dance they did with their tongues what their bodies yearned for.

"God, Samantha, you're so sweet!" His hands moved up and down her back, caressing and making her skin feel as if it were on fire. Then he cupped her breasts and thumbed the nipples into rock-hard peaks.

"Jack," she said on a sigh of longing.

"I want you, Samantha."

Samantha couldn't think, couldn't formulate a response to the provocative declaration. She could only feel. And what she felt was good, so very, very good.

He unhooked her bra and gazed worshipfully at her breasts, his eyes darkening with passion. "You're beautiful. Perfect, like ripe peaches." He moved to taste her. "Sweet. I was right." Jack kissed her again, and she moved against him, wanting, needing what only he could give, what she'd been dreaming of for years. "I want you, Samantha," he said again. "Do you want me, too?"

"Yes," she finally choked out. "I want you very much."

Did I just tell Jack I wanted him?

Samantha tried to clear her head, to make sense of what was happening. Friends didn't do this. But when his warm hand touched her belly she couldn't think about anything but the need building inside her.

"You're so soft, so perfect."

Jack made short work of her jeans and underpants and soon she was lying before him completely naked. At first she felt self-conscious. He was gazing at her like a hungry man at a banquet. But then he shrugged out of his pants, and her attention was diverted toward much *bigger* things.

Caressing the hard planes of his chest, Samantha felt the soft hairs beneath her fingertips. Her hand moved lower, and she heard him suck in his breath. His stomach was washboard flat, attesting to the sit-ups and push-ups he did every morning.

"You've got perfect breasts, did I tell you that? And such large nipples." He began toying with them, and Samantha's thighs flooded with desire.

"Jack," she whispered, reveling in the compliment even if deep inside she didn't believe it. Her boobs were nothing to write home about.

His lips replaced his fingers and he sucked her nipples, then began kissing every inch of her heated flesh until she could no longer form a coherent thought, much less an objection. When his mouth reached the juncture of her thighs and he parted her legs to taste her most intimate place, Samantha had to anchor herself to the bedsheets, for fear of flying off to the ceiling.

"I can't remember ever being this hard before," he admitted.

I can't remember ever being this hot before!

"I don't want to hurt you." His hand moved between her legs to make sure she was wet and ready for him, and then he very carefully positioned himself over her to enter. "I can't wait any longer. I can't—" He plunged in.

Wow! was her first thought, then she swallowed hard and her breath quickened. "Ohmigod!" Samantha cried out, her breathing rapid now, her body bathed in sweat, as Jack moved in and out of her in a controlled rhythm that had her heart pounding loud in her ears as he took her higher and higher.

"Stay with me, sweetheart. This is going to be so good, so goddamn good." His body was bathed in sweat; droplets of moisture clung to his upper lip and forehead as he forcibly restrained himself from going too fast.

He smiled a sweet smile. "Are you doing okay?"

"Yessss!" Samantha increased her movements to match his, their bodies moving together in perfect harmony. As they climbed to that place where the air got thin, she couldn't draw a breath and began to see brilliant stars before her eyes. "Oh! Oh! Oh!"

Jack pushed hard, one last time, and the stars exploded. Samantha climaxed, just before he did.

Floating back down to earth, they lay in each other's arms, cocooned in a warm, wonderful feeling of euphoria and contentment. And that's how they remained, for the rest of the night, not giving a thought to what tomorrow might bring.

CHAPTER SEVEN

THE SUN STREAMING through the window woke Jack the following morning. He squinted, then stretched, and as he did so his arm came into contact with something soft and warm—Samantha's breast.

Glancing over, his eyes widened in horror as the memory of the previous night came flooding over him. "Holy shit!" Samantha was asleep beside him. She was naked—naked and smiling, like she was having the most delicious dream. But, of course, it hadn't been a dream. None of it. He remembered the liquor, the kissing, the— "Holy shit!"

Easing himself out of bed, he reached for his pants and rubbed the back of his neck, trying to ease the throbbing of his head, which felt like a time bomb about to explode.

He took full responsibility for what happened. For what *shouldn't* have happened. He cared a great deal about Samantha, cherished their friendship, their easygoing relationship.

Samantha Brady was the kind of woman a man

could trust, the kind who would always stick by you when things got tough and you needed support and comfort. But she wasn't the kind of woman you take to bed and make mad, passionate love to. She'd been hurt in the past by a selfish jerk. Jack didn't want to treat her in the same shameless fashion.

A woman like Samantha expected things from a relationship. She had girlish fantasies about Prince Charming and babies, and though she protested that marriage wasn't for her, he knew she was only kidding herself.

Samantha would make a wonderful wife for some lucky man. But he wasn't that man!

"Samantha, wake up!"

"What? What is it?" She refused to open her eyes. "Go away. It's early. I don't want any bagels."

"Wake up! Something terrible has happened. You're not in your own bed. We're in a motel. We've just spent the night together."

That got her attention because she opened her eyes wide, pushed down the covers, stared open-mouthed at her nakedness, shrieked and then pulled them back up. "My head hurts."

"Yeah, well…so does mine. I think we need to talk."

"Are you trying to tell me that we did something beyond sleeping last night? To be honest, I can't remember much of anything."

"Well, aren't you lucky?" He shook his head and sighed deeply. "We made love, right there in that bed you're lying in." And it had been wonderful, from the little he remembered about it—wonderful but disastrous.

Clutching the covers tightly to her chest, Samantha looked confused and dismayed. "But how? Why? I mean—We've never done that before."

"We've never drunk two fifths of Jack Daniel's before, either. I think that had a little something to do with it." But dammit! She'd been so totally alluring and sexy, not to mention kissable. Still, that wasn't an excuse for what he'd done—what they'd both done.

"I'm sorry. This is my fault entirely. I take full responsibility. I didn't mean for anything like this to happen," he said. "I was drunk off my ass, unable to control myself."

Samantha looked almost flattered by the admission. "Look, it happened. We'll just forget about it and not talk about this again. We've known each other a long time, Jack. We've gotten through worse things. We'll get through this, too."

"Do you think so? Because I wouldn't want what happened to mess things up between us, Samantha. You're my best friend. And I care about you." Too much, but he wouldn't allow himself to overthink that right now.

She smiled sweetly at him. "You're mine, too, Jack. And nothing's going to mess things up between us. I'm not a virgin. I've had sex before, with men I didn't like nearly as well as I like you, so let's just forget it, okay? It was a mistake, pure and simple."

He nodded, a surge of relief rushing through him. Having a romantic relationship with Samantha would never work, not in a million years. They were good at being friends and roommates, but anything more than that was inconceivable. Hell, they didn't even like the same movies.

"I'll run down to the motel's office and see what time the tow truck's due to arrive. Why don't you take a shower while I'm gone? I'll take mine when I get back."

"All right."

Donning his shirt, he paused at the door. "And we won't talk about this again?"

She smiled back at him. "About what?"

Jack had the urge to kiss her just then, but sanity prevailed and he rushed out of the room before he could change his mind.

JACK AND SAMANTHA might not have discussed what had occurred the previous night, but it was there just the same, sitting between them like a big, fat, ugly pink elephant on the ride home.

They hadn't talked much, about anything, and Samantha was starting to feel uncomfortable, wondering if Jack was going to treat her differently now that they'd slept together. Though apparently they'd done very little sleeping.

Men were weird about sexual encounters. They often felt proprietary, guilty or worse, angry, believing that the woman in question had somehow trapped them into a situation they didn't want.

Is that what Jack thinks? That I'm trying to trap him?

"I'm glad the sun's out, aren't you?" she asked, attempting to ease the tension.

"Yeah," he replied, but didn't glance over at her.

"The car seems to be working okay, doesn't it?"

"Yeah."

"Are you excited about getting your real estate business off the ground?"

"Yeah."

She sighed with irritation. "Can I paint your bedroom pink with yellow cabbage roses?"

"Yeah."

Okay, she was in major trouble. Or, she should say, *they* were in major trouble, because Jack hated it when she went into his room and tried to decorate. The man was obviously not himself.

"Are you going to talk to me or not, Jack Turner? I'm getting tired of the yeahs."

He glanced sideways at her, a confused expression on his face. "Did you say something? Sorry. I was just lost in thought."

I couldn't guess about what.

"I told you, having sex was no big deal. I can't remember much about it, so it couldn't have been very memorable." She was glad he couldn't see her fingers crossed in her lap. The little she could remember had been wonderful, totally wonderful, a fantasy come true. But now her girlhood dream was turning into a nightmare of major proportions.

"No need to get insulting. You sure seemed to like it at the time."

"How would you know? You were drunk, too."

"I just do. You were moaning so loudly I was afraid the people next door were going to bang on the wall."

She gasped and felt her cheeks heat with embarrassment. "What an outrageous thing to say! I never moan. I'm quite certain about that."

"I'm just being truthful."

"How do I know that? I can't remember anything. Most likely you're embellishing, just to feed your stupid ego. Men do that. You all think you're God's gift to women."

"There's no point discussing this with you—you're irrational."

"Irrational, my ass! And we're not supposed to be

discussing this anyway. We made a deal, remember?"

"Fine."

She crossed her arms over her chest. "Fine."

CHAPTER EIGHT

THINGS HAD GONE from bad to worse since they'd spent that fateful night at the motel. In fact, it had gotten so tense between them, Samantha feared she was losing her best friend.

"Jack," Samantha called out, making her way down the hall toward the bathroom, where she knew he would be showering at this time of the morning. Usually Jack sang stupid songs at the top of his voice, but the past few days she hadn't heard him vocalizing. "Have you seen my hairbrush? I can't seem to find it, and I've looked—"

He pulled opened the bathroom door and his shocked expression stopped her in midsentence.

"What's wrong?" she asked, trying not to notice that the towel wrapped around his waist was tenting out. "Are you sick?"

"Why are you walking around half-naked? Don't you have a robe you can put on?"

She stared openmouthed at him. "What the hell is wrong with you this morning? Did you wake up on the wrong side of the bed? I've been walking around this apartment in my underwear for the past six years, and you've never said a word before about it. Now all of a sudden it bothers you?" Her brow wrinkled in confusion. "Why?" She wouldn't allow herself to think he was sexually attracted to her, despite their romantic encounter and the fact that the barber pole he hid under his towel was getting quite prominent.

"I—" His face was turning an unbecoming shade of red; he looked totally flummoxed and very uncomfortable as he adjusted the towel around his waist. "I just think it would be better if we both kept our clothes on, that's all."

She gazed at his bare chest, still dripping with droplets of moisture from his shower, and knew exactly how that warm flesh felt beneath her fingertips, how soft his hair had been when she'd caressed his—

Don't go there, Samantha.

"So it's okay for you to be naked, just not me, is that it?" When he didn't answer she added, "I have my underpants on, in case you're interested." His gaze lowered, zeroing in on her crotch and the yellow patch of hair that showed through the thin material of her white cotton panties.

He swallowed, staring as if mesmerized, then said, "You should be more circumspect."

"Why? You've seen me naked. I've got nothing left to hide."

Why am I being so perverse?

Because he pisses me off, that's why.

And because she'd spent another sleepless night after waking up from one of those hideous dreams where Jack was lying on top of her naked body and doing all sorts of delicious things to her. Her body had been bathed in sweat and she'd been throbbing in all the wrong places. And to make matters worse—there was no Jack. Which tended to make an even-tempered person slightly insane.

Horny, thy name is Samantha.

"Yes, I've seen you naked, so unless you want to get that way again—"

"Am I supposed to take that as a threat?"

"I suggest you cover up and quit flaunting your—"

"Flaunting! How dare you? I've never flaunted a day in my life. It's not my style, and you know it."

He looked as if he were about to say more, but instead turned on his heel and walked into his bedroom, slamming the door behind him.

"Well, how rude!" Samantha declared, heading to her own room to get dressed and wondering if she and Jack were going to be at odds over every little item now that things had apparently changed between them.

Hell, for years people—well, hippies, anyway—had been advocating "make love, not war." So why, now that she and Jack had made love, did they seem to be at war? The whole thing perplexed her, but she'd do her best to fix things with Jack. She hated being at odds with him. He was, after all, her best friend in the world.

And she…well, she used to be his.

JACK ENTERED the apartment that same day after work and the first thing he did was sniff the air like a bloodhound. Something smelled delicious, and he guessed that Samantha had prepared his favorite dinner: spaghetti *pomodoro*.

He supposed she was as sorry about this morning as he was. They rarely argued, even though they disagreed about a great many things. But the sight of her in her skimpy bra and panties had tested not only his self-control, but also his ability to think rationally—to think like a friend and not a lover. He was a man who prided himself on self-restraint and willpower, but a man could take only so much half-naked Samantha.

"Jack, is that you? I'm in here."

"Yeah, it's me." He set his briefcase down on the hall table and followed his nose into the kitchen, where Samantha stood at the stove, adding basil and garlic to her concoction. She looked pretty. Her blond hair curled riotously around her face; the steam rising from the pot made her cheeks rosy.

Coming up behind her, he reached around and presented her with the bouquet of yellow mums he'd purchased from a street vendor on the way home. "Sorry I was such an ass this morning. Forgive me?"

She turned, clutching the flowers to her chest, a look of surprise and pleasure crossing her face. "Oh, Jack, they're beautiful. Thank you! And me, too. I mean, I'm sorry, too."

"Are you making pasta *pomodoro,* I hope?"

"Yes, and you'd better be hungry because I've made enough to feed a third world country. We've also got salad and garlic bread. And for dessert...tiramisu, which I bought at the Italian bakery around the corner."

Jack's stomach grumbled. "I can't wait. I'm starving. We were so busy today I didn't have time to eat lunch."

"So everything's going well?" she asked, placing the flowers in a glass vase and setting them smack-dab in the middle of the table.

His smile was full of pride. "We got three new listings today, and I'm about to write my first contract. Tom was right—this endeavor of ours is going to be a huge success."

She threw her arms about his waist and hugged him, and Jack inhaled the clean scent of her, mingled with garlic. It was intoxicating…and dangerous. "I'm so happy for you. I just knew you'd be great at running your own business."

Realizing where his thoughts were heading, he extricated himself from her hold and stepped back. "Thanks. I appreciate your support."

Samantha looked at him strangely, but didn't say anything.

"How was your day? Did you finish those ads I asked you to put together?" He'd hired Samantha to prepare his advertising copy. She was very creative and could think outside the box, unlike some of the firms he'd spoken to.

"I hope you like them. I've never written ad copy before, but I think they're good, if I do say so myself."

"I'm sure they'll be great. I told you—you're a talented writer."

Samantha continued setting the table. "I got another rejection letter on my book today. That makes two this week. I guess I'm not as great as you think. I'm not sure it'll ever sell. Maybe I should just chuck my novel into the garbage and write something else."

"If you're asking for my opinion, the answer is no. It's a good book. Some savvy editor is going to buy it. These things take time—you'll see. You've got to have patience."

"I was hoping to sell it so I could build my nest

egg. My savings are dwindling, and I'm not getting as many hours as I want at the coffee shop."

"But you're earning a decent living. You've sold a bunch of magazine articles, and I'm paying you for the ads. It's not like you're not working."

"Babies are expensive. I need to earn even more. I've been thinking about getting another job, maybe waitressing at night or—"

"That's a lousy idea. How will you find the time to write your book and care for a child if you're working all the time?"

Samantha heaved a sigh. "I don't know. I just know I need to earn more money. I may have to hire a babysitter or pay for preschool at some point. I want to be prepared."

Jack fought against the need to take her into his arms and offer to care for her. "You're a grown woman," he said in a voice harsher than he intended. "You'll figure it out."

"I guess. I—"

"You're the one who decided to have a baby, remember? You'll just have to figure out how to make it work. No one else can do it for you."

Her eyes misted with tears, making him feel like the meanest bastard on earth. After a moment, she stiffened and said, "I intend to, with no help from anyone, including you. As I said, I just need to work harder. If you'll excuse me, I'll go and do just that."

"But what about dinner? I thought we were going to eat now."

"You go ahead. I'm not very hungry." She turned on her heel.

"Samantha, wait!" But she just kept on walking, and Jack had the strangest feeling that things between them had been forever altered by that one night of lovemaking, and he didn't know how to make things go back to the way they were before.

"THANKS FOR coming over, Patty. I wasn't sure whom else to call."

Taking a seat at Samantha's kitchen table, Patty lifted the coffee cup Samantha had just filled to her lips. "I was taking today off anyway—Elizabeth Arden calls—so it's no big deal. What's the problem? You sounded awful on the phone. Don't tell me you're finally pregnant and regretting it already? It's too early in the morning for that kind of news."

Samantha sighed. "I wish. It's still my dream to have a child, but the insemination procedures didn't work and I haven't heard back from the adoption agency. Actually, I asked you over to discuss something else."

"You seem upset. Has something happened?"

"It's Jack. Things are really bad between us at the moment, and I don't know how to fix it." She stirred three teaspoons of sugar into her cup, wishing it were melted chocolate.

"Well, since you're not sleeping together, it can't be a lover's spat, so... Uh-oh. What's that awful look on your face? You look positively guilty. Don't tell me—"

"Afraid so. Jack and I spent the night together. We made love."

"You're kidding! But you told me—"

"It was all a terrible accident, and it's ruining our relationship. Things just aren't the same between us anymore."

"I wish something that terrible would happen to me," Patty confessed, smiling to herself.

"This is serious, Patty. Please don't make light of it."

"Sorry." She sobered instantly. "Tell me what happened."

Samantha explained about the trip, the car trouble and the booze.

Patty's eyes widened, then grew knowing. "No wonder you did the deed. You were both shit-faced! So how was it? And don't spare any of the details."

"From the little I can remember, pretty wonderful. Apparently I made a lot of noise."

Samantha's friend laughed. "Good lord, Samantha! Only something like this would happen to you.

The rest of us aren't lucky enough to just fall into bed with a great-looking guy like Jack Turner."

"What am I going to do, Patty? The past few days have been awful—tense silences, stupid arguments and lots of small talk. I don't think Jack and I have laughed once, and that's just not like us. We're usually so free and easy around each other. I just hate what's developed, and all because of having slept together, of having sex. I almost hate the word."

"Bite your tongue! Life isn't worth living without sex."

"Maybe not for you, but it's ruined my life."

"Do you want my advice, Samantha?" Patty's expression grew serious. "Because if you do, I'm going to tell it like it is, and I'm not going to pull any punches."

Like that was something new?

"That's why I asked you over. I thought maybe if we put our heads together we could come up with some sort of solution—a way to fix things."

"What you should do, hon, is move out of this apartment. It's time you started living life on your own. You should cut your ties with Jack, give up that silly idea of having a baby and get on with your plan to become a published novelist."

Samantha's mouth dropped open, then snapped closed. "But—"

"An intelligent, attractive woman like you doesn't

need a man or child to complete her. Everything you need is within you. You're smart and savvy. You just need more self-confidence and chutzpah. You need to believe in yourself, in your talent as a writer."

This wasn't the kind of advice Samantha had been seeking or wanted. She didn't want to move out. She wanted to fix things with Jack, to make their lives uncomplicated and fun, like they'd been before, not the taut, tense situation they had become.

And she still wanted a child.

"I'm not like you, Patty. You're a self-possessed, in-your-face kind of woman. It's admirable that you can go toe-to-toe with the big boys. But I'm just not cut out for that.

"I like my life, such as it is. I agree that I should probably find an additional job, so I can contribute more to our living arrangement, and I've suggested that to Jack. But as far as leaving…" She shook her head. "I don't think so. And as for having a child… Well, I'm just not ready to give up on that idea, either."

Patty shook her head. "But, Samantha—"

"I realize that I haven't been very successful at conceiving and that I probably won't be able to. But I'm still hopeful that one of the adoption agencies I contacted will come through."

"Oh, Samantha. Are you going to live your whole life waiting for things to happen? If so, you could be waiting a long time. You should be out there making them happen, not wasting your life on events that may never come to pass."

Samantha felt hurt by her friend's comment. Even though Patty had always been blunt, she had never been intentionally cruel. "Is that what you think? That I'm wasting my life on dreams?"

"There comes a point in life where you have to take control of your own destiny, not wait for it to drop in your lap like manna from heaven. Jack is the perfect example—he's out turning his dream of being an entrepreneur into a reality."

"Just because my dreams are different from yours and Jack's, doesn't mean they're not valid or worthwhile. I've worked hard to achieve my goals, in spite of what others may think. I'm almost done with my manuscript and will be sending it off. And I've seen a specialist in order to conceive a child, but I ran out of money, so now I've got to take a different approach.

"I don't intend to give up. I intend, as the saying goes, to have my cake and eat it, too. And I intend to fix things with Jack."

Her friend smiled kindly. "Just be careful you don't end up with indigestion, honey."

Samantha felt the acid reflux even as they spoke.

CHAPTER NINE

JACK GLANCED UP from the sales contract to find Tom Adler hovering over his desk, a thoughtful, curious expression on his face. He'd hoped for a little space today to get his feelings for Samantha sorted out, but Tom wasn't likely to leave until Jack acknowledged him.

"Hey, partner! How's it going?" Jack asked.

"For a man who's just written a three-and-a-half million dollar contract, you don't look very happy. What's up? The Fosters haven't changed their minds, I hope?"

Tossing down his pen, Jack leaned back in his black leather swivel chair and heaved a heartfelt sigh, knowing his friend was right: this should have been one of the happiest, most fulfilling moments of his life. But it was marred by the recollection of the wounded look on Samantha's face when she'd left him standing in the kitchen last evening. She'd gone to her room after their discussion and hadn't emerged by the time he'd left for work this morning. And he still felt like a shit about the whole turn of events.

"No, it has nothing to do with the contract." He paused, and then confessed, "I slept with Sam."

Tom's eyes widened to the size of saucers, then his mouth dropped open before he found his voice. "I had no idea you were gay. Or are you bisexual? Because you should know, I'm straight as an arrow."

It took Jack a few moments to try to figure out how Tom had formed such a ridiculous conclusion, and then he remembered. "Sam's a woman, Tom. I'm not gay or bisexual, so breathe easy. Your virtue is safe with me."

"Sam's a woman! No shit! How come you led me to believe otherwise? That was damn sneaky of you."

Jack shrugged. "You drew your own conclusions, and I thought it best to let you think what you wanted to."

"So I wouldn't hit on her, right?"

"Something like that."

"Sam must be quite a looker, if you were afraid of a little competition. Otherwise you wouldn't have been hiding her from me. You wanted the woman for yourself, didn't you?"

"Samantha's very pretty, but also vulnerable and somewhat naive. She needs to be protected from men like us, which makes what I did even more reprehensible. I should be shot."

"So how was it? The sex, I mean?"

"That's not the point. I fucked everything up between us. We've been best friends since grade school and now we're barely speaking."

"That's tough. I'm sorry, man."

"I'm confused. I don't know what to do. Sometimes I think I should just do the honorable thing and—"

"Whoa!" Tom held up his hands, his eyes filling with panic. "I hope you're not thinking what I think you're thinking because that wouldn't be very smart. We've been in the dating trenches a long time, Jack. Don't go getting serious and stupid on me now. We're both confirmed bachelors. Marriage isn't an option for us, and you know it."

"But Samantha's my best friend. I feel conflicted, not to mention guilty as hell about what's happened. And it's my fault, all of it. If we hadn't had so much to drink, if I hadn't suggested we play that stupid game—"

Christ! What was I thinking?

He hadn't been thinking, not clearly anyway.

"I've really messed things up. And I'm worried that if Samantha and I keep living together, it's going to happen again. I see her in a different light now. There's no going back to the way things were before."

Shaking his head, Tom began to pace across the oriental carpet that covered fifty-year-old oak planking, and listened while Jack explained about the night at the motel and how crazed he'd been at the sight of Samantha in her underwear.

"I have feelings for her, Tom," Jack admitted. "I'm just not sure what those feelings are." But they went deep—and they scared him.

"Of course you do," his partner agreed, grinding to a halt in front of him. "But that's friendship and responsibility, not love. I think under the circumstances the best thing for you to do, since you're feeling conflicted and all, is to ask Samantha to move out. Removing temptation is a surefire way to avoid repeating past mistakes."

"I can't do that! We're best friends."

Tom shrugged. "I don't have all the answers, buddy. And I've got to go." He checked his watch. "I've got a listing appointment across town in thirty minutes."

Jack just wanted to forget the whole miserable episode had ever happened, but that was impossible now—now that he'd seen Samantha naked, kissed her, made love to her. Now he knew how silky her skin felt beneath his hands when he caressed her, how clean her hair smelled when his nose pressed into it, how she made soft, mewling sounds when in the throes of passion, the way her body trembled beneath him when she climaxed.

Jack knew everything about Samantha, except what to do about her.

SAMANTHA HAD JUST placed a pan of brownies in the oven when she heard Jack's key in the door. She was tempted to retreat to her room again. His comments of the previous night had wounded, and she hadn't yet forgiven him for it.

Unlike the pasta *pomodoro,* the brownies were not a peace offering. She intended to eat every single one of them herself. Chocolate was a wonderful restorative, and her roommate was no longer brownie-worthy.

"Samantha," he called out. "Are you in the kitchen? I smell something awfully good. What are you making?"

"I'm baking brownies."

He entered the room, his grin full of anticipation. "For dessert tonight?"

She shook her head. "No. They're for me."

"Oh. I see." But his perplexed, disappointed expression said he didn't. "We need to talk, Samantha. Do you have a few minutes?"

She shrugged. "I guess." A nervous flutter began in the pit of her stomach. Jack wore his business face, so Samantha knew this was going to be more than a friendly chat about his workday.

"Let's go into the living room. I think we'll be more comfortable in there," he suggested.

Uh-oh. The seriousness of the impending conversation just went up a notch. Though she hated leaving the brownies, Samantha followed Jack, seating herself on the red suede chair, and waited for the bomb to drop.

"I've spent most of today thinking about our situation."

"What situation is that?" she asked, feigning ignorance.

"You and me. What happened between us."

Samantha sighed. "You are making way too much of what happened, Jack. I told you—as far as I'm concerned it was a no-strings-attached mistake. Let's just drop it and move on."

"As much as I'd like to do that, I can't. Our night together has changed everything."

She scrunched her forehead. "But why? Don't you still want to be friends?" A feeling of panic rushed through her.

"Of course I do," he said, running impatient fingers through his dark hair. "You're very important to me." She breathed a sigh of relief, until he added, "Which is why I've come to a decision."

"A decision?"

"I'm moving out."

"What?" Her eyes widened. "I can't believe I'm hearing this."

"There's an empty apartment across the hall. I've decided to move into it."

"But, Jack, this is *your* apartment. You shouldn't be the one moving out. That should be me."

"I've made up my mind, so there's no use trying to talk me out of it."

"But why? That's crazy! I don't understand."

He shook his head. "I've already thought this through. Since I own this building, it won't be a hardship or any added expense for me to move."

"But what about the income you'll lose by not renting out the other apartment?"

"I can sustain it. And I'll continue paying the utilities and expenses on this one, too."

She shook her head adamantly. "I can't let you do that. It wouldn't be fair. The only reason I agreed to live here rent-free was because I was cooking and cleaning for you. If I'm not contributing, I can't stay here."

But where would she go?

Her options were few. Moving back home would be the same as admitting defeat. Patty's lifestyle was too unconventional to contemplate, so she wouldn't be a good choice for a roommate. And without a fabulous paying full-time job, she'd end up on the street in no time. New York City was nothing if not expensive.

"Yes, you can. What happened was my fault, and I take full responsibility for everything. And the fact that I can't move beyond it is also my failing. If you

want to make a contribution, you can continue helping me with the ads and whatever else the firm may
need you to do."

Tears filled her eyes. "Jack, please don't do this.
We're friends—we can work things out. We always
have before." She was devastated. It felt her heart
was being ripped from her chest.

"The time apart will do us both good. You'll see.
You can walk around here buck-naked, have your
girlfriends over whenever you want and you won't
have to listen to me complain. The separation will
give us time to salvage our rapidly deteriorating relationship."

"Do you really think things are that bad between
us? I know we've hit a few bumps in the road, but—"

Good grief! It felt like she were getting a divorce.
And she wasn't even married!

"I'll be living right across the hall. If you need
anything, you know where to find me. But we won't
be in each other's pockets. We'll have time apart to
adjust to what happened. Hopefully, things will
eventually return to normal."

"Normal is highly overrated. I like my life in up-
heaval. I'm not sure I know how to live it any other
way."

His sad smile touched her heart. She knew this
had been a difficult decision for him; a stupid one,
but still difficult.

"Since I'll be moving out tomorrow, you might want to reconsider sharing your brownies with me. You know how much I love them."

She shook her head. "Forget it. It's time you learned what life without me is going to be like. And I don't think you're going to like it one bit."

JACK MIGHT NOT have liked living apart from Samantha, but Samantha absolutely hated it. For a woman who had never put demands on him, except for the occasional "honey-do" project, like painting a cabinet or repairing a clogged drain, she was still at a loss to understand why he'd moved out.

It was true things had gotten slightly uncomfortable after the *episode,* which is how she now thought of that fateful night at the motel, but they would have learned to adjust and go on. It certainly wasn't the end of the world, as Jack made it out to be.

It had been almost two weeks since he'd made the decision to leave, and though she saw him almost every day, it wasn't the same. Their conversations were stilted. The camaraderie they'd once shared had been replaced by wariness on his part.

Though Samantha had to admit that from a purely sexual standpoint it was easier not having to see Jack in the flesh, so to speak, his absence hadn't lessened the frequency of her erotic dreams. They'd even gotten more intense. So had her need to talk to him about nothing and everything, which is why she'd gotten rather inventive at finding reasons to visit him at his apartment.

Checking her watch, Samantha figured Jack would be home from work by now. He rarely stayed at the office later than six. She picked up the brownies she'd baked, glanced in the mirror to make sure she didn't have leftover salad greens stuck in her teeth, and headed across the hall.

Knocking on the door, Samantha waited for him to answer. She thought she heard voices. Perhaps he was on the speakerphone with a client, or had his TV up too loud.

When the door finally opened it wasn't Jack who answered, but an attractive twenty-something redhead with a fabulous figure and a luminous smile. Great teeth, too. Samantha, who had a slight overbite, hated her on sight.

"May I help you?" she asked with a pleasant smile.

Dumbstruck for a moment, Samantha finally found her voice. "Hi! I'm Samantha from across the hall. I've baked brownies for Jack—they're his favorite." She thrust the aluminum pan at the woman, who seemed startled at first, but then grateful.

"Thanks. I'm Amanda Peters. I'm cooking dinner for Jack tonight and these brownies will be just perfect for dessert. Would you like to come in? Jack's in the shower, but he should be done soon."

Feeling her cheeks heat at the proprietary nature of the remark, Samantha shook her head. "No thanks. I've got to get back to my dinner." It was a lie, pure and simple, but there was no way she was going to watch Jack and his latest bimbo coo at each other. "Just tell Jack I said hi." She turned on her heel and beat a hasty retreat to her apartment, closing the door behind her and leaning heavily against it.

Jack had a new girlfriend—one he hadn't told her about. They used to share everything, and it hurt thinking that he'd kept secrets from her.

Admit it, Samantha! What really hurts is that Jack is making love to another woman, sharing his life, but not with you.

"I don't care!" she told herself, heading straight for the kitchen and the quart of chocolate ice cream that awaited her there. "We're just friends. Nothing's changed," she told her refrigerator.

But it had.

Jack had changed.

Samantha was miserable.

And life as she now knew it sucked.

DRAGGING HER weary body out of bed, Samantha answered the doorbell the following morning to find the object of her sleepless night standing outside her door. Her heart raced at the sight of him, but she quickly issued a cease and desist order. After all, it was just Jack.

"Good morning. Hope I didn't wake you," he said, looking very handsome in a navy wool sport coat and gray slacks.

She glanced bleary-eyed at the wall clock, which made her cringe. It was only seven-thirty. "I was sleeping, until you rang the bell. Don't you have a key?"

"I wanted to drop off your pan. Thanks for the brownies. They were great." He handed her the pan.

"You're welcome." *NOT!* "I met your new girl-friend."

"How'd you like her? Amanda's a friend of Tom Adler's."

The memory of the perfectly coiffed, impeccably designer-dressed Amanda Peters made Samantha slightly nauseous. At the moment, she was standing in the hallway of the apartment dressed in a pair of blue flannel pajamas decorated with white sheep, which had seemed adorable when she'd purchased them, but now felt pathetic. Couple that with her un-ruly mane of hair, and she looked pretty damn sad—a disaster, really.

"She seemed nice," she finally said when he cleared his throat. "Do you want to come in? I'll put on a pot of coffee."

He shook his head. "Can't. I've got an appoint-ment to show houses at nine, and I've got to pull lis-tings before the clients show up."

"Oh." Could she feel any more miserable or pathetic?

"How're you doing? Have you adjusted to our new living arrangement?"

She forced a smile. "I don't know why I ever thought having a roommate was such a great idea. It's been wonderful having all this space and freedom these past two weeks."

Disappointment flashed in his eyes, and Samantha wished she'd just kept her mouth shut. It was a big lie anyway. "Are we still going to your parents' house for Thanksgiving?" he asked, a look of uncertainty on his face. "I wasn't sure if you'd changed your mind."

"Of course we're going, just like every year. Mom called the other night to confirm, and I told her we'd be there."

"Good. And I'll be sure to rent a more reliable car this time."

Ignoring the reference to the *episode,* she asked, "Will you visit your parents this time? For what it's worth, I think you should."

"Probably. It's a holiday, after all. But to be honest, I'm not looking forward to it. I have a feeling it's going to be very uncomfortable for all of us."

"Speaking of being uncomfortable, I don't want my family to know about what happened between us, or the fact that we're now living apart. It would only create confusion." And she was confused enough as it was. Having to explain what had occurred to someone else would be impossible. She barely understood it herself.

"I totally agree. It's no one else's business." He shoved his hands in his coat pockets. "Well, I guess I'd better get going."

"Okay. See you later," she said, out of habit, and Jack got a funny look on his face.

"I have a date tonight, so you probably won't."

Samantha felt her cheeks warm. "I meant—see you around. Bye." She practically shoved the door in his face so he wouldn't see the tears running down her cheeks.

"Damn you, Jack! Why did you have to go and ruin everything?"

Damn you, Samantha! Why did you have to go and fall in love with your best friend?

JACK HATED doing laundry. But now that he was no longer living with Samantha, the dreaded chore had fallen to him. Tuesday evening found him standing morosely in front of the dryer in their basement laundry room.

The wet clothes he held were making his shirt soggy. Opening the dryer door, he shoved the washed clothes into the plastic basket, only to yank them out again. "Damn!"

The dryer was full of female clothing. He had just hooked his finger around a pair of black lace panties when the door opened and Samantha walked in, looking quite indignant.

"What are you doing here?"

"Laundry."

"And why are you touching my underpants?"

His eyes widened as he studied the provocative panties. "These are yours?" He smiled. "Very pretty. I didn't think you went for—"

She reached out and grabbed them out of his hand. "I'll empty the dryer and be on my way." She bent over to pull the garments from the dryer, affording Jack an excellent view of her tight, round bottom.

"Take your time." Was that a thong peeking out of her waistband? He swallowed.

She gazed over her shoulder and straightened. "What are you looking at?" But the furious expression on her face told him she knew and remembered, too.

"I thought you sent your clothes out to be laundered," she stated.

"I did at first, but it's gotten too expensive."

"Maybe your new girlfriend will do your laundry for you."

He grinned. "I can think of better uses for Amanda when she's with me."

Samantha's face flamed and her blue eyes blazed. "Well, I won't keep you. Sorry you had to wait for the dryer." She hefted her basket and began to walk away.

Jack suddenly felt stupid and sorry for the comment he'd made. "Samantha, wait!"

She ground to a halt and turned. "Did I forget something?"

He shook his head. "Would you like to go and grab a pizza? I haven't eaten yet, and—"

"No thanks, Jack. I've got things to do, like fold my laundry." She escaped out the door before he could protest.

Dammit, Turner! You're a goddamn fool!

CHAPTER TEN

THE WEEKS LEADING UP to Thanksgiving continued without incident. Jack was still dating Amanda, Samantha was still feeling miserable about it, and the weather had turned seasonably cold.

The day before Thanksgiving, Samantha and Jack arrived at her parents' farm a little after one. Jack parked the car, mumbled something about looking for Ross and then disappeared, while Samantha dragged her overnight bag up to the house to surprise her mother.

She needed to talk to someone. She and Jack hadn't spoken more than a handful of words on the way up.

A fractured heart wasn't much fun. Though Samantha had gone that route before with The Bastard, this time it was different. This time the hurt went much deeper. She was positive her heart had split into a thousand tiny jigsaw pieces, but the pieces no longer fit together as they should. She was disjointed, at loose ends—restless, yearning, needy—and she didn't dare voice aloud what, or rather *who*, she needed.

The voice inside her heart told her she was in love with Jack; the voice inside her head told her to shut up and get over it.

Samantha entered the house as quietly as she could, being careful not to bang the screen door behind her, and was immediately assaulted by the scents of nutmeg and cinnamon. Following her nose, she found her mother at her usual place in the kitchen, next to the stove. "Hi, Mom! I'm home."

Lilly turned and her face lit with surprise. "Samantha! I wasn't expecting you this early." She glanced over her daughter's shoulder. "But where's Jack? Don't tell me he didn't come with you?"

"Jack's outside looking for Ross. And then he plans to drive over to see his parents. He'll be here eventually."

Content with the explanation, Lilly went back to the pot of cranberry sauce she was cooking. Once she was satisfied that the mixture had thickened enough, she turned off the stove and faced her daughter again.

"Let's sit and have a cup of tea. I'm pooped from all this cooking. Lord, but it gets harder every year to put on these big meals."

"But they're always so delicious, Mom. I can't wait to taste your stuffing again. Nobody makes turkey stuffing the way you do."

Pleased by the compliment, Lilly placed two cups of hot tea on the table, then sat, heaving the weary sigh of someone who'd been on her feet since early morning. "So tell me what's been going on. I sense you and Jack are at odds with each other. Am I right?"

Alarm bells went off in Samantha's head. Her mother was too astute for her own good. "No," she said quickly. "Why do you ask?"

"You seemed distracted the last time we spoke on the phone, sort of down. Do you need to talk to me about anything? I'm a good listener."

Here was her chance to tell her mother everything, but Samantha couldn't. She wasn't ready to face her family's disappointment yet. "You know how it is between me and Jack, Mom. We argue, and then we make up. It's no big deal."

"Well, dear, I know from living with your father that men can be hardheaded, and I'm sure Jack is no exception. I just hope whatever is between you two won't spoil the holiday. Jack has a good heart, but I'm sure his unorthodox upbringing has taken its toll."

"Jack's stubborn, that's all." He hadn't given an inch regarding their present living arrangement, though she'd hinted a few times that she wasn't enjoying her solitude. In fact, rather than strengthen their relationship, as he'd originally thought, it had only served to make things worse.

Samantha wondered if he had used what had happened between them to suit his own purpose. After all, six years was a long time to live together if you weren't married. Perhaps he'd grown tired of her. He certainly didn't seem sad or upset that they no longer hung out together or shared their lives. She, on the other hand, had not adjusted at all, which made her borderline pathetic.

JACK DROVE DOWN the narrow dirt road leading to Silver Lake and parked near the water's edge. It was a clear, cold day. A flock of Canada geese circled overhead, then landed on the surface of the water, taking a respite from their journey south to warmer climes.

As a kid, he'd sought refuge at the lake numerous times to escape the screaming matches between his parents. Today he needed a comforting, familiar place to sort out his thoughts and feelings, about them, and most especially about Samantha.

Samantha still occupied the majority of his thoughts. He missed her like crazy—missed laughing with her, seeing her and eating dinner with her every night. There hadn't been a day since he'd left that he hadn't thought about calling her or dropping by their...*her* apartment.

They continued to run into each other in the hallway several times a week but when they did they spoke of mundane things like the weather or his new business—a business he might not have started if it hadn't been for her.

She'd asked for his help on a few occasions. Once the garbage disposal had gotten stuck, and another time she'd found a mouse beneath her bed. The memory of that night still made him smile.

"Dammit, Samantha!" Jack shook his head and heaved a dispirited sigh. There had to be a way to fix things; he just hadn't figured it out yet. But he was determined to keep Samantha in his life. She meant too much to him to allow this estrangement to continue.

He was afraid—afraid of losing his best friend, afraid that he would never look at her in the same way again…as just a friend. Why had everything gotten so damn complicated? Why couldn't he forget the night they'd made love and move on? It seemed she had.

Jack had plenty of questions, but no answers. That seemed to be true in other parts of his life as well.

At the moment, he had to deal with the pressing matter of Martin and Charlotte Turner. He'd procrastinated long enough. What would he say to them? He hadn't spoken to his mother in months, and his father in a lot longer than that.

He knew it was time, though the idea of driving into the lake and forgetting the whole thing was very tempting.

"IT SURE IS GOOD to see you again, Princess. I've missed you."

"Thanks, Dad! It's good to be home," Samantha said, and it was true. Home gave her a sense of peace and contentment and lightened the weight of her problems like no place else on earth, if only momentarily. "I've missed sitting on the porch with you. We haven't had a good chat in a long while, have we?"

They rocked the front porch swing in unison, staring up at the diamond-studded night sky.

"Weather's getting a bit nippy for porch sitting, don't you think? Shouldn't you put on something warmer? I'd hate for you to catch a chill."

Samantha was numb to the core, but she wasn't about to admit that to her worrywart father. "I'm fine. This jacket is down and very warm."

He didn't look convinced. "You're sure? I don't want my baby girl to catch cold."

"So, how are things going?" Samantha asked to change the subject. "Are you and Lucas getting along?" There'd been a time when her father and brother had been at odds with each other. Lucas was the opinionated sort who thought he knew everything there was to know about apples. Of course, that didn't set well with her father, the utmost authority on apples and just about everything else. Disagreeing with Fred Brady was like talking to a brick wall. The man had turned passive-aggressive into an art form.

"Me and Lucas are too much alike to ever have a smooth sail, I guess, but we do fine. I've been giving him a lot more responsibility in running the farm, and he's listening to direction for a change. The orchard will be his one of these days—Ross has no interest in apple farming—so I figure he needs to learn, just like I learned from my dad."

"That makes sense," Samantha agreed. "And speaking of Ross…"

Fred shook his head. "Your brother doesn't have the heart for farming. Ross needs to find his own way. No one else can do it for him. He's unhappy, though he does his best to hide it from everyone." He turned to gaze into his daughter's face. "And what about you, Samantha? Are you happy in New York City? You know you're always welcome to move back home, if you're not. I worry about you living in that cesspool."

"I'm still enjoying the city, Dad, though I'm worried my book won't sell." She paused. "And—"

"And what?"

Thinking better of what she was about to admit—that she and Jack were having problems—she shook her head. "Oh nothing. Sometimes I just wish for things that are too impractical." *Like a baby, a big fat book contract, and... Jack.*

"There's nothing wrong with wishing and hoping. If folks didn't have dreams and aspirations this country wouldn't be what it is."

"That's true. But sometimes I dream too much. There's such a thing as practicality. I don't think I have enough of that."

Her dad smiled, patting her knee. "Princess, one of these days when you least expect it life's going to intrude, kick the rug right out from under you and knock you right on your behind. It happens to everyone. So for now, be content to be a dreamer. There's plenty of time for reality."

"But I'm thirty-one, Dad, and I've done nothing productive with my life. I feel like such a loser sometimes."

"Who says you haven't done anything productive? How many people can say they've written a book? That's quite an accomplishment, young lady." For a man who'd been dead-set against her moving to New York to pursue a writing career, that was quite an admission.

"But what if no one buys it?"

"They will."

"How can you be so sure? I've got enough rejection letters to wallpaper my bathroom."

He smiled and patted her knee. "Because I know

you, Samantha. You always achieve what you set out to do. It's part of your nature. You have your mom to thank for that. Lilly can be damn stubborn at times."

Samantha knew that to be true. It had been her mother who'd convinced Fred to let his youngest child spread her wings and do her own thing. "I'm so glad you and Mom are my parents. You guys are the best." She leaned over and kissed his grizzled cheek.

Wrapping his arm about her, her father said, "We'll always be proud of you, Princess. Your mother and I know that you'll never do anything to hurt this family. You're too sensible, levelheaded and kind to do otherwise. You've always been our shining star."

Samantha swallowed, wondering if she'd ever be able to live up to her Dad's expectations. They were lofty, and at the moment, she was down about as far as a person could be.

CHAPTER ELEVEN

JACK PULLED UP to his parents' house on Sycamore Lane and was surprised to find the lawn neatly mowed and yellow and purple pansies blooming in red clay pots on the front porch steps. He had to check the numbers on the mailbox post just to make certain he hadn't made a mistake.

Nerves churned his gut as he made his way up the walk to the front door. He paused a moment, took a deep breath and then knocked. The door opened almost immediately to reveal his mother, looking relaxed and pretty in a yellow sweater and green wool slacks.

"Jack!" Charlotte squealed, tears filling her eyes. "It's so good to see you. I wasn't sure you'd come."

"Hello, Mom. I'm staying at the Bradys' for the Thanksgiving holiday. I thought I'd come over to visit for a bit. That is, if you're not too busy."

"Too busy for my own son? Don't be silly. Come in."

Jack remembered a time when his mother *had* been too busy for him. She'd been preoccupied with catering to her husband's many binges, or the cure-alls for his drinking. But noting the joy on her face, he opted to keep that resentment to himself. After all, the past could not be undone…any of it.

"Is Dad here?"

She nodded. "He's out back replacing the roof on the garden shed." Her smile grew wide. "He's a new man, Jack, a *changed* man. I know you won't believe it, but your father has given up the bottle for good this time."

"No, I don't believe it, but I'm happy if things are under control for the time being. I'm happy for *you*, Mom."

"Alcoholism is a sickness, Jack. I've learned a lot by going to Al-Anon and by reading various books on enabling addiction. I guess I was just as sick as Martin."

Jack didn't know how to respond, so he kept his mouth shut.

"How long will you be staying? I suppose you'll be eating Thanksgiving dinner with Samantha and her family? I see Lilly at church most Sundays and keep tabs on you that way."

"I'll be here for the weekend. I've started my own real estate company, so I've got to be back in the city for my Monday morning appointments."

His mother's eyes widened. "Aren't you the successful one? Are things going well?"

"I'm doing okay." He grew instantly suspicious. "Why do you ask? Do you need money?" He reached for his wallet as he'd done a hundred times before, but his mother stopped him, hurt flickering in her eyes.

"No, we don't need your money. Martin is working at Home Depot and I'm a substitute teacher, so we're making ends meet."

Jack was unable to hide his surprise, but if his mother noticed, she didn't comment.

"Do you want to come say hello to your father? I know things haven't been good between you two, but I'm hoping things will be different now."

Charlotte looked so hopeful that Jack didn't have the heart to tell her she was wasting her life on a man who was never going to change. "I guess, but I can't stay long. The Bradys are expecting me."

His mother nodded, but looked upset. "I understand. Hopefully, when you come to visit next time you can stay longer."

Without committing or commenting, Jack followed his mother outside to where his dad was working on the shed. Martin was up on the ladder, nailing shingles onto the roof and singing at the top of his lungs. The first thing Jack noticed was that his father still had a great voice, but also that he had aged tremendously. His dark hair was completely white, and he was thinner and frailer than he'd remembered.

"Martin, come down here," Charlotte called out. "We have company."

The older man turned, his face lighting with joy at the sight of his son. "Jack, it's good to see you!"

Jack's palms began to sweat as he felt years of anxiety and dislike coming to the forefront, but he fought hard to maintain control of his emotions. "Hello, Dad. I see Mom's put you to work."

Martin Turner smiled. He'd been a handsome man in his youth, with aspirations of the stage, but the ravages of hard liquor had taken their toll, as evidenced by the bags under his eyes and the unhealthy pallor of his complexion.

"Charlotte finds plenty for me to do. Guess she figures if she keeps me busy I won't drink, and it's working. Haven't touched a drop in almost eight months."

Charlotte smiled proudly at her husband, who winked in return.

"That's great, Dad," Jack said, putting out his hand to shake his father's and feeling very uncomfortable when the man pulled him into an embrace. As a boy, he would have given anything for a hug from his dad, but Martin Turner hadn't been the demonstrative type.

"We've missed you, son. It's good to see you. You're looking fit as ever."

Jack noticed that his dad's eyes were clear. His

hands weren't shaking, and he seemed in control of his speech patterns; the usual slur that Martin acquired when he'd had too much to drink was missing. "You look good, too, Dad."

"Charlotte, do we have any iced tea?" his father asked. "Jack and I are going to sit on the patio a bit and get caught up. How does that sound, son?"

"I can't stay. I told Mom—"

"We won't keep you long, boy. I know this is hard for you, and I feel very sorry about what I've put your mother and you through all these years. You'll never know how sorry."

Charlotte glanced at her son with sadness in her eyes, then she hurried into the house to fetch the tea.

Martin gazed fondly at his wife's retreating figure. "I couldn't have gotten through these past months without the help of your mother, and AA. Both have been a godsend."

Jack didn't bother to hide his skepticism. "But you've had both at your disposal many times before. What makes you think this time will be different?"

His father shrugged. "I just do. Can't explain it, but I finally figured out that I was killing myself with the liquor and that if I didn't want to die, I needed to stop."

"Just like that?"

"Just like that. I know you're skeptical, son. Can't blame you for that."

"I won't deny it. I've heard this same story too many times before, had too many promises broken." Not to mention his heart. He didn't intend to make the same mistake twice. "I hope for Mom's sake that you're telling me the truth," Jack said. "She deserves better than what you've put her through."

"What I put you both through, you mean. I know I made your lives a living hell. I can't change the past, only make the present and future better. I hope you'll give me that chance. Will you?"

The question hung in the air for what seemed like an eternity. Jack wasn't sure how to answer. He'd traveled down this road too many times before, and always hit a dead end.

AFTER THE BIG holiday dinner of roast turkey, stuffing, yams and all the usual fixings, the men gathered in front of the television to watch football games, as they did every year, while the women cleared the table and washed the dishes. Samantha hadn't yet figured out why women were delegated to the role of housemaid while the men got to relax and enjoy the afternoon. Didn't seem quite fair to her, but that's the way it had always been and her mother wasn't about to change tradition now.

After the last dish was wiped and put away, she took the opportunity to steal a few minutes to herself and went outside to take a walk.

She and Jack had hardly said more than two sentences to each other since he'd returned from visiting his parents. But if anyone had noticed, they hadn't mentioned it, for which Samantha was grateful. The last person she wanted on her case was her mother.

Walking down the gravel path to the orchard, Samantha noticed how barren the trees appeared without their leaves and fruit. Come spring, the buds would burst again with life, but for now the trees were resting during the cold November days and nights.

"Samantha, wait up!"

Her heart quickened at the sound of a male voice, until she recognized it as her brother's. She couldn't help but be disappointed, not to mention curious, to find Ross heading in her direction.

"Hey, sis!" he called out. "What are you doing out here by your lonesome? Did you and Jack have a fight or something? You guys have been real quiet this trip."

She shrugged, hoping to stem her inquisitive brother's questions. "Jack and I see each other all the time. When I come home I like to visit with the family. I can talk to him anytime."

He seemed to buy her explanation. "Gotcha. Guess you two are always tripping over each other. Can't blame you for wanting a little space. Bet Jack feels the same way."

The statement hit her like a punch in the gut. "Did he say that?"

Ross shook his head. "No, but sometimes I get the feeling that he feels closed in. Not that he doesn't love having you for a roommate, don't get me wrong. I just think that it's kind of tough having a woman around when you're dating. You know…lack of privacy, that sort of thing. I doubt he brings many of his dates home."

"I usually make myself scarce when he does." Which wasn't quite the truth. She'd been around on a few occasions when Jack had brought his girl-friends home, and it'd been awkward for both of them when he'd made the introductions, and then dragged the flavor-of-the-week into his bedroom. Samantha always tried to ignore the sounds of plea-sure emanating from the next room, but the walls were thin and she had a natural curiosity. If she closed her eyes, she could pretend Jack was making love to her, but then she'd awaken to the reality that she and Jack didn't have that kind of a relationship and never would.

"I guess you could be right," she admitted finally.

"Don't you feel weird when the shoe's on the other foot?" Ross asked.

"I don't date that much. And when I do, we usu-ally go out."

"How come you're not dating? A pretty woman

like you, all those men in the Big Apple, and you don't date? Are they blind or just stupid?"

Samantha smiled. Ross mostly irritated her, but there were times, like now, when she found him very sweet. "Thanks for the vote of confidence. How come you're not inside with Ellen? She might feel awkward being alone with Mom."

"Are you kidding? They're like old friends. I'm sure they don't even miss me."

"So everything's fine with you two?"

"Sure. Why do you ask?"

"No reason. Just a feeling I had."

"I admit I get bored—there's not much going around here. Jack invited me to New York. I'm thinking about it. Maybe I'll visit and get my Christmas shopping done while I'm there."

Panic filled her voice. "But you can't! I mean— we don't have the room, and things are in chaos right now." Ross's brows drew together in confusion. "You know Jack's just started a new business and I'm trying to finish my book?" she went on to explain. "And with the holiday coming I think it would be too hectic." There was no way she could have her brother come for a visit. Not now.

Disappointment filled his eyes, and she felt like the worst sister in the world. It was obvious he'd been seeking a place of refuge, to escape. From what, she wasn't certain.

"It was just an idea. I don't want to intrude if I'm not welcome."

"It's not that, Ross. It's just…bad timing."

"Sure. Fine. Whatever. I wasn't inviting myself. Jack's the one who issued the invitation." He turned on his heel and stalked off, leaving Samantha alone to ponder the mess her life had become, and all because of one magical night.

ROSS CONTINUED on to the pond and seated himself on the wooden bench. His life had been one big screw-up ever since he'd broken his leg and ruined his promising football career.

His restlessness was damaging his relationship with Ellen, a woman he respected and cared about. They'd met while he'd been recuperating in the hospital. She'd been visiting the patients on the orthopedic ward. Her sunny disposition and kindness had attracted him from the first moment they met, and as soon as he'd been released, he'd asked her out.

At the time, he'd been looking for a woman to settle down and start a family with. He thought he wanted the simple life, the life he'd grown up with, and Ellen fit the bill to a tee.

But he missed the excitement of travel, of being in the limelight and participating in something bold and exciting. Playing in the NFL had been his boyhood dream and something he had worked hard all his life to achieve.

Now he was back to being just Ross Brady from Rhinebeck again—part-time high school football coach, part-time apple farmer, part-time boyfriend and full-time fool.

What the hell was he going to do with his life?

CHAPTER TWELVE

"I CAN'T BELIEVE you have so many people on your Christmas list," Samantha told Patty one Saturday afternoon in mid-December. They were shopping at Bloomingdale's and she had only purchased one measly gift for her dad, while Patty's bags were overflowing with merchandise.

This was going to be a meager Christmas, no doubt about that. She had no extra money to spend on gifts, and what money she'd been earning from freelancing and writing ads for Jack's company wouldn't be enough to allow for extravagances. She supposed she could give everyone gift certificates from Starbucks with her employee discount, but that didn't really appeal.

"How can you afford to buy all those presents?" Samantha asked. "You must have spent a small fortune."

Hefting her shopping bag to a more comfortable position, Patty smiled. "These are mostly for my male friends. I like to get them each a little something to remember me by."

"Like what? Thongs? Flavored condoms?" She grinned at her friend's smug expression, but then was suddenly overtaken with a bout of nausea, a panicked look crossing her face. "My lunch is starting to back up. I need to get to the restroom before I barf all over Bloomingdale's."

"I doubt anyone would be too thrilled about that, including me. Go. I'm going to check out the cosmetic counter while you heave ho. I'm sorry you're not feeling well. Do you think it was the quiche?"

Samantha paled and made a frantic beeline for the ladies' room, where she promptly gave up her lunch, three times over.

Beads of perspiration erupted across her forehead, and she rested her head against the cool wall of the metal bathroom stall, waiting for the nausea and light-headedness to subside. After the worst was over, she rinsed her mouth with the small bottle of Scope she always carried in her purse, reapplied her lipstick and went in search of her friend.

Patty was at the Estée Lauder counter, testing the latest fragrances. "I feel so much better. I guess it must have been something I ate," Samantha told her. Though she couldn't understand why she'd become ill. She had an ironclad stomach and rarely got sick from anything she ate. In fact, Jack used to tease her about it, back in the day when he was still teasing her.

Samantha saw Jack almost every day in one fashion or another, but it wasn't the same as before. For instance, they always went Christmas shopping together, but that wasn't going to happen this year. When she'd suggested that very thing and tried to plan a day when they could go, he'd claimed he was too busy with work and would do his shopping online.

At least he wasn't dating Miss Perfect anymore. Amanda Peters had fallen by the wayside like so many others—herself included—and Jack was unentangled at the moment, which almost made it more frustrating because Samantha figured he now had the time to tangle with her.

"What do you think of this fragrance?" Patty held out her wrist so Samantha could sniff, but she made a face at the obnoxious odor.

"The smell of that perfume makes me want to heave again. Are you about done?"

Patty's eyes filled with suspicion, as she looked Samantha over from top to bottom. "Are you sure there isn't more to this sickness of yours than you think, Samantha? You've been looking a little peaked lately."

"What do you mean, more? I probably have the flu or something. What else could it be?"

Not one to beat around the bush, Patty said, "Do you think you might be pregnant?"

Mouth agape, she stared at Patty as if she'd lost her mind. "Pregnant? Are you kidding? The doctor said it would be almost impossible for me to conceive because of my ovary problem. How could I be pregnant?"

"Well, the timing would be about right. And *almost* isn't a definite. And if I recall correctly, you and—"

Samantha grabbed her friend's arm. "Don't say what you're thinking! *That* would be a total disaster."

Ohmigod! What if it's true? What if I'm pregnant with Jack's child?

Her last period had been in September. But she'd figured that was because she'd been under a great deal of stress lately.

"No matter how unpalatable the thought, you have to consider the possibility. After all, you did have sex with the man."

Two old ladies who were shopping nearby turned to look at Samantha disapprovingly. She blushed an unbecoming shade of scarlet. "*Sssh!* I don't want the whole world to know my business. Let's discuss this somewhere more private." Not that she wanted to even acknowledge the possibility.

"There's a coffee shop across the street. We'll go

there," Patty suggested, and Samantha followed behind her, like a woman on the way to an execution, which seemed apt, because if Patty were correct and Samantha were pregnant, she was as good as dead.

Seated at a table in the small café, she waited while Patty ordered two coffees, then said, "This would be the worst thing that could ever happen to me and Jack, Patty. He would never forgive me if he knew I was carrying his child. He doesn't want children. He's made that point clear time and time again."

"Well, then he should have used a condom before having sex with you. You reap what you sow, as the saying goes. You weren't the only one who was irresponsible. Jack deserves half the blame."

"Thanks. I'll be sure to use that argument if your suspicion turns out to be correct."

"And why didn't you use a condom? Don't you carry them in your purse?"

Embarrassed, Samantha nodded. "Of course." It was the eternal optimist in her. "But we were drunk and protection was the farthest thing from our minds at the time. I know it's not a good excuse, but it's the only one I can come up with at the moment."

How many babies were conceived with similar pathetic excuses?

"How long has it been since you've had your last period?"

"September. I'm pretty sure about that. It's been at least three months. In all the turmoil, with Jack moving out and everything, I hadn't been keeping track. Guess I didn't want any reminders about how infertile I was."

Her friend smiled kindly. "Guess you're not that infertile after all. Well, don't worry. I know someone who can take care of your problem. He's an excellent physician, and very discreet."

Samantha looked aghast. "You mean an abortion?" When Patty nodded, she shook her head. "No! I would never do that, especially to Jack's child. If it's true that I'm pregnant, this baby could be an answer to my prayers. And I'd be having the baby of someone I care very deeply about, not some stranger's."

"Someone who obviously doesn't care very deeply about you," her friend retorted. "I'm not saying this to be mean, Samantha, but you can't possibly be entertaining the idea of having this child. There could be legal ramifications. Jack would most likely sue for joint custody, and he'd be well within his rights to do so."

"That's what I have you for, counselor. And I don't give a rat's ass. If I'm pregnant, then I'm going to consider it a gift from the Almighty and be grateful. Jack doesn't have to be responsible, financially or otherwise. This will be my child. In fact, if it does turn out that I'm pregnant, I'm not going to tell him. What's the point? He's made his feelings clear on the matter."

"As your attorney, I must counsel you that that would be very unwise. As I said, the legal ramifications could be considerable. But first things first," the ever-practical lawyer said. "We need to stop at the drugstore on the way home and purchase a pregnancy test, see if we even need to be having this conversation. After all, maybe it *was* food poisoning."

Staring into her coffee cup, Samantha didn't respond. Now that she'd accepted the possibility that she could be pregnant, she wanted it to be a reality.

ARMED WITH A home test, oodles of encouragement from Patty that everything would turn out okay and the knowledge that being pregnant was only a slim possibility, Samantha entered her apartment a short while later and headed straight for the bathroom, eager to get the ordeal over with. Hard to believe that this morning her biggest worry had been how to pay for Jack's Christmas present—if they were even exchanging gifts this year.

They'd always exchanged their presents the night before leaving for her family's farm, where they spent the Christmas holiday every year. It had become a tradition. She probably should have uninvited him, but that would have raised too many red flags with her family—not to mention with Jack.

Samantha didn't have a credit card and was often short of cash, just like this year, so she usually just baked Jack cookies or made fudge. One year she'd knitted him a scarf, which ended up lopsided and about six feet long, but he liked it anyway. He'd worn it to her parents' house, which was nothing short of endearing, though she hadn't seen it since and thought it was probably warming some homeless person's neck.

Entering the bathroom, she assembled the contents of the kit on the edge of the sink and seated herself on the toilet. And waited. But she was so nervous that nothing happened. And no matter how hard she squeezed, prayed and pushed, she couldn't make anything come out.

"I'll drink water," she said, knowing that sometimes talking to herself helped calm her nerves. So she drank five Dixie cups worth and waited again, singing all the stanzas she knew of "Turn the Beat Around." Still nothing.

"Dammit!" She took a deep breath. "Okay, just relax. You're too tense. Take deep breaths." Finally after a few minutes, which seemed like hours, she was able to produce the desired results and perform the test.

Her hand shook as she held the stick and waited.

Then her eyes widened as she watched the tip turn from blue to pink, indicating she was...

"Pregnant! I'm pregnant!" Her heart started pounding loud in her ears, and all of a sudden she felt like she might throw up again. She jumped up and spun around, depositing whatever was left in her stomach into the toilet bowl.

Yep. I'm definitely pregnant.

As if in a trance, Samantha walked into her bedroom and plopped down on the bed, hardly able to believe that she, Samantha Brady of infertility fame, was going to have a child—a flesh and blood baby to call her very own.

It was nothing short of a miracle.

"Ohmigod!" She leaned back against the pillows and closed her eyes as the import of what had just occurred hit her with the force of a sledgehammer. Samantha knew very little about caring for a small child. She'd done some babysitting, but that was it. And as far as she knew, babies didn't come with instruction manuals.

Would she be able to support herself and a child adequately enough? That was her biggest concern. She'd be a single mother, alone and independent for the first time in her life. And it scared the hell out of her. But she knew she could do it. She could do anything once she set her mind to it, her father was right about that. She'd just have to find more freelancing jobs, increase her hours at Starbucks and sell her book.

Okay, so she had a plan. But she still didn't know what to do about Jack. She swallowed hard. If he found out she was pregnant with his child, he would never forgive her, not in a million years. He would think she'd gotten pregnant on purpose. He would twist everything in his mind, and she would come out the seducer, the manipulative, evil woman who had stopped at nothing to get herself with child.

After all, Jack was dead-set against her having a baby and knew how much she wanted one. But how could she keep such an important event from him? Jack had a right to know he was going to be a father.

Shit. I am in so much trouble.

Not to mention that she had no idea what she would tell her parents, especially her dad, who thought she could do no wrong. He would not be thrilled to find that his little princess had fallen off her throne. And with no Prince Charming in sight to catch her!

Samantha would be seeing her mom and dad over Christmas, along with Jack, but she wouldn't confide her secret then. No sense ruining everyone's holiday. She'd just wait to tell them in the New Year…and dread the weeks leading up to it.

Now that she'd made the difficult decision not to tell anyone about the baby, Samantha wondered how she was going to keep such a secret all to herself. Jack was the one person she'd always confided in— the one with whom she shared her most intimate thoughts and dreams. And he was the one person she wouldn't be able to tell…at least, not right now. Perhaps she could wait awhile, and then break the news to him gently.

Yeah, like that's going to put him in a better frame of mind!

Glancing down at her stomach, Samantha was relieved to find she wasn't showing yet. She might look a bit pudgy, but not three months pregnant. And she could chalk up the extra weight to too many brownies.

She and Patty had been invited to Jack's company Christmas party, and she needed to pretend that everything was normal, business as usual, par for the course.

Only her world had just been turned topsy-turvy. She was going to have a baby. She was going to be a mother. She was going to be alone. She was going to—

Drive herself insane.

"I can do this!" she told herself with more confidence than she felt. "I can make it all happen just like I've always dreamed."

So why am I so scared?

CHAPTER THIRTEEN

JACK WATCHED Samantha across the room and at that moment, no one else existed for him. She was dressed fittingly for a Christmas party in a red knit jersey dress and looked positively radiant.

Compared to Patty, who was standing next to her and wore gobs of makeup to accentuate her features, Samantha wore very little enhancement and outshone every other woman in the room. Her beauty came from within. He could see it in her smile, the brilliance of her sparkling blue eyes and the luster of her hair. She was a naturally beautiful woman.

She smiled and waved when she saw him, and Jack's heart gave a little twitch as he crossed the room to greet her and her friend. "Hello, ladies. You're both looking lovely this evening. Thanks for coming to our little soiree."

"Thanks for the invitation," Samantha said.

"Yes, thanks." Then Patty added, "I hope you don't think I'm being rude, Jack, but would you mind pointing me in the direction of the food? I haven't eaten a thing all day and I'm starving."

Knowing Patty's penchant for devouring whatever was in her midst, be that men or food, Jack pointed to the long buffet table at the back of the room. "Help yourself."

"Are you coming, Samantha?" Patty asked, rather pointedly, and Samantha shook her head.

"No. I'm not hungry. I ate before we came. I'll grab something later, but you go ahead."

"Suit yourself," the woman said before walking away, and Jack was relieved to have Samantha all to himself, which seemed totally illogical since he'd purposely distanced himself from her for weeks.

But dammit! He missed her.

"You look very pretty tonight. There's something different about you. Is that a new dress?"

Samantha appeared discomfited by the question and shook her head emphatically. "No. This is the same dress I wore last year."

He nodded, still trying to figure out what was different about her. "So, how have you been?"

"Fine."

"I heard from one of the tenants in our building that you'd gotten sick at Bloomingdale's. Apparently Mrs. Castor—you know, from 3B—had gone into the ladies' room and overheard someone in the stall throwing up, then you walked out and she recognized you."

Color filled her cheeks. "It was nothing, just a touch of food poisoning. I'm fine now."

"That's good. Are you sure you don't want something to eat? Tom ordered enough food to feed a small country. And I promise it won't make you sick."

Samantha's gaze flitted around the room. "Is Tom here? I'd like to meet him. We've spoken on the phone a few times, but I've yet to meet him in person. He has a wonderful phone presence. It's no wonder he sells so well."

Feeling that old panic rush through him, Jack wondered if Samantha would find Tom attractive and want to date him. There was no doubt in Jack's mind that his partner would think she was a knockout.

Glancing around the room, Jack spotted Tom by the bank of windows, talking to Patty, who hadn't wasted any time in finding the most eligible bachelor at the party. "He's over there by the window. I'll introduce you, if you like."

Following Jack's gaze, Samantha nodded. "He's very handsome. How come you never tried to set us up?"

"Is he?" Jack feigned innocence and shrugged. "Tom didn't seem your type. He's too smooth, too sophisticated."

She stiffened, and it was clear that he'd insulted

her without meaning to. "And what am I? Some country bumpkin?"

"No, not at all. But you're sweet and a bit naive, so I thought—"

"Naive? Well, isn't that judgmental of you? I'll have you know I'm quite worldly. I may not have grown up in the big city, but I've adapted quite well. I can travel on the subway all by myself, and I don't hang out in the park at night."

Her sarcasm was sharp. "There's no need to get bent out of shape. The truth is, Tom's a womanizer and I didn't want him hitting on you and breaking your heart."

"Like you've never done that, I suppose?"

Hurt filled her eyes, but he refused to acknowledge or respond to the question. "Come on. If you're so insistent on meeting Tom Adler I'll introduce you. But it looks like your friend's gotten there first."

Samantha smiled tightly. "We'll see about that."

Taking her hand, Jack led her to where the chatting couple was standing. He made the introductions, then gritted his teeth when Tom said, "I've heard so much about you, Samantha, only I'd been led to believe by our devious friend here that you were a man."

Patty burst out laughing, but Samantha didn't find the comment the least bit amusing.

"What?" Her eyes widened. "Jack told you I was a man?"

"Well, not in so many words, but he didn't correct my false assumption that his roommate was male. I was quite shocked when he told me the truth. Guess Jack wanted to keep you all to himself. Can't blame him for that."

Tom winked at Samantha, and Jack shot him a lethal look. "Samantha's her own woman. She doesn't belong to anyone."

"That's right. I'm a free agent. Footloose and fancy-free."

"So am I," Patty offered, eyes twinkling as she directed her question at Tom. "Perhaps you'd like to engage in a little *ménage à trois?*" She grinned at Samantha's horrified expression.

"That might be your style, Patty," Jack said, eyes narrowing, "but it's not Samantha's."

"How would you know what Samantha's style is? You're not living together anymore. For all you know she could be banging the entire New York Giants football team and enjoying the hell out of it."

"Patty!" Samantha said, eyes wide and filled with disbelief. "Stop saying such outrageous things."

Tom laughed. "I'd already figured that Patty was brash and outspoken. Guess I wasn't far off the mark."

The redhead smiled and clutched his arm. "Too much woman for you, Tom?"

"On the contrary, counselor, you're just my type."

The two walked off, leaving Samantha and Jack staring after them.

"They deserve each other, if you ask me," Jack said, not bothering to hide his annoyance.

"Well, no one did. Just because Patty isn't your type doesn't mean other men don't find her attractive. And I could say the same for myself, too."

"Who says I don't find you attractive?"

She shrugged. "I think it's pretty obvious, don't you? We lived together for six years and there wasn't a spark between us until that night we got drunk. Then you took what was purely animal instinct and made it out to be something else, probably to further your own ego."

His lips thinned. "You don't know what you're talking about, so you should keep quiet."

"I'll say whatever I want, and you won't tell me differently, Jack Turner."

At this point, several of the guests had turned to look at the sparring couple glaring at each other like dueling swordsmen.

"Great. Now everyone will be talking about us. I hope you're happy. Some of these guests are my clients."

"So what? Why are you always so concerned about what everybody thinks? Is your reputation that precious to you?"

"What the hell is that supposed to mean?"

"It means I'm leaving. That's what it means."

"But you haven't eaten."

"No. But I've had my fill just the same. See you around, Jack." With that, she stalked off, looking indignant, regal and very determined to escape.

Even as he fumed, Jack felt a twinge of admiration for Samantha and he wondered, not for the first time, why he was fighting so hard to keep her out of his life when all he really wanted to do was kiss her.

TEARS STREAMING DOWN her face, Samantha bolted for the elevator as if the devil himself were on her heels. It was clear to her now as it had never been before that Jack would never see her as anything but sweet, naive Samantha Brady from Rhinebeck, New York—former classmate, former roommate, former lover, former, former, former...

Jack was embarrassed by her very existence. That's why he hadn't told his friend the truth about her. The ridiculous story he'd made up about Tom being a womanizer was a crock of— Samantha didn't need to be hit over the head with a two-by-four to figure out that she and Jack would never work as a couple. Hell, they didn't work as friends anymore.

In the taxi on the way home, she pressed her hands against her abdomen and was grateful that she'd decided not to tell Jack about his...*her* baby. Jack Turner wasn't a part of her life anymore. The sooner she quit mooning over a man she could never have, the sooner she could get on with her life.

And she wouldn't be alone, as she'd previously feared. She'd have a baby to love and nurture, a child to raise to adulthood, a person who would love her unconditionally for who she was and be content with that. A woman couldn't ask for more than that.

Patty was right about one thing: a woman didn't need a man in her life to make it or her complete. She only needed herself.

CHAPTER FOURTEEN

SAMANTHA SPENT the weeks leading up to Christmas finishing her manuscript and sending it off to several publishing houses. Now with a week left to go until the holiday, she was baking cookies to take home to her family.

Unable to muster up much holiday cheer, she had decided not to put up a tree or any other decorations this year. She'd just sent greeting cards to a few of her out-of-town friends and wrapped the presents she'd purchased—a tie for her dad, which he would most likely never wear, cologne for her mom and socks for Lucas and Ross.

As yet, she hadn't bought anything for Jack, and it was doubtful she would. His behavior at the office party hadn't put her in a very generous mood, and she was still put out with him. He'd phoned a few times and left messages, but she hadn't returned any of his calls. Samantha had done a lot of thinking and a whole lot of soul searching since that night, and she'd come to the conclusion that she needed to move on with a life that didn't include Jack, as difficult as that would be.

Peering through the oven's glass door, Samantha checked the latest batch of sugar cookie cutouts. She was about to prepare the icing when the phone rang.

"Hello, dear," her mother said when she answered, and Samantha felt mildly disappointed that it wasn't Jack, even though she'd promised herself she wouldn't care anymore.

Old habits die hard, especially with pathetic, pregnant, lovesick women.

Forcing a smile into her voice, she said, "Hey, Mom! Do you have the tree up and decorated? I can't wait to see it." Her parents always cut down at least a twelve-foot Douglas fir, even though her father usually ended up cutting several inches off the bottom to get it to fit in the living room.

"Oh, Samantha, it's so lovely. I think it's our prettiest one yet."

She smiled at her mom's traditional enthusiasm for each year's family tree. "My presents aren't very grand this year, so I hope you guys won't be too disappointed."

"Just having you home is present enough, dear, you know that. And having Jack here with us will make the holiday even more special. Is he looking forward to coming?"

"I suppose so. He hasn't really said."

"Are you and Jack still at odds, dear? I've been worried about you two."

It was a second chance to set the record straight, to tell her mother that she and Jack were no longer living together and that she would be having his baby come summer.

"Everything's fine, Mom. You shouldn't worry."

"Well, this is the season for forgiveness, so I hope you two have worked out whatever was bothering you at Thanksgiving. We're all looking forward to seeing you, especially Ross, whose boredom has grown to new heights. I do worry about that boy."

Tears filling her eyes, Samantha wanted more than anything to confide in her mother about Jack and the baby, but she knew she couldn't. Not yet. "I know we'll have a great time, Mom. We always do. And I wouldn't worry about Ross. He's a big boy. He'll figure things out eventually." There came a point in everyone's life when they had to grow up, whether or not they wanted to. That time had come for Samantha, and it would for Ross, too.

"I suppose," Lilly said, not sounding at all convinced. "I'm hoping to talk your father into going caroling this year. He's always such a grump about it."

"I don't think any of us enjoys standing out in the freezing cold and singing our hearts out for neighbors who would just as soon be watching television."

"Oh quit being so cynical. You sound just like Fred. You know the neighbors love it."

Samantha rolled her eyes, wondering what land of denial her mother was living in. Suddenly, a familiar odor assaulted her senses. "Oh no! My cookies are burning. I gotta go take them out of the oven, Mom."

"Okay, dear. Give Jack a kiss and hug from me. We'll see you in a few days."

Samantha hung up the phone, sighing deeply, then hurried to the stove. She'd have to tell her parents the truth about everything, sooner rather than later, and that would be difficult, on many levels.

Fred and Lilly would expect her to tell Jack about the baby. They would want her to do the proper, traditional thing and marry him—something Samantha had no intention of doing—which was why she'd been contemplating not telling them that the child was his. If she let them think the sperm donor was anonymous, she'd have a much easier time of avoiding complications. Of course, she'd also be lying.

No sooner had Samantha taken the cookies out of the oven when she was once again interrupted by a knock on the door.

"Good grief!" Wiping her hands on her jeans, she hurried to answer the insistent pounding. Flinging open the door, she was about to yell at whomever it was when she discovered Jack on the other side. He was smiling and holding a precious puppy. The dog had a big red bow tied around his neck and was licking Jack's hand fast and furiously. "Jack! I wasn't expecting you." Her heart skipped several beats, making her feel breathless. "And who is this adorable creature?"

"Merry Christmas, Samantha," he said, handing the puppy to her. "This is for you."

"But—" She stared into the black-and-white face of the Boston terrier puppy and her heart melted, as did any reservations she might have had about receiving a dog as a Christmas present. Samantha was a sucker for puppies, and Jack knew it.

"Well, aren't you the cutest little thing?" Her question was answered by an enthusiastic licking of her face.

"I think he likes you."

She held the dog out in front of her and looked him square in the eye. He was petite, pink-cheeked, and she was in love. "What's his name?"

"He doesn't have one yet. I just picked him up from the pet store this morning. I thought you should be the one to name him since he's yours."

Samantha stared long and hard at the puppy, and then cuddled it to her chest, where he nestled against her, seeking warmth. "I'm going to call him Jake— Jacob Brady. It's got a nice Irish ring to it, and he looks like a scrapper. Jake's a good name for a scrapper."

Jack reached out into the hall and produced a shopping bag full of puppy food and other pet supplies, as well as a metal crate for the puppy to sleep in. "The pet store guy recommended you use this at night and when you go out of the apartment. He said it'll make it easier to housebreak him."

"Thank you! I'm so thrilled. I don't know what to say. But I love this little guy already."

Was Jack expecting a thank-you kiss? Samantha hoped not, because she just couldn't put herself through that, not now.

Looking pleased and relieved, Jack set up the crate, while Samantha fetched food and water, then they put little Jake into the crate on top of a foam pad, where he promptly went to sleep. "Guess the poor little guy's a bit tired out," he said. "The cab ride from the pet store was a bit harrowing. He hated all the horn honking. I don't think Jake's a native New Yorker."

Gazing fondly at the puppy, then at Jack, Samantha did her best not to cry. Jack's thoughtfulness was one of the things she loved best about him.

"I don't have your Christmas gift yet. I'm sorry. We usually don't exchange until the night before we leave for my parents' house," she reminded him, hoping the explanation seemed plausible and feeling ashamed at her earlier pettiness.

"I know. But I figured you and Jake needed time

to get used to each other before we dragged him off somewhere strange."

So he was still planning to go. Samantha felt relieved and anxious, all at once. "That was smart thinking. It'll give us a chance to bond."

Jack sniffed the air, and his eyes lit. "You've been baking cookies, haven't you?"

"Come into the kitchen. I just pulled a batch of slightly burned cookies from the oven. I was going to toss them, but you can eat them instead. I know you're not picky."

He grinned, and her heart executed an Olympic-calibre flip. "I love your cookies, burned or not." He seated himself at the table, and Samantha set a plate of very brown sugar cookies in front of him. "These aren't frosted yet, so you'll have to tough it out."

Jack devoured three of the cookies in the space of just as many seconds. "Mmmm. Good. Are you making fudge this year, too? I love your fudge."

She nodded. "But not until right before we leave, or I'll eat it all."

He laughed. "I remember last year you—" And then he stopped. "Guess things are a bit different this year."

More than you'll ever know, Samantha was tempted to blurt. "How are things at work?" she asked to ease the discomfiting moment. "Are you still busy?"

Reaching for the glass of milk she'd just poured, he shook his head. "It's not as hectic as it was. Things have slowed a bit, but we expected that, what with the holidays and all. People don't have time to look at houses right now.

"How about you?" he asked. "Are you still working on your book?"

"Nope. I'm proud to say it's done and out."

"Congratulations! And I firmly believe that it's just a matter of time until it sells."

"At this point, I'm not holding my breath. If it happens, it happens." Though she'd been praying a lot. Selling her manuscript would be the answer to some of her financial concerns. Not that she expected to receive a million dollars for it, but anything was better than nothing, at this point. And knowing she had a book contract would offer a modicum of security. "I intend to keep submitting the book, and I'm also working on some new magazine articles."

"Really? That's great. What about?"

One was about unwed motherhood for the *Sex and the City* generation, but she didn't want to tell Jack that. "Oh, I'm toying with several ideas at the moment. They're still in the formative stage."

Sitting at the table, chatting with Jack about her work and other mundane matters, seemed so natural. It was the one thing she missed above all else.

"So, are you dating anyone new?" she couldn't help asking.

"New? No, no one new," he replied, and she felt vastly relieved. It didn't seem right that the father of her unborn child would be seeing other women—or having sex, for that matter. If she was going to practice celibacy, then he should, too.

Brain and other organs to Samantha: *Why are we practicing celibacy?*

"Because it's the right thing to do," she said without realizing she'd spoken her thoughts aloud.

"Are you dating anyone?"

"Ah, no one in particular. I've been too busy working and getting ready for Christmas."

"Things are back on with Amanda Peters. You remember her, don't you?"

She should have known. Jack was not into celibacy. It had been wishful thinking to believe that he wouldn't want to date anyone else. Not that they'd ever dated, but having sex should count for something.

Her hands started to move toward her abdomen, but she forced them down to her sides. "Mom's ecstatic that you're coming for Christmas. Though you shouldn't feel obligated to come, if you have plans with Amanda."

"I wouldn't miss it," he replied, before asking, "Any news about Ross and Ellen?"

"Not really. He's still at loose ends. Mom didn't

mention Ellen, so I'm not sure what's going on there."

"Maybe I should invite him to come down for New Year's Eve."

She looked horrified at the suggestion. "You can't do that! Then everyone would know that we're not living together and would ask all kinds of questions. Remember we agreed to keep what happened just between us?"

Eyes filling with disappointment, he said, "It's going to come out sooner or later, Samantha. I can't put Ross off indefinitely. He's mentioned visiting a time or two. We're best friends, and we like to hang out together."

"Well, he can wait a little while longer, until we can make up an excuse why we're not living together anymore, like maybe you're engaged." The thought sent a stabbing pain into her heart.

He laughed. "I have no intention of getting married. But maybe we can use that same excuse for you."

"It's very doubtful that I'll be getting engaged in the near future."

"Why's that?"

Because men don't marry pregnant women, that's why.

And you're already taken.

"I'm not in the marrying mood at the moment.

I've decided to put all my efforts toward achieving my career goals."

He looked at her strangely and she felt her face heat. "I'd better get a move on, if I'm going to finish my shopping," he said. "The stores will be packed so close to Christmas and I hate crowds."

"But I thought you were buying all your gifts online this year. At least, that's what you told me."

"Did I?" He shrugged. "Guess I changed my mind."

Her eyes narrowed. "Well, don't let me keep you."

"Glad you liked my present, Samantha. I'll see you in a few days. Be packed and ready to go at the crack of dawn, so we can beat the traffic heading north."

"I'll be ready. And thanks again for Jake. I love him."

She watched him leave, then heaved a sigh. She knew it was better this way, but why did it have to hurt so damn much?

"I DON'T KNOW WHY I let you talk me into this every year, Lilly. You know I hate traipsing around in the cold and snow, singing Christmas carols to neighbors who could care less. I'm a farmer, not a songbird."

"Oh, Dad, lighten up," Samantha chastised, winking at her mother, who sort of resembled the abominable snowman, with her multiple layers of clothing and heavy wool coat. "If we have to sing for our supper, so should you. Isn't that right, Jack?"

Smiling, the man standing next to her nodded his confirmation. "Absolutely. Besides, Fred, I don't want to be the only other male making a fool out of himself."

"But you do it so well," Samantha teased, and he chucked her under the chin.

"Hey, don't forget me," Ross chimed in. "I'm feeling like a bigger ass than usual."

"That's impossible, Ross," Samantha kidded, knocking her brother in the arm. "You're always a big ass. Right, Ellen?"

The small woman standing next to her brother seemed to fade at the question, and Samantha was fairly certain that this would be the last holiday those two would spend together. "I guess," she replied in a small voice.

"Hush up, everyone!" Lilly demanded. "We're at the Sadlers. Get read to sing 'Away in a Manger.' And no laughing or there won't be any pecan pie when we get home."

"Oh, Mom," Ross said in a three-year-old singsong, hugging his mother around her shoulders. "You're a harder taskmaster than my old NFL coach, and that's saying a lot."

"Just see that you do what you're told, Ross Brady. I mean it about the pie. Not one piece, if you don't behave."

Samantha and Jack exchanged looks, and then burst out laughing. It was the first time they'd truly laughed together since Jack had moved out. It felt glorious, and oh so right.

"That goes for you two, as well," Lilly cautioned the couple, which made them laugh even harder.

"Are we having fun yet?" Fred wanted to know, and his wife showed him, by tossing a snowball and hitting him right in the back of the neck. Then she burst out laughing.

He gazed at her with disbelief on his face. "Dammit, Lilly! What's come over you?"

But instead of replying, she hurled another snowball at his head, hitting him squarely in the face.

Fred growled. "Paybacks are tough, woman." He began chasing the screaming woman around the yard, pelting her with snow, until everyone was laughing hysterically, including Fred and Lilly.

By the time the cold and weary carolers arrived back at the house everyone was in a jovial mood. Even Ellen had eventually enjoyed the moment and pelted Ross with several snowballs, running off before he could retaliate.

"I hope the fire is still going," Samantha said, entering the front hallway and shedding her outerwear, which she hung on a hook on the wall. "I need to defrost." Her teeth started chattering.

And just like old times, Jack wrapped his arm around her affectionately and pulled her close to his side. "You need to put a bit more meat on your bones, woman. That's why you're always cold."

She smiled up at him, then suddenly her eyes widened. They were standing under the mistletoe, and her heart began to race. Jack's eyes darkened with passion; hers filled with terror.

"Kiss her, Jack," Lilly demanded. "You're standing beneath the mistletoe. If you don't, it'll bring bad luck to all of us."

"Quit being so superstitious, Mother," Samantha retorted, trying to back out of Jack's reach, but her movement only made his grip tighten.

"I don't need any bad luck right now," he whispered. "Do you?"

Swallowing with some difficulty, she shook her head. And then Jack's lips covered hers in a soft, melting kiss. Time seemed to stop. She could feel his heart beating as fast as her own, and they lost themselves in the moment, until someone—Ross, she thought—broke through their veil of passion.

"Hey, no need to put on a vulgar public display, Jack. That's my sister you're kissing."

They broke apart almost guiltily, and stared at each other for a moment, then Jack grinned mischievously. "You should do more kissing and less talking, Ross. The world would be a better place if you would."

Not to be outdone, Ross grabbed Ellen's arm and dragged her under the now vacated mistletoe and kissed her briefly on the lips. There was little passion in the action, and the disappointment in the woman's eyes was evident.

"You call that a kiss? Jake gives better kisses than that," Samantha told her brother, making Ellen's face redden. "And speaking of my dog, where is—?" And then she spotted Jake; he was curled up in a corner of the sofa, sound asleep. Her mother had thought the crate cruel and had freed him. Not that she could blame her. Jake was the most adorable puppy ever created. And if she could only get him to stop pooping and peeing every fifteen minutes, her life would be borderline perfect.

Well, if not perfect, then at least manageable.

SAMANTHA HAD a difficult time falling asleep that night, and she'd spent a lot of her waking moments wondering if Jack had been similarly affected by the kiss they'd shared.

She had felt his response. Samantha hadn't imagined it. She'd also felt him harden against her belly, so at least she could take some solace in the fact that he wasn't immune to her charms entirely. He didn't need a fifth of Jack Daniel's to find her appealing.

And the kiss had only served to strengthen her need to have him close. Beneath the covers her hands moved to rest on her abdomen, and she took comfort in the fact that Jack's baby grew within. She might not have Jack, but at least she had a small portion of him, a reminder of the glorious night they had spent together.

There were times like this, when the night was still and quiet, that she could close her eyes and conjure up memories of the night they'd made love. Jack had been tender and solicitous of her needs. She had been driven mad with desire. And it now seemed incomprehensible that she would never again be in his arms or feel that way, never experience the depth of passion they'd created.

There might be another man for her down the road, though Samantha doubted it. From now on, she would measure every man she met against Jack— against the way he'd kissed, held and made love to her. And they would all come up short. Samantha loved Jack, and that love would remain with her until the day she died.

If only she could tell him about the baby. But Samantha knew if she did, it would only serve to pressure him into marrying her; Jack would want to make things right. And he was dating someone else now. If his relationship with Amanda continued and grew serious, and then he was forced to break it off because of the baby, he would end up hating her for trapping him into a loveless marriage.

A tear spilled from the corner of Samantha's eye, and she punched her pillow at the pure injustice of the whole situation, wondering if religious orders accepted women with babies. Probably not.

CHAPTER FIFTEEN

JANUARY WAS supposedly the month for new beginnings, but you couldn't prove that by Samantha, who'd just received the latest in a string of rejection letters—one from a publisher who'd expressed real enthusiasm for her writing.

"Dammit!" she swore, tearing the letter into shreds and tossing it on the floor while tears of frustration spilled onto her cheeks. "Damn! Damn! Damn! I hate writing! I hate the whole stupid publishing industry!"

Jake chose that moment to pee on her Skechers, which seemed somehow fitting to Samantha since everyone was pissing on her lately. "Jake, you naughty boy!" She grabbed a paper towel and cleaned up the mess, then picked up the offending creature who'd followed her into the kitchen, intending to scold him further. But he licked her face, tears and all, and she didn't have the heart to do it.

The doorbell rang just then and Samantha heaved a deep sigh. Wiping her face with the back of her hand, she debated whether or not to answer it. She'd been avoiding Jack since they'd returned from her parents' house, fearful that if he looked too closely he'd figure out what had put her into such a funky, emotional mood.

Like most women in her condition, her hormones were out of whack. There were days when she felt totally insane. She cried for no reason, felt both uncontrollable rage and periods of euphoria and had bouts of such deep depression that she feared she would never get through the next month, let alone all nine.

The persistent caller continued ringing the bell, then a familiar irritation-filled voice called out, "I know you're in there, Samantha, so open the damn door!" Only Patty could demand action with such authority.

Relieved it wasn't Jack, but hating the possibility that her friend had come to lecture—Patty's arguments could be brutal and persuasive—Samantha opened the door.

"What took you so long? And what the hell is that?" Patty asked, pointing at the small black-and-white puppy Samantha cuddled in her arms. "What an ugly creature. Where did you find it?"

"Jake is not ugly—he's adorable. And I didn't find him, he found me. He was a Christmas present from Jack."

"Oh, that explains it then." Patty peered closely at the animal who bared his tiny teeth in response and barked at her. "Watch it, buster! I eat dogs like you for breakfast."

Whining pathetically, the puppy retreated, seeking refuge by burying his muzzle in Samantha's armpit. "Now you've gone and scared him. If this is the way you treat men, it's a wonder you have any dates at all."

Her smile full of confidence, Patty replied, "I keep my men in line. If you don't relinquish the upper hand, they can't take advantage of you."

Patty might never allow a man to hurt her again, Samantha thought, but she wasn't likely to ever form a close relationship either. "Come in. I was just about to make lunch. Can I fix you something?"

"No need." Reaching into her Burberry plaid tote, which Samantha knew had cost the lawyer at least five hundred dollars, Patty produced a paper bag. "I've brought lunch. I stopped at the deli on the way over. And for the expectant mother… Ta-da!" She held up a plastic-wrapped chocolate chip cookie.

Smiling, Samantha wished others could see this softer side of Patty, but knew her friend went out of her way to hide it. It just didn't fit with the tough-as-nails image she'd created for herself.

"How thoughtful of you! Not that I need to eat more sweets. I stuffed myself on dessert while I was at my mom and dad's."

"Sounds like you had a great time."

"We did. It was fabulous." *Especially the kiss with Jack.* "Did you have a nice Christmas, too?"

Her friend shrugged. "I went to a few parties, but spent Christmas Eve and Day at home, reading briefs and dining on Chinese takeout."

"How awful. I mean—don't you have family nearby?"

"I have a married brother who lives near Buffalo." She made a face of disgust. "But I can't stand his stupid wife and bratty kids, so I stay at home, where I can celebrate in peace and quiet."

"Well next year you'll have to come home with me and spend an old-fashioned Christmas, complete with all the trimmings. It's usually chaotic and noisy, but we have lots of fun—and the food is fabulous."

"Sounds nice, thanks. Maybe I will," she said. When she noticed the pile of torn paper on the floor, she added, "You know, for someone who spends most of her day working at home, you're a lousy housekeeper."

Following her gaze, Samantha shrugged. "It's another rejection letter. I'm so pissed off and depressed that I can't sell my stupid book. My life really sucks."

"It's the life you've chosen, so quit whining and let's have lunch. I'm starving and I don't have that much time. I've got a hearing this afternoon."

Patty had a way of putting things in perspective. Knowing from past experience that there was no use in arguing, Samantha led her into the kitchen and while Patty fetched the plates, Samantha filled two glasses with soda and grabbed the napkins.

"Thanks for buying lunch. I really appreciate it."

"You need to get out more. You shouldn't be spending so much time alone in this apartment. It's not healthy for you, or the baby. If you do nothing else, go for a walk and window shop. You'll gain too much weight if you just sit around here and eat all day. I'm sure Jake would like to accompany you."

Jake, who was wagging his stumpy tail, seemed to agree.

"I know you're right. I just haven't felt motivated to do much, including exercise."

"Are you still barfing?"

Samantha nodded. "Yes, but not as much as before."

"That's good. So what did your parents say about the baby?"

There was a long silence, and then Samantha swallowed hard before shaking her head. "Okay, don't get mad, but I haven't told them yet."

Patty, who never avoided confrontation of any kind, appeared to be disappointed. "Oh, Samantha, that's so foolish. You need family support at a time like this. You've got to tell them."

Setting down her turkey sandwich, Samantha sighed. "How can I? They think I'm perfect. My dad calls me his little princess. Can you imagine what they'll think of me when they find out I'm going to have a child, and without the benefit of a husband? I'll be the black sheep of the family, and that's always been Ross's role."

"But you were going to have one artificially anyway, so what's the difference? Pregnant is pregnant."

"It just seems different, that's all. Jack's the father, and my parents adore him. They'll put pressure on us to marry, and I'm not going to allow them to force Jack into anything, which includes marrying me. At any rate, he's dating someone else right now. And let's be honest, if this pregnancy is anyone's fault, it's mine."

"Look, honey, you're going to have to bite the bullet and tell your parents about the baby. In another month, you won't be able to keep this a secret from anyone, including Jack, and you're going to need all the help and support you can get when he eventually finds out."

"But—"

Patty shook her head. "You're a grown woman, Samantha, and you've got to face the consequences. There's a way out of this mess, but you're not willing to take it."

"I told you—"

"Okay, I can accept that—abortion isn't for everyone. But you've got to accept responsibility for what you've done, for the sake of your unborn child and for your own well-being."

Samantha stiffened. "I'm perfectly fine."

"You are not! Have you looked in the mirror lately? Your hair is matted and snarled, you've got dark circles under your eyes. You're a mess, girl, and you've got to clean up your act. If you need moral support to face your parents, then I'll go to Rhinebeck with you. Will that help?"

Samantha was so grateful for the offer she launched herself off the chair and moved around the table to hug Patty. "I can't thank you enough. I've been dreading having to do this by myself. I've felt so isolated these past ten days."

"Because you've isolated yourself. I know you've been avoiding Jack, but you shouldn't be avoiding life, honey. You've got to embrace this new development and go with it."

"But I'm afraid. What if I screw it all up? Freelancing is great—it allows me to work from home. But I need to earn more money."

"Then supplement your income until your book sells. There are plenty of jobs in publishing you can do. You've just got to wrap your mind around the possibilities and take a chance."

Her friend made sense, and Samantha decided to

make a list of job possibilities that very afternoon and work on her budget. "I don't know what I'd do without your friendship, Patty."

"Just wait till you get my bill. You won't be feeling so magnanimous then."

Samantha laughed, and then so did Patty. "I'm going to get through this. I just know it."

"That's the spirit. You just keep telling yourself that. Women are by far the stronger sex. Why on earth do you think God made women the birth givers? Do you really think a man could stand all that pain?" She shook her head. "Men are wusses. The only thing they're good *for* and *at* is sex. And some aren't even good at that. I could tell you stories that would make your toes curl."

"I'd rather hear about what's made you so bitter toward men. You must have been hurt by someone, but you've never talked about it."

Patty looked uncomfortable. "It's not something I like to talk about. It's part of my past—a time when I was stupid and vulnerable."

Samantha reached out and touched her hand. "If you feel you can trust me, I'd like to know."

Heaving a sigh, Patty said, "I've never told a soul about this, Samantha. But I do trust you, and I think it's time you knew a bit more about what makes me tick."

Samantha nodded, but remained quiet.

"I was engaged once to a man who I loved above all else. We met in college. He was one of my professors, and ten years older than me, and I thought he walked on water. I was young, naive and quite flattered by the attention he gave me. Long story short, we had a wild, wonderful affair that no one on or off campus knew about—or so I thought. I kept it from my family and friends, and he kept it from his…wife. But I didn't find that out until later."

Samantha's eyes widened. "Just like The Bastard!"

Patty nodded. "But unlike the bastard who duped you, I got pregnant. And when I told Roger, he was ecstatic. We made plans for our future, picked out a name for our baby and did all the things expectant parents do. And then one day his wife confronted me at the college library, where I was studying."

"Oh my God! What did you do?"

"I dropped his class the next day, then transferred to another school to finish my undergrad work. I was completely devastated, could hardly drag myself to class, day after day, but I managed to continue and finally get my degree."

"And the baby?"

"I lost it. A miscarriage. I was alone in my apartment when it happened. I've never experienced so much pain, either physically or emotionally, since. So you see, I'm done with men. I will never let another man use me like that again."

Samantha drew Patty into her arms. "I'm so sorry. I knew something terrible had happened for you to be so disillusioned about love."

"I don't dwell in the past. It's not healthy or productive. I've moved on. And so should you, Samantha."

She sighed. "I guess you're right."

"Honey, I make my living by being right. Now, let's figure out a date when we can go and visit your family. The sooner the better, okay?"

Samantha nodded. "But don't say I didn't warn you. My parents are likely to go ballistic when they hear the news." She couldn't bear to imagine what her father would think, or Ross and Lucas. Her big brothers had always been overprotective to a fault. It was another one of those damn Brady traits.

"You leave them to me. I've handled a lot of difficult situations in my lifetime, and I'm still here to talk about them."

"That's true. But you've never gone ten rounds with Fred and Lilly Brady." And that was one confrontation Samantha wasn't eager to witness.

FOUR DAYS LATER, Samantha was packed and ready to go. She glanced at her watch—it was nearly nine. Patty had rented a car and would be arriving at any moment to pick her up for their drive to Rhinebeck.

Butterflies were beating her stomach into a frenzy

when the doorbell rang and Jake barked. "Okay, sweetie. We're going bye-bye now."

But when she opened the door it wasn't Patty but Jack standing on the other side, and she wished she could melt into the floorboards. He was the last person she wanted to see right now, though his smile had her pulses racing just the same. "Hello. This is a surprise," she said finally.

"Hope I'm not intruding. I brought over some bagels. Thought we could have breakfast together," he said, holding up a white paper sack and looking eager at the prospect. "We haven't spent much time together since Christmas."

She was tempted to remind him that that was what *he* wanted, but she didn't want to make a scene just now. Good arguments took a while to develop, and she was short of time. "I'm really sorry, but I'm on my way out. Patty will be here at any moment."

His face filled with disappointment. "Oh. I didn't know."

"How could you?"

"Do you need me to take care of Jake?" The puppy rushed over to him and began devouring his shoe.

"Thanks for the offer, but we're taking him with us."

"Hey, little guy. How're you doing? You've grown since the last time I saw you." He began to scratch

Jake behind the ears, and the dog fell immediately into puppy ecstasy.

Samantha could relate. She had only to close her eyes to relive every passionate moment in Jack's arms.

"He's almost housebroken, thank goodness." Well, except for her Skechers. For some reason, the dog did not like her new tennis shoes.

"So where are you girls going? On a shopping expedition to the outlet malls?" It was then he noticed her suitcase and his smile disappeared.

"Patty's been dying to meet my parents, so we're driving up to Rhinebeck for a few days."

"I wish I'd known. I would have rearranged my schedule and come with you. You know how much I love visiting your family."

"It's a girls-only type of thing. We thought we'd visit, do some shopping with my mom, that sort of thing."

"Oh, I see." But the disappointment on his face said he didn't. "Well, I hope you have a great time. Here," he said, handing her the bagels. "You might get hungry on the way up. Patty doesn't strike me as the type to stop for inconsequential things like food."

"She's not the ogre you think she is."

"Have a good time, Samantha, and stay safe. Guess I'll talk to you when you get back."

Samantha watched Jack disappear down the hall

and suddenly felt guilty for lying, about everything. But she was certain she was doing the right thing by keeping the truth about the baby from him. He'd only be burdened by it, and he had a lot on his plate right now, with the new business and all. He didn't need to worry about her, and she knew without a doubt that he would. Not to mention, there was the very real problem of Amanda Peters to consider.

"I'm doing the right thing, Jake," she told the puppy, who was busy biting the laces on her tennis shoes. "Jack will be better off, and so will we. You'll see."

Now if she only believed that, everything would be hunky-dory.

FOR AS LONG AS Samantha could remember, it had been a tradition with the Bradys to call a family meeting when anything of importance needed to be discussed.

Ross had called one before accepting his NFL contract, and Lilly had, too, prior to going ahead with the plans to remodel the house. Lucas had declared his intention not to finish college at a family meeting, and Fred had sought everyone's opinion before purchasing a new tractor for the farm.

Thus far, Samantha had been the only holdout—the only one who hadn't asked for approval before heading off to New York to pursue her career as a novelist. But today, with Patty looking on, her face filled with encouragement, that was about to change.

She sat in the overstuffed blue-and-white gingham chair by the fireplace and wrung her hands nervously as she regarded the various members of her family, whose faces reflected their surprise and curiosity that she'd called for a meeting. "I asked to meet today to discuss something very important— something that's happened to me."

Concern suddenly replaced interest on her mother's face. "You're not sick, are you, dear? Please tell me you're not."

"No, it's nothing quite that dire. But what I have to tell you is going to change everything for me as well as have a serious impact on this family, so I wanted to do it in a family meeting."

"Go ahead, Princess, just get it out," her dad urged. "Whatever it is, it can't be that bad. And we're here to help."

If only she could believe that, Samantha thought, but she knew her dad wasn't likely to be so accepting once he heard her news.

"Yeah, just spit it out," Lucas agreed.

Heaving a deep sigh and praying silently that she wouldn't be burned at the stake or have a red letter *A* branded into her forehead, Samantha sucked in her breath, before saying, "I'm pregnant. I'm going to have a baby."

There was a moment of stunned silence, then Lilly's face lit with joy. "But that's wonderful, Samantha, if a bit unorthodox. I assume it's Jack's child? I mean, I can't picture you with anyone else."

"Wonderful? Are you insane, Lilly? Our daughter just told us she's pregnant," Fred said to his wife.

"But I'm certain it's Jack's. Isn't it, Samantha?"

Samantha cast Patty an *I told you so* look and nodded. "Yes, Mom, it's Jack's. But it's not what you think."

"What the hell does that mean?" Ross wanted to know, not looking at all pleased by the revelation. "And where is Jack? Why isn't he here to tell us this news? Is he ashamed for taking advantage of my little sister?"

"Ross is right," Fred agreed. "Why isn't Jack here to explain why he's taken advantage of my little girl?"

"It's not what you think, Dad," Samantha repeated. She had feared Ross's response would be volatile, and she didn't want anything to come between his friendship with Jack.

"Then what the hell is it?"

"Be quiet, Ross, and let your sister finish," Patty admonished. "You're acting like some overprotective Neanderthal."

"Well, I think this is wonderful news, Samantha, despite the unusual way you went about it," her mother declared, earning an outraged look from her husband. "Now you and Jack can get married, just like we've always hoped you would. We'll have the wedding here. Your father and I will pay for everything. Isn't that right, Fred?"

At first, Samantha's father said nothing, but as his wife continued to look at him pleadingly, he heaved a sigh. "Of course we'll do what's right by Samantha. She's our only daughter. But that doesn't mean I approve of the way she and Jack went about this."

He turned to look at his daughter. "You should have gotten married first. I expected better of you, Samantha."

"Jack and I are not getting married," she tried to explain, "so you needn't make any wedding arrangements. He doesn't even know about the baby. I haven't told him, and I'm not sure I'm going to."

Her mother's face registered surprise.

"What? Are you serious?" her father asked, not bothering to hide his shock. "How can you not tell Jack? He's the baby's father! He has a right to know."

"What happened between us was an accident. We were on the way home after the harvest festival weekend and the car broke down." She went on to explain about the motel, and the Jack Daniel's that Ross had generously provided, and left the rest of the tale to their imaginations.

"Don't blame this on me," Ross said, crossing his

arms over his chest in a defensive posture. "I didn't ask you to drink the booze or have unprotected sex. So, are you going to keep the baby?"

"Yes, I'm keeping it. I've always wanted a child, and this baby is the answer to my prayers."

"But you're not married, Samantha. How can you have a child without a husband?" her mother wanted to know. "The baby will need a father."

"The baby *has* a father. *Jack* is the father," Fred stated quite emphatically. "You have to do what's right, Samantha. You can't keep something like this from Jack. It wouldn't be legal. I'm sure your lawyer friend here told you that. You and Jack must get married and quickly."

"Patty and I have discussed it. And I'm sorry, Dad, but I intend to have this child on my own. I'm not going to ask Jack for child support or anything else. What happened was my fault, and—"

"That's a crock of shit and you know it! Jack is as much if not more to blame as you," Ross argued, his face reddening in anger. "I should kick his ass for taking advantage of you while you were drunk. What kind of a man does that?"

"Stop it! You'll do no such thing. What happened with Jack was consensual. He didn't take advantage of me. I was a very willing participant."

At the admission, her father stood, casting Samantha a look of disbelief and disappointment, and stalked out of the room without saying a word. Samantha guessed she had been knocked off the pedestal for good.

"You've really fucked things up this time," Lucas said. "Now you've gone and upset Dad."

"Watch your language, son," Lilly chastised. "I'll not have you using such vulgarity in this house."

Patty rose to her feet. "I'm not a member of this family, so I don't really have a right to speak, but Samantha is my best friend and I'm going to anyway. Samantha was reluctant to come here and tell you about the baby, but I encouraged her, told her you'd be supportive. You're her family, after all, and families are supposed to support one another."

"It's okay, Patty. I dropped quite a bombshell on them today."

"Hell, yes, you did," Ross agreed.

But Patty would not be dissuaded. "The coming months are going to be difficult for Samantha. She's going to need your love and encouragement to get through them."

Lilly finally spoke. "Samantha is the baby of this family, so naturally we are somewhat shocked and yes, disappointed, by what she had to tell us. But we all love her. That will never change."

Rising from her seat, Lilly crossed the room to where her daughter sat, with tears streaming down her face. "I still love you, dear. Don't ever doubt it.

And I'll be the best grandmother to this baby I know how. I just wish you and Jack could have worked things out, that's all."

Samantha clasped her mom's hand. "Jack doesn't want to get married, Mom. He's told me that a million times. I can't trap him into something he'll come to hate me for. That wouldn't be right. Besides, he's seeing someone. For all I know, it could be serious." The very idea made her heart ache.

"But if he knew about the baby…"

"I don't want a man to marry me because I'm pregnant. I want a man who will love and cherish me. A baby just isn't a good enough excuse to get married these days."

"Nothing's a good enough excuse to get married, if you ask me," Ross stated.

"My sentiments exactly," Patty concurred, and Ross took a second look at the attractive woman seated next to him.

CHAPTER SIXTEEN

"LOOKS LIKE the Holden contract is going to stick," Tom told Jack one snowy afternoon in mid-January. "They had three separate cases of buyer's remorse, but it finally went through. Thank God!"

Jack nodded, but didn't look up from his work. "Good to hear it."

"You don't seem very pleased that I've saved our firm from utter ruination and bankruptcy." Tom's exaggerated boasts finally stole Jack's attention and he smiled.

"Guess you expect a dinner or something, huh?"

"At the very least a bottle of champagne and a couple of hot chicks."

"I can provide the first. All out of the second, I'm afraid." Jack had finally broken it off with Amanda and wasn't dating anyone else. For some reason, women didn't interest him at the moment. Well, maybe one woman, but Samantha wasn't speaking to him much these days, and he missed her like crazy.

"Whatever happened to Samantha's sexy friend, Patty? I've called her a few times, but she never seems to be home."

"Patty eats men like you for dinner, then spits out the leavings, my friend. I don't think you want to get involved with her. She's a hard case."

"On the contrary," Tom protested, "I found her to be quite soft, that one evening we spent together. And she was hot as hell between the sheets."

"I wouldn't know. I've never had any desire to sample the wares."

"So how are things between you and Samantha? Have you talked to her lately?"

Jack shrugged. "Not really. I think she's avoiding me." He'd sensed that for weeks now, but didn't know why. They'd gotten along well over Christmas. Well, as good as could be expected under the circumstances. They'd had fun caroling, and Samantha had even accompanied him to his parents' house to deliver some Christmas gifts. He'd tried not to think about the kiss they'd shared, but he hadn't been able to get it out of his mind. Her lips had been soft and so very sweet.

"But that's what you wanted, right? I thought you decided that you two would never work as a couple."

Tom's comment brought Jack back to the present. "I know I said that, but now I'm beginning to feel differently about it. I was probably too hasty and scared after what happened between us. I should have been more rational, taken the time to think things through, instead of going off half-cocked."

His friend smiled knowingly. "From the looks of it, you're not going off, half or full. Maybe you need to take care of that problem first. You might see things differently once you're not horny."

Jack wondered what had possessed him to discuss his personal life with Tom. His playboy partner might be a damn good salesman, but he had an immature way of looking at women and relationships. Jack had been like that once, a lifetime ago.

"I think I'll drop by Samantha's tonight and see how she's doing," he said. Maybe he'd surprise her with a box of chocolate-covered caramels, which she absolutely adored.

"I can't figure you out, Jack. You finally get what you want, but now it's not what you want at all. I think before you do anything else, you need to figure what the hell you *do* want, and whether that includes a relationship with Samantha."

So maybe I'm the one with the immaturity problem.

"You're probably right. Turner/Adler is doing great, thanks in large part to you, so I've got no complaints there, but my personal life sucks. I'm not even dating. Most women bore me."

"I could set you up, if you like. I know a lot of—"

Jack shook his head. "That's just it. The idea sounds totally unappealing. Dating and casual sex were fun once, but I want more than that now."

"You mean, like marriage?"

Jack almost laughed at the horrified expression on his friend's face. "Hell, I don't know. I'm not keen on getting married. My parents had an awful marriage." Though it seemed better now, there were no guarantees when it came to love and marriage and he wondered how long this period of contentment between them would last. Most of his friends' marriages had ended in divorce.

"Everything I know about relationships and parenting I learned from my mom and dad. And that's not saying a hell of a lot."

"That's not quite true, Jack. I'd wager that most everything you've learned about relationships has been because of Samantha. Think about it. She's the one you bonded with all those years ago, and she's the one you want now. If I didn't know better, I'd say you were in love with your best friend."

"Of course I love Samantha. She's like a sister to me."

Tom scoffed. "I've seen the way you look at her when you think no one else is looking. If you looked at my sister that way, I'd knock your teeth down your throat."

"I'm not in love with Samantha. We're just friends."

"Coulda fooled me. If I were you, Jack, I'd do a little soul searching. You might be surprised by what you find."

JACK DID A GREAT DEAL of thinking on the way home that night, but he hadn't come to any conclusions where Samantha was concerned. How did a man know when he was truly in love? There weren't any guidelines, and even if there were, they wouldn't have fit into his and Samantha's relationship.

Theirs was a comfortable, give-and-take connection. They'd always loved each other, but it had been a different kind of love—the warm, enduring kind, not the heart-palpitating, sick-to-your-stomach kind that was always depicted in movies. At least until that night in the hotel. He shook his head, still confused by it all.

The streets were crowded as he hurried along, bumping shoulders with cashmere-coated executives intent on getting home and women carrying handbags large enough to pass for suitcases. January's bitter wind slapped his cheeks, but he felt warmed by the notion that he would see Samantha tonight.

Did that mean something?

Only that you're an idiot, Turner.

As Jack neared his apartment, he thought he recognized Ross standing in front of the building, and wondered if his friend had finally taken him up on his invitation to visit.

He hoped not.

Not that Jack didn't want to see Ross, but now wasn't the right time. Now he needed to be with Samantha, talk to her and maybe make sense of his feelings.

"Ross!" he called out despite his misgivings, waving and hurrying to catch up to him. Whoever it was didn't hear or acknowledge him, just kept walking into the building, so Jack figured he must have been mistaken.

But it turned out he was right. Ross Brady stood by the bank of mailboxes, opening Samantha's with a key. "Hey, Ross! When did you get in? It's good to see you, buddy. Though I must say I'm a bit surprised."

The man turned, but there was no friendly smile or warm greeting from him. "A few days ago. Look, I gotta go. Samantha's waiting for me."

"A few days—! But how come you didn't come by? We could have gone out, had some fun."

"From what I hear, you've already had your fun," the man retorted before hurrying up the stairs.

"Ross, wait!" But he didn't stop, and Jack felt even more confused by his comment. He couldn't imagine what Ross was referring to, unless—his gut clenched. Unless Samantha had told her family what had happened between them.

But why would she? That didn't seem likely.

Samantha had gone out of her way to warn him off the subject. Maybe she had wanted to give her version of events first. And if that were the case, he was going to be royally pissed off.

"I JUST RAN INTO JACK," Samantha's brother said, entering her apartment. She was folding laundry, most of it Ross's, and listening to Aerosmith.

Ross had been living with her for almost a week, after inviting himself to stay. He'd used the excuse of her pregnancy, saying she needed a support system, but Samantha suspected he was infatuated with Patty and had come to New York to escape from his relationship to Ellen and start things up with the sexy attorney.

He didn't say how long he'd be staying and hadn't talked at all about his almost-fiancée, except to say that he and Ellen were taking a break. Samantha wondered if Ellen was aware of that, or of Ross's attraction to Patty. She doubted it. On the other hand, Patty knew all about Ellen from her time spent with the Bradys. Lilly had given the poor woman an earful.

"I hope you weren't rude to Jack. I told you that you had to play by my rules if you were going to live here." Ross was all bark and no bite, except when he was protecting his sister, so she wasn't taking any chances.

"Don't worry. I didn't touch a hair on his precious head, though I sure as hell felt like it. I don't like the idea of his having taken advantage of my little sister."

"Get over yourself, Ross. I'm a grown woman, in case you haven't noticed. And Jack's not the first man I've had sex with, so quit being stupid."

"Jack's supposed to be my best friend. How else do you expect me to feel? He betrayed our friendship. I thought I could trust him."

Join the club, Samantha felt like saying. "I'm as much or more to blame as Jack for what happened. But I'm not sorry about it. Not if it means having the baby I've always wanted. I'm just sorry that this situation is going to ruin whatever friendship Jack and I have left when he finds out about it."

"Why didn't you tell me that he'd moved out of the apartment? Why did you keep it such a big secret? Jack might be my best friend, but you're my sister. I would have kept your confidence. You should have trusted me."

"I'm sorry, Ross, but I couldn't take the chance. I didn't want to upset Mom and Dad, and I didn't want to answer a bunch of stupid questions, like the ones you're asking me now. If you'd like me to return the favor, we can discuss why you ran away from Rhinebeck and Ellen."

Ross's face grew florid. "I get the picture."

"Good. But at some point you're going to have to make a decision as to what you're going to do about her. You can't just let the poor woman hang in limbo. You owe her more than that."

"That's my business, so butt out."

"Not while you're living here, it's not. I have more important things to think about than your inability to commit to a relationship. I'm going to have a baby, and I don't need to worry about another one, namely you."

"What are you, my mother?"

"No, I'm your sister. And since you invited yourself to stay here and be my protector you'll just have to put up with my meddling. I've found that the more my hormones rage, the more I like to butt in."

"Well isn't that just great? But I don't want your advice. I can handle my own life."

"Oh yeah. You've done a bang-up job of it so far. And if you've come here to try and woo Patty Bradshaw, it's not going to work. She's not interested in lasting relationships. She lives for the moment and is content with that."

"Maybe she just hasn't met the right guy."

Samantha rolled her eyes. "And you're him?" She laughed. "I don't think so. Sports are your whole life and I doubt Patty knows the difference between a football and a hockey puck. You two have nothing in common."

Ross grabbed his jacket and said with a disgruntled look on his face, "I don't need this shit. I'm outta here."

"What about dinner?"

"You eat it. I'll grab something while I'm out."

"They don't serve food in the kind of bars you frequent."

He slammed the door behind him, and Samantha heaved a sigh. It wasn't going to be easy having Ross as a roommate, especially in her present condition. She had no patience for stupidity, and her brother was being pretty damn stupid at the moment. They'd never seen eye to eye on anything, probably because they were too much alike, a depressing thought at best.

Samantha pushed thoughts of Ross to the side, knowing she had more pressing things to deal with at the moment, like feeding her dog. "Jake, where are you?" she called out. Ross wasn't the only one who hated confrontation. The puppy tended to hide whenever Samantha and her brother got into one of their verbal sparring matches. "It's time for dinner, sweetie."

Entering the kitchen, Samantha began to open the can of puppy food, which smelled like rotting liver. As soon as Jake heard the can opener, he came bounding into the room and skidded to a halt in front of his water dish, wagging his stubby tail and looking hopeful. "I thought you might be hungry," she said, setting the bowl of food down in front of the eager pup.

The smell of the dog food made her nauseous, and Samantha felt bile rising to her throat. "Not again!" She made a beeline for the bathroom and promptly gave up the remnants of her lunch.

A few moments later, the front door opened, but the stereo blaring in the background and Samantha's preoccupation with vomiting didn't allow her to hear that someone had just entered the apartment.

"Samantha! Samantha, are you here?"

Samantha's head was still hanging over the toilet bowl when she felt someone watching her. She turned it slightly to find Jack standing at the bathroom door's threshold, frowning.

"The front door was unlocked. I thought we'd talked about that. And your watchdog isn't much of a watchdog. Jake didn't even bark when I came in. What's wrong? Are you sick again? You've been sick to your stomach a lot lately. What gives?"

She heard suspicion in Jack's voice and experienced a moment of panic. It was then she decided she had two choices: make up another excuse about why she was puking her guts out, or tell Jack the truth about the baby and risk ending their relationship—a relationship she very much wanted and needed in her life.

Some choice.

Wiping her mouth with the washcloth that Jack handed her, Samantha righted herself. "Thanks. I didn't know the door was unlocked. Ross must have left it open."

"Speaking of Ross, I came over here to speak to you about him, but I think we might have more pressing matters to discuss. Am I right?"

A lump the size of a grapefruit forming in her throat, Samantha nodded, dreading the confrontation that was imminent. Jack would be furious when she told him about the baby, and his enraged side was a scary thing to behold. He didn't get mad often, but when he did it was time to get out of Dodge.

"Let's go into the living room and sit down," she suggested, and Jack followed her into the front room, where they seated themselves on opposite ends of the sofa. "Would you like a beer? Ross just picked some up."

"No thanks. What's Ross doing here anyway? And what's his problem anyway? He was rude as hell to me when I ran into him earlier."

"Sorry about that. I tried to explain that what'd happened between us wasn't your fault, but Ross is determined to remain stubborn. I'm afraid he's mad at you."

"Great. So I'm assuming he knows we made love?"

Love. It was an interesting term for what they had done, and Samantha wished it were true, for she was truly in love with Jack and cherished the memory of their time together as lovers.

"I've told my family everything that happened between us, Jack. I had to."

"But I thought we agreed to keep that just between us. Why the change of heart?"

"Because they would have found out soon enough, that's why."

His brow wrinkled in confusion, and then as comprehension dawned, his gaze fell to the slight bulge beneath Samantha's tee shirt and his eyes widened. "You mean…?"

"I'm pregnant, Jack. It happened the night we were together at the motel. If you recall, we didn't use a condom."

Jack was visibly shaken. "Christ! That was totally irresponsible of me."

"Of us, you mean. But if you recall, we weren't thinking too clearly that night." A major understatement if ever there was one.

"I'm confused. I thought you told me that you couldn't get pregnant. Were you lying? I know how badly you want a child, but to—"

"I didn't lie, and don't you dare say I did," she replied with no small amount of anger and disappointment that he'd accuse her of such a thing.

"The doctor told me that the likelihood of my getting pregnant was slim at best. Just my luck to have had sex with a man who has super-charged sperm." Jack had always been a strong swimmer; apparently his sperm were, too.

Rising to his feet, Jack began to pace, rubbing the back of his neck to ease the tension there. After a few moments, he said, "Why were you trying to keep this from me? We've always shared everything, Samantha. Why didn't you tell me about the baby? How long were you going to wait? Until the kid entered college?"

"Because I knew you didn't want a child. You've made it clear over the years what you think of marriage and family. And I don't intend for this baby to be a burden to you. I'm going to have this child on my own. *We* don't need you to be involved."

His face registered surprise, and then anger. "Are you crazy? How can I not be involved? I'm the baby's father."

"You are merely the sperm donor, and that's how you must think of it. We just used a different method for conceiving, that's all. You're not responsible for this baby in any way."

Jack rocked back on his heels as if slapped. "I take my responsibility a whole lot more seriously than that, Samantha, and you know it. What kind of a man do you think I am? I'm not going to walk out on my own child."

She knew he was thinking about the remote, unfulfilling relationship he'd had with his father, but she would not let that sway her. She had to be strong, for the sake of the child, and herself.

"As far as I'm concerned, you already have. You walked out of this apartment and my life months ago, rejected our friendship and all that we had together. Why would I think that we could parent a child together when we couldn't even make it as friends?"

His face turning three shades of purple, Jack replied, "That's my child you're carrying. I damn well will be involved. I have rights."

"Maybe you do, but you don't deserve them. Now please leave. You're making me upset."

"And just what the hell do you think you've made me? I find out after months of deception that you're pregnant. You weren't going to tell me, were you?"

She shook her head. "Probably not for a while. I didn't see the point in it. Besides, you're with someone else now. I figured you wouldn't want the complication to ruin things between you and Amanda Peters."

"I'm not seeing Amanda anymore."

Taken totally by surprise, all Samantha could say was, "Oh."

"Did your parents go along with this plan of yours not to tell me about the baby?" He seemed astounded by the possibility—astounded and deeply hurt.

"Of course not. They want us to get married, but I told them that was out of the question."

"Why?"

Samantha's mouth opened and closed, then she said, "Because I don't want to marry you, that's why. And I know for sure that you don't want to marry me. You don't love me. And I won't marry a man who doesn't love me. I have more self-respect than that."

"I can't believe that after all these years and everything we've meant to each other, you would want to kick me out of your life. Out of my child's life."

His wounded look tore at Samantha's heart, but she knew a clean break was the only way. "It would be too difficult any other way, Jack. And that brings up another point. I can no longer accept your generosity as far as this apartment goes. I intend to start paying more of the expenses."

"With what? Don't tell me you've sold your book? Is that what this is all about? Suddenly you're published and have found your independence?"

"Don't be an ass. I'm not published, except for my magazine articles. But I'm looking for a job in publishing. I'm hoping to proofread or copyedit to supplement my income, at least until my book sells." She'd probably be receiving her first royalty check at a home for the aged.

"What makes you think you're qualified?"

"Publishing houses are always looking for free-lancers like that. I can do either one. I have a promising interview on Monday. If I'm hired, I plan to work from home, where I'll be able take care of the baby."

"You've got it all worked out, haven't you? But you're forgetting one thing—that child you're carrying has a father. I won't be tossed aside like some hired stud with a thank-you and a pat on the head. Just you remember that."

Jack stormed out of the apartment, slamming the front door behind him. Then the floodgates opened and she allowed the tears she'd been holding back to flow. Soon, she was in a full-fledged hysterical state, sobbing her eyes out for what might have been but never would be now.

The puppy hurried over to comfort her and she picked Jake up, snuggling him to her chest. "I love you, Jack Turner," she whispered, patting the dog who'd settled down on her lap. "And I'll probably die an old maid because of it."

But at least you'll have a child—Jack's child.

It was true. She'd have the baby she'd always wanted, but never the man she loved.

CHAPTER SEVENTEEN

JACK WAS STILL reeling from his confrontation with Samantha as he paced the confines of his living room. He was furious with the stubborn woman for trying to cut him out of her and his child's life. He felt as if he'd just been sucker punched. He was going to be a father and the mother of his unborn child wanted nothing to do with him.

Jack and Samantha, close confidantes and life-long friends, were no more. And that saddened him even more than Samantha's high-handed manner in proclaiming him a nonentity—*a sperm donor,* for chrissake!

He wanted to rail at her, to release the anger and frustration he felt at her duplicity and stubbornness. Their years of friendship should have counted for more. Where was the trust, the honesty they had always shared? How could she believe he had walked away from their friendship?

Because that's exactly what I did.

If he were truly honest, he had to admit that he'd

run like a scared rabbit because he couldn't face the possibility that he was in love with his best friend.

Of course, now that it was too late, now that there was no hope that they would ever be together, he knew he was unequivocally and madly in love with the exasperating woman, and there wasn't a damn thing he could do about it.

Samantha had stated quite clearly that she wanted nothing from him—no money, no support, no father for her baby. He'd hurt her, and she was getting her revenge.

How could I have been so blind? So damn stupid?

All this time Samantha had been right under his nose and he'd never seen her as anything but a friend and companion. Even after their glorious lovemaking, he'd denied her, dismissing what was between them. He'd had a thousand different reasons for doing so, for wanting to lessen the desire he felt, but for the love of God he couldn't remember what they were now. Now nothing seemed important except finding a way to win Samantha over, and not just because of the baby.

In truth, the thought of having a child terrified him. Jack wasn't father material. He'd been raised in a dysfunctional family by a remote man who hadn't known the meaning of love, or, if he had, had been too drunk to realize it.

Where were the skills he needed to parent? How

would he learn how to be a good father? Those were usually lessons a man learned from his dad, but Jack hadn't been that lucky.

Even now, though they were getting along in a civil fashion, Jack didn't feel the deep sense of love and affection he should. Too much water had gone under that bridge, too many disappointments and heartaches for him to just forgive and forget. Maybe in time, if his father stayed sober, there would be a chance for them; he just didn't know.

Just like he didn't know if there would be a chance for him and Samantha.

Pressing his hands against the sides of his head, Jack felt tears well in his eyes, but he blinked them away. It wasn't manly to cry. That's what he'd been told over and over again as a child. *"Be a man, son, and stop your sniveling,"* his father would say as he hoisted the belt up over his head, slapping it across Jack's backside during one of his drunken rages. *"Only girls cry. Quit being a girl, you damn sissy!"*

Jack sniffed, swore and rose to his feet. Men might not cry, but they sure as hell drank, and he intended to get shit-faced before this day was through. And then when he stopped feeling sorry for himself, he'd figure out a way to get back in Samantha's good graces.

Samantha might be stubborn, but so was he.

"I CAN'T BELIEVE you told Jack the truth. That was either very brave or very insane of you, Samantha."

Samantha smiled halfheartedly at Patty and forked a piece of roasted chicken into her mouth. She had very little appetite for the celebratory dinner her friend insisted on paying for, but after finally landing a job as a copy editor she felt she couldn't hurt Patty's feelings by refusing the kind invitation.

Her last interview had been that morning, and she'd been hired on the spot, much to her surprise and delight, not to mention relief. Her supervisor had sent her home with several manuscripts to edit and she was anxious to dig into them and prove her worth.

"Is everything all right? You look like you're a million miles away."

"Sorry. I was thinking about my new job." Her mind returned to the matter at hand. "As for telling Jack, it was the only thing I could do, Patty. I owed him that much. And I'm not very good at lying, anyway. Eventually, he would have found out about the baby. You know that."

"Yes, and legally you really had no choice. Like it or not, Jack's the father. So how did he take the news? Is he ecstatic at the idea of becoming a father?"

"You know he's not, though he didn't seem as horrified as I'd been expecting. He even seemed willing to marry me, if you can believe that. Though, of course, that's not even a remote possibility." Not without love, and Jack had made no avowals to that end. Foolishly, she had held out hope that he would. But the sad fact was Jack couldn't say what he didn't feel. He wasn't in love with her, and that was that.

Patty snorted in disbelief. "Too bad he wasn't of a similar mind *before* he found out you were carrying his baby."

Unable to dispute that, but unwilling to continue their present depressing discussion, Samantha decided to change the subject to the topic she knew was Patty's favorite: Patty herself. "Ross has a crush on you," she said, and the woman smiled knowingly.

"I figured as much. He's called my office several times. So far I haven't returned any of them."

"So far?" Samantha's eyes widened. "You mean you might?"

Patty and Ross? Good grief! The world wasn't ready for such a hideous combination of egos.

With a lift of her shoulders, Patty said, while continuing to eat her filet mignon, "I find your brother very attractive. Does that surprise you?"

Samantha wasn't surprised; she was shocked, but chose not to let on. "I figured as much. Ross is very good-looking. And he's got that macho thing going for him. I guess if I wasn't his sister, I'd think he was attractive."

"Would it bother you if I dated him?"

Hell yes! Samantha wanted to shout, but didn't, saying instead, "Ross is practically engaged to Ellen Drury. I'm not really sure how I would feel about it, to be perfectly honest. I don't think he's made a clean breast of things with her, though he told me they were taking a break. But somehow that just doesn't ring true. And I wouldn't want to see Ellen get hurt. I like her."

"I don't care about his other women. I just want to sleep with him. I'm not looking for anything long-term, you know that. I'd like to take Ross to bed, not marry him."

"But I'm not sure that's what Ross is looking for at this point in his life. He talks a good game, but—"

"He's a man, isn't he? Men are always looking to bed good-looking women. Trust me, I know what I'm talking about."

"That's not what I meant. Ross is vulnerable right now. He doesn't know what he wants out of life, and he's running away from the decisions he needs to make. I'm not sure dating you is going to help that situation. It would only muddle things for him."

"How do you know? Maybe he'll realize after dating me that he really loves Ellen and wants to marry her."

Samantha doubted that very much. "You're

Ellen's total opposite. She's quiet, reserved, almost mousy. You're smart, beautiful and exciting. I can understand why my brother is attracted to you, but I don't think he'll be happy with someone who isn't looking for a committed relationship. Deep down where it counts, Ross has traditional values. He wants to get married and have children."

"People change. Perhaps that's what Ross wanted in the beginning, but he may have decided to go the single route instead. He knows I'm not interested in marriage and family. I made that clear back in Rhinebeck."

"Maybe, but I don't want him getting hurt."

"I'm only going to sleep with him, not shoot him in the head and leave him for dead."

"You use men up, Patty. I've seen it happen. You date them, make them fall in love with you, then discard them. It's a game to you. But this is my brother we're talking about."

Hurt filled Patty's eyes. "Are you saying you don't want me to date your brother? I find that very hurtful. After all, we're best friends, and Ross is a big boy who is capable of making his own decisions. I'm sure he can decide what he wants or doesn't want from a relationship."

"I'm not going to interfere between you and Ross any more than I have already. And my intention was never to hurt you, but to protect my brother from getting hurt. He thinks he has all the answers, but Ross doesn't know what he wants. That's all I'm saying."

"Will it make you feel better if I say that I'll let him down gently?"

Samantha smiled softly. "No one knows better than I how kind and generous you are. You've been a wonderful friend. I don't want you getting hurt, either, especially now that I know what you've been through."

Her friend laughed at the absurdity of Samantha's statement. "That will never happen again, on that you have my word. It's so much easier to avoid messy complications by keeping your feelings intact and your heart inside your chest. I never wear mine on my sleeve, honey. Not anymore."

Samantha sighed. "Like me, you mean?"

"I know you're in love with Jack and have been for years, even if you never realized it. But there's going to be someone else out there for you, Samantha. Once you get over Jack, the world will be full of possibilities."

"There aren't a lot of guys out there willing to date women with babies."

"You don't need a lot, Samantha—you only need one."

Yeah, but the one she needed was no longer available.

GLANCING OUT the window, Samantha studied the heavy clouds and wondered if it was going to snow. February always brought the heaviest snowfalls to the city.

She was halfway through the third of the manuscripts she'd been given to copyedit and had formed three conclusions: all authors were not created equal, you could become published even if your writing sucked, and her novel was much better than any of the books she had read thus far.

Now she just needed to convince someone else of that.

Reaching for another of the chocolate chip cookies she'd baked that morning, Samantha refocused her attention on the manuscript and munched. Eating cookies while reading made the lackluster writing much more palatable—palatable but very fattening.

The phone rang, and she reached across Jake's head to answer it. "Sorry, buddy," she said to the dog, who was sleeping and didn't acknowledge her existence.

"Hello, Samantha."

"Mom!" Samantha's heartbeat quickened. She hadn't heard from either of her parents since she'd dropped her bombshell and had been worried that her news had caused a permanent rift between them. "How are you?"

"At the moment, I'm freezing. I'm standing on the sidewalk in front of your apartment building, using Lucas's cell phone. I didn't want to come up without calling first."

Filled with disbelief, Samantha rose up on her knees to take a closer look at the sidewalk below. "I see you. But what are you doing here?"

"If you don't mind, I'll explain all of that as soon as I come inside. I'm getting frostbite out here."

A few minutes later, Lilly Brady appeared in the flesh. She was towing a small suitcase behind her, clutching her purse, as if she expected to be mugged at any moment, and she looked cold down to her bones. Her nose was red, her cheeks chapped and it looked as if her eyelashes were stuck together.

"Come on in. I'm so happy to see you!" Samantha threw her arms about her mother and kissed her icy cheek. "You *are* frozen. I'll make some tea to warm you up."

"Thank you, dear. I should be used to the cold by now, but I've been standing out on that sidewalk trying to figure out how to use Lucas's stupid phone and it took me quite a while."

"But why didn't you call from the station?"

"I didn't want to bother you. And Ross—" She glanced around. "Is your brother here?" Samantha shook her head and her mother continued, "Ross isn't reliable. He kept me waiting once for over an hour at the train station in Rhinebeck. And do you know why? So he could check his e-mail," she explained, not waiting for her daughter to answer. "Can you believe it?"

Unfortunately, Samantha could. Ross was a real egocentric. Being a football star had given her brother more than big shoulders; it had swelled his head to gigantic proportions. But when his career ended so abruptly, she and the rest of the family had made allowances for his bad behavior, knowing how devastated he'd been by the accident.

Ross had wanted to play football since the age of five. He ate, drank and slept the sport, and he'd finally won a football scholarship to play in college and had been drafted by the New York Giants shortly before graduation. The whole family had been ecstatic and very proud of him. Through hard work and determination Ross had persevered to realize his dream.

But then Ross had broken his leg in several places and his whole personality changed. He was no longer an affable, easygoing guy, but instead had allowed bitterness and disappointment to give him an unattractive edge. He'd grown indifferent about life and the people who surrounded him, including his own family.

Brushing the disturbing thoughts of her brother aside, Samantha asked, "Have you eaten, Mom? I've got some chocolate chip cookies, or I can make you a sandwich. I haven't started dinner yet."

"Cookies are fine," Lilly replied, following her daughter into the kitchen and studying her surroundings. "Your apartment's nice. It's much larger than I expected."

"It's decent by New York standards. But it's not mine. Jack owns it, along with the entire building. I'm just renting from him."

"I see," Lilly said, taking a sip of the hot tea and sighing deeply. "This is heavenly. I can feel myself defrosting as we speak."

Samantha smiled. "Excellent. So what brings you to New York? And where's Dad? Did he come, too?" Her father abhorred big cities, so getting him to visit usually took an Act of Congress or a threat from his wife.

"*You* brought me to New York, Samantha, you and the baby. And no, I'm sorry to say Dad didn't come with me. Fred still hasn't come to terms with the idea that his baby girl is going to have a baby and raise it on her own. That's going to take a bit more time. But don't worry. Eventually your father will come around. He loves you, and I know he's always wanted to be a grandfather."

"I'm sorry to be a big disappointment to everyone." The fact that her father thought badly of her cut Samantha to the quick. She couldn't bear the thought that he was disillusioned and disheartened by her actions.

"You took us by surprise, dear, but I've grown used to the idea. In fact, I'm actually excited at the prospect of becoming a grandmother. I'm going to spoil my first grandchild rotten. I hope it's a girl. The clothes are so much cuter."

Reaching out, Samantha squeezed her mother's hand. "Thanks, Mom! I needed to hear that."

"How are things with Jack? Does he know about the baby yet? I'm sure once you tell—"

"He knows, Mom. And nothing's changed. We're not together and have no plans to be."

"But you love him! I see it in your eyes. And I know he loves you."

"Maybe like a sister, but that's just not enough for me. I want the whole enchilada or nothing."

"You've got a tough road ahead of you, Samantha. Being a single mother won't be easy. But I'll be here every step of the way. So tell me, have you seen a doctor? It's very important to have proper prenatal care."

"I have. Dr. Phillips said everything was fine. I have another appointment next week."

"Oh darn." Lilly's face filled with disappointment. "I won't be able to stay that long. I promised your dad I'd only stay a day or two. He's such a baby when he has to fend for himself."

"I'm just happy you came, even if it's a short visit. Ross is staying in the guest room, but you can sleep in my room with me. The bed is fairly large and I don't snore."

"That's fine, dear. It wasn't my intention to impose, but I just couldn't stand leaving things up in the air between us. So I decided that the best thing for me to do was to follow my heart and come visit."

"I'm glad you did, but why haven't you called before this?"

Her mom's cheeks tinged pink. "I needed to sort out my feelings, I guess. And I've had a lot going on in my life—the church bazaar, refereeing squabbles between your father and Lucas and listening to poor Ellen go on about Ross. But I know none of that is a good excuse for not calling, and I'm very sorry. I should have been a better mother."

"You're the best, Mom. Never doubt it. So what's up with Ellen? Does she know why Ross is here in New York?"

Lilly made a face of disgust. "She suspects, but isn't certain. Ross told her he was coming to see you, support you in your time of need, so to speak. He didn't mention when he was coming home, and Ellen is worried that he's not. I guess things haven't been good between them, as we'd suspected."

"Ross is infatuated with Patty Bradshaw. I think he came here to see her."

"Oh no! Ellen will be devastated. What am I going to tell the poor thing? I'm not sure what she'll do when she finds out."

"The truth, I guess. She deserves to hear it, and she won't from Ross's lips—he hates confrontation." Which was odd, considering the sport he had chosen to play.

"Your brother can't help it if he's screwed up at the moment. He's had a difficult time since his injury."

"We've all been making excuses for Ross far too long. He's milked the loss of that football contract to gain all the sympathy he could. But it's time he stands on his own two feet and owns up to what's expected of him. He can't keep running away from life forever, Mom. None of us can."

Her mother heaved a sigh. "That's very true. Your father and I have done Ross an injustice by making excuses for him. Your brother has been very good at making people feel sorry for him, but if he's dumping that lovely girl for a flashy New York lawyer, then this is where the pity stops."

"I'm happy to hear you say that."

"Where is your brother, by the way?"

"Out buying new clothes. He's asking Patty out on a date."

"So he's really going to betray Ellen, even though they're practically engaged?"

"Looks that way. Ross craves excitement, and Patty is that."

Her face a mask of disgust, Lilly said, "In my day, men dated flashy women but married the steady, nurturing types. I guess that doesn't hold true anymore."

"Ross claims that he doesn't want to get married, though I doubt he's told Ellen that. It really ticks me off that he's been stringing her along like this."

"That boy's a fool. He doesn't know what he wants or what a terrific woman Ellen is. He's always been blinded by superficial things that didn't matter—a pretty face, a pair of big boobs."

"Mother! I've never heard you say boobs before."

"I'm not as backward as my children think, Samantha. I've been on this earth a lot longer than you or your brothers, and I've learned a few things along the way."

Refilling the plate of cookies, which were nearly gone, Samantha poured more tea into the cups. "Care to enlighten?"

"Men often miss what's most important in life— the love of a good woman, contentment and friendship. If your brother thinks he'll find that in a woman like Patty, he's sadly mistaken. Don't get me wrong—I've got nothing against your friend. But it's obvious that she's not Ross's type."

"I've told him as much, but he's determined to make an ass out of himself."

Samantha thought about Jack, about everything he was throwing away because he didn't love her, and sighed deeply. "Why does life have to be so difficult? Why can't things just fall into place?"

Lilly clasped her daughter's hand. "I think God wants us to work for what we really want, so we'll appreciate it that much more when we finally get it."

"But sometimes things just aren't meant to be, Mom."

A knowing look crossed Lilly's face. "And sometimes they are, Samantha."

CHAPTER EIGHTEEN

THE DRIVE TO Rhinebeck seemed to take forever, no matter how fast Jack drove the SUV he had borrowed from one of his tenants. Not yet dawn, there was little traffic, and he allowed his mind to wander and ruminate over the frantic call he had received earlier this morning from his mother.

"Jack, it's Mom. Something terrible has happened. Your father—"

"Is he dead?" A lifetime of memories flashed before him, and he bolted upright, bracing himself for the worst. He had thought about this day a thousand times over, wondering if he would feel sadness and guilt when the time came. Astonishingly enough, he felt both.

"No. Not yet. But it's very serious. Martin is in the hospital. He began hemorrhaging internally late last night. It was awful, Jack. I've never seen so much blood. The sheets were soaked in it."

His father was still alive. Jack sighed deeply in relief.

"What do the doctors say? Do they have a diagnosis?" His father's years of drinking had finally taken their toll on his body. News of his hemorrhaging didn't come as a shock, only the fact that it had taken so long for his father's organs to give out.

"They've stopped the bleeding for now and are running a bunch of tests, doing biopsies, that sort of thing. I was hoping you could come, just in case—" The rest was left unsaid, but his mother's meaning was clear: his father was not expected to live.

"I'll be there as soon as I can. Try not to get too upset, Mom. We'll get through this, you'll see."

In a tear-filled voice, she said, "I love you, Jack. And so does your father."

Jack had played that conversation over and over again in his head, knowing he had made the only decision he could—the right decision. His mother needed him. And he needed to see his father. He couldn't let the man die with so much left unsaid between them.

But what would he say when the time came? That he loved him? That everything that had happened in the past was now forgiven?

A good son would forgive and forget. A good son would let go of his anger and hurt and move on, be supportive of his family.

But was he a good son?

AN HOUR AND a half later, Jack entered Mercy Hospital and made his way quickly to the ICU, where Martin Turner was being treated for a still-undiagnosed ailment.

Directed to his father's room by a gray-haired nurse, Jack paused in the doorway to find his mother seated next to the hospital bed praying over his father's still form. She looked exhausted, her face filled with sadness and worry, and his heart twisted, as it had so many times before in similar situations.

"Mom," he whispered, entering the room, and she looked up, her eyes lighting with relief.

"Thank God you're here, Jack. There's been no change. Your father's been sedated and isn't likely to awaken for quite some time, if ever."

He moved to stand beside her and wrapped his arm about her shoulders. "*Ssh!* You shouldn't talk like that. You of all people know what a fighter Dad is. He's been down this road before. We all have."

"But never like this, Jack. Look at him. His face is so ashen he already looks dead." She began to sob softly.

Jack did look, his gut clenching at the sight of the man he'd professed to hate for so many years—the man who had oxygen tubes stuffed up his nose and some type of intravenous solution pouring into veins that previously thirsted for liquor.

The tyrant of his childhood looked shrunken and old. The pallor of death surrounded him and there was no certainty that God or the devil wouldn't have their due before this day was done.

"Just keep praying, Mom. It's all you can do at a time like this." When she nodded, he added, "I'm going to talk to the doctor, and then I'll be back. Send the nurse to get me if there's any change or Dad wakes up, okay?"

His mother reached out and squeezed his hand. "I know this is very difficult for you, Jack. I'm so proud you've been able to put aside your differences, and—"

"Mom, he's my father. Of course I had to come. The other stuff doesn't matter now. I'm a grown man, and I've come to terms with my childhood." *Had he?* Jack wasn't really sure, but he intended to make the effort, considering the present circumstances.

"Your father loves you. He talks about you all the time, asks me if I've heard from you. I know he's sorry for the way he treated you. I'm sorry, too. Sorry I wasn't there for you when you needed me. I wasn't a very good mother. I—"

His mother's words of apology went deep, piercing his heart because of the sad truth they held. "That's in the past, Mom, and there's no sense in talking about it now. We've got bigger issues to face at the moment. I'll be back in a few minutes. Do you want some coffee? I'm going to get a cup—hopefully it'll help me wake up."

"No, honey. I'll be fine. But don't be gone too long, just in case—" He kissed his mother's cheek and saw the fear in her eyes before escaping out the door.

Jack was in emotional overload. First, there was the news of his impending fatherhood, the argument with Samantha and now this. He wished he'd been more of a praying man. He could use God's help right now.

He wanted to call Samantha, to ask her to come to the hospital. He needed to be with her, to hear the soothing sound of her voice and hold her hand in his. But she'd made it clear that he wasn't welcome in her life any longer. So he'd have to face his difficulties alone, as he'd forced Samantha to face hers.

Being alone sucked. Why had it taken him so long to realize that?

"DO YOU THINK I should come?" Samantha's mother had just called with the news of Martin Turner's hospitalization, and Samantha was beside herself with worry, mostly for Jack. She knew this would not be an easy time for him. "Jack might need a friend right now, Mom. I should be there."

"It's still touch and go, dear. Martin has lapsed

into a coma, Jack and Charlotte remain at his bedside and there's nothing you'd be able to do, even if you came."

"But Jack—" She couldn't bear the fact that he was going through such an ordeal by himself. She knew better than anyone what he was dealing with—and now he had the added burden of the baby to think about.

"The emotional upset might not be good for the baby, Samantha," her mother cautioned, and Samantha's hand flew to her abdomen.

"I hadn't thought of that."

"Well, you'd better start thinking about it. I'm sure Jack wouldn't want you to put yourself or the baby at risk. Don't worry. I'll let him know we talked and that you're concerned. I'll have him call you just as soon as we know something more definite."

She hung up the phone, feeling more alone than she'd ever felt in her life. Jack was gone, her father wasn't talking to her, Ross remained in a snit because of her refusal to bless his relationship with Patty, and the only companion she had was a black-and-white puppy who wasn't a great conversationalist.

A hot-fudge sundae was the only cure for what ailed her at the moment. She had just removed the carton of vanilla ice cream from the freezer when the phone rang again.

Hoping it was Jack, she rushed to answer it, stubbing her toe on one of Jake's chew toys and cursing a blue streak at the pain that resulted. "Hello," she answered in a not-too-friendly tone.

"May I speak to Samantha Brady, please?"

Samantha rolled her eyes, which were still watering. "Look, if you're hoping to sell me something, I can tell you flat out that this is not a good time. So—"

"It's Ellen, Samantha. Ellen Drury. Have I called at a bad time?"

"Ellen?" She was stunned to hear from the woman and felt embarrassed that she'd been so abrupt. "I'm so sorry, Ellen. I didn't recognize your voice. I just stubbed my toe and it hurts like hell."

"I'm sorry. You might try putting some ice on it."

"I'm going to put ice cream on it instead, after I shove a large portion of it down my throat."

"Oh, dear. I have called at a bad time, haven't I?"

Ellen's voice was soft and small, and Samantha felt like she'd just kicked a helpless kitten. "No, really, it's fine. How are you?" As if she didn't know.

Damn Ross's cowardly hide!

"Confused, mostly. I was hoping you might be able to help me sort out a few things."

"Have you spoken to my mother?" Please say yes! Please say yes! She didn't want to be the bearer of bad news.

"Not recently. I've been out of town. My aunt died."

Swearing inwardly that her mother hadn't told Ellen about Ross's indiscretion, she conveyed her condolences and then said, "I'm not sure if I can help or not. But I'll try, of course."

"How's Ross? Is he doing okay?"

"Ross is fine. He's not here at the moment, though, if you called to talk to him." Actually, she doubted her brother would be back this evening. He'd spent every night this week away from the apartment, and she didn't need a crystal ball to tell her where he'd been.

"I didn't call to speak to Ross. I wanted to talk to you, if you have time to chat."

Samantha sucked in her breath, dreading the questions she knew would be forthcoming. "Of course I have time. Is there a problem?"

"Ross left Rhinebeck rather abruptly after your last visit here. We haven't been getting along very well, and I think he wants to end our relationship. I was just wondering if he'd said anything to you about it."

Hearing the uncertainty and sadness in the woman's voice, she chose her words carefully. "Not really. He told me you two were taking a break. I assumed it was mutual." Samantha couldn't bear to tell her the truth—that the man Ellen loved had betrayed her, that the man she loved was an idiot.

"It's more like Ross is taking a break from me. I think he's infatuated with your friend. He spoke about Patty Bradshaw constantly after you left, then told me he was going to New York to stay with you. I just put two and two together."

Heaving a deep sigh, Samantha said, "I'm not going to lie to you, Ellen. Ross is dating Patty. I think it's just a fling, but I know that's not going to make you feel any better. My brother's an ass and needs to grow up. But he's still my brother and I love him, so I'm not sure what else I can say, except I'm sorry. You don't deserve to be treated like this."

Ellen was quiet for a few moments, and then she asked, "Are they having sex?"

Samantha crossed her fingers behind her back. "I don't know."

"I guess that's that, then."

"What do you mean?" She couldn't believe Ellen was willing to give up so easily. "I thought you loved Ross. Are you just going to give up and let another woman have him?"

"I do love Ross, with all my heart and soul. Don't ask me why, because he's treated me pretty badly these last six months. I guess I just feel that if I could get him to open up, tell me what's really bothering him, that things would be different between us. I know a woman can't change a man, but I'm convinced that Ross is hiding his true self, that the man everyone sees isn't the man he really is. I know deep down Ross cares for me. If only—"

"Then fight for him, Ellen. If you love him that much, you shouldn't give up."

But isn't that what I've done with Jack?

"But how can I? I'm no competition for Patty Bradshaw. I saw her in town when she was visiting your family. She's beautiful. I can see why Ross is attracted to her. She's everything I'm not."

"You're a lovely, smart woman, Ellen, and you need to quit short-changing yourself. Patty might have Ross temporarily, but you've been with him these past two years and that counts for a lot. You have something, a special something that attracted my brother. He wouldn't have stayed with you if he didn't truly care. I really believe that."

"But what good does that do me now? He's gone."

"The good news is he's not that far away. You could come to New York and give Patty some competition." No one was more surprised than Samantha to hear herself suggest such a thing, but she was sick and tired of the underdog never winning, herself included. And she was also a big enough person to admit when she was wrong, and she'd been wrong about Ellen.

Ellen might not be flashy or exciting, and her personality and Ross's might be different, but maybe the young woman would actually be a calming influence on her brother and would make him an excellent wife.

"Be serious, Samantha. I'm a schoolteacher, she's an attorney. My clothes are from J.C. Penney, and I'm quite sure that Patty has never shopped anywhere less than Barney's. How can I possibly compete with such a fashionable, successful woman?"

"You don't need to spend a fortune to look glamorous. You could do a makeover—maybe cut your hair, wear some makeup, buy some new clothes—if you wanted to try and win my brother back."

"I don't know. It's not my style."

"Well, it's up to you, Ellen. I'm not saying it'll work, but it couldn't hurt to try. I hate to see you give up without a fight. After all, you just admitted how much you loved Ross. So why would you want another woman to have him?"

"I appreciate your advice. I'm not sure what I'm going to do, but if I decide to come to New York, I'll let you know."

"That's fine."

"And Samantha... Please don't tell Ross that we spoke. If I do come, I want the element of surprise."

"I won't breathe a word."

"Thank you. You've been very nice to me over the years. Your whole family has. No matter what happens between me and Ross, I hope we'll always remain friends."

"Ross doesn't deserve you, Ellen."

"He's a good man. And I just want him to be happy. Ross deserves that."

Ross deserved a kick in the butt, but Samantha didn't bother to tell Ellen that. Her brother was making a huge mistake. She just hoped when he realized that, it wouldn't be too late. Ellen wouldn't wait forever. No woman should have to.

Do you hear that, Jack Turner?

IT WAS NEARLY midnight and Jack's mother had gone to an adjoining room to lie down for a while. She was exhausted; the day's events had taken their toll. The night duty nurse was stationed at a desk across the hall, and for the first time since he'd arrived, Jack found himself alone at his father's bedside.

Martin was still comatose and had been for many hours. His organs were starting to shut down. The doctors didn't hold out much hope that he'd survive the night.

Jack stared down at his father's lifeless form. He wanted to reach out to him, to hold his hand, but he couldn't do it. Too much had happened between them. And though deep down he loved his father, he didn't think he would ever forgive him. Not even now when he knew the end was near.

"It's Jack, Dad. I'm sure you're surprised that I came. I'm pretty surprised myself. But I wanted to be here for Mom. I wish I could say that I feel a whole lot differently about everything that's happened in the past, about us, but I can't. And I'd be lying to you and myself, if I did.

"You need to be strong now, Dad, for Mom's sake. She loves you very much, always has. Try hard to beat this. Mom needs you to be there for her."

I love you teetered on the tip of Jack's tongue, but no matter how hard he tried, he couldn't say the words. "I'm proud that you stayed off the booze these past months. I want you to know that. And that I got to know you as the father I'd always hoped you'd be. I hope that'll be enough for you, because it's all I can give."

Jack was astonished to find tears rolling down his face, and he wiped them away with the back of his hand. He cried for the child he once was, for the man he wanted to be and for the father he never really knew or understood. "Goodbye, Dad," he whispered. "I hope the next life treats you better than this one did."

SAMANTHA WAS SURPRISED to find her brother seated at the breakfast table when she entered the kitchen the following morning. "Well, good morning. I didn't know you were home." She poured a cup of coffee and sat down at the table across from him. Ross looked bleary-eyed but otherwise content.

"Patty had an early appointment this morning, so I didn't spend the night."

"I think we should talk, Ross. I'm really concerned about what's going on with you and Patty."

He put aside his newspaper and reached for his coffee cup. "What's going on is really none of your business, Samantha. I told you that once before. I'm a big boy and I can make my own decisions. I sure as hell don't need you making them for me."

"If you want to break it off with Ellen, then you should go home to Rhinebeck and do just that. It's not right to string her along. She has feelings. And you have a history together. I'm surprised you would be so callous toward her. Don't you care that she's probably upset?" She chose her words carefully, trying not to let on that she'd spoken to Ellen.

"Ellen's always upset about one thing or another." He sighed. "Look, she's a good woman. I know that. But she's not what I need right now. I'm not ready to live up to her expectations."

"Ellen would make a wonderful wife and a terrific mother, and I know deep down that's what you want."

"You don't know anything, so quit trying to put words in my mouth. I haven't been this happy since I lost my football contract. Why can't everyone just leave me alone and let me live my own life?"

"Because your life impacts others, that's why. Because there are consequences to face when you make the wrong decisions. Because Patty Bradshaw

is not going to be the woman you'll spend your de-
clining years with. She will have moved on by then,
Ross. I've known her a long time. She isn't interested
in anything but sex."

His brows rose. "And what's wrong with that?
Maybe I'm not ready to settle down. Everyone wants
to tell me what to do, but maybe I'm not ready to do
what you all want. I need my freedom right now. I
need excitement. And yes, I need sex. Ellen was
conservative as hell in bed, while Patty is totally un-
inhibited and wild. I've never felt so—"

She held up her hand to cut him off. "Please spare
me the details. I'm not interested in hearing them,
especially at this hour of the morning. There's more
to life than sex and excitement, Ross, and Ellen isn't
going to wait forever for you to make up your mind
about what you want. I hope you don't screw up your
life any more than you have already."

"You sound as if you know something I don't.
Have you spoken to Ellen?"

Samantha crossed her fingers under the table.
"No, we haven't seen each other since Christmas.
But being a woman, I know what women are like."

"Forgive me for saying this, sis, but you haven't
exactly been scoring any touchdowns with your own
love life. You've made a mess of things with Jack,
you've got a baby on the way, and our father isn't
singing your praises these days. All in all, I don't

think you should be handing out relationship advice."

His words felt like a slap, but Samantha was determined not to let the hurt show. "I know I haven't always sung Ellen's praises, but I realize now that I was wrong about her. You have a wonderful woman who loves you, an opportunity to make a good life together and have a passel of kids, and you're throwing it all away on a pipe dream that's never going to come true. Trust me, if I were in your shoes and had someone who loved me as much as Ellen loves you, I wouldn't be sitting here having this stupid conversation with my ungrateful, pigheaded brother."

Ross sat there in stunned silence.

"And from now on you can do your own laundry and clean up your room. As you've so recently pointed out, I'm not your mother and I don't intend to be treated like her. Start pulling your weight around here, Ross, or find somewhere else to live. I love you, but you're a lazy pig."

Samantha stomped out of the kitchen, plopped down in front of her computer and realized she felt good. Kicking ass was very freeing, and she discovered, as her fingers started moving over the keyboard, that the writer's block she'd been experiencing for weeks was gone.

She might not have a husband on the horizon, but she did have a job, a baby on the way and a new book to write. It was more than some women had, and she felt pretty damn lucky at the moment. Of course, her hormones being what they were, that was likely to change at any moment.

CHAPTER NINETEEN

MARTIN TURNER never awoke from his coma. His burial took place on a snowy February afternoon, with only a handful of people in attendance.

Now, three days later, Jack was driving back to New York City with Samantha by his side. She and Ross had made the trip to Rhinebeck to attend the funeral, but her brother had opted to stay behind to take care of some "personal business," so she had reluctantly accepted Jack's offer to drive her home.

"Thanks again for coming, Samantha. I wasn't sure you would. I know my mother appreciated that you were there."

"I'm happy I came, even though my mother's given me nonstop grief over it." Lilly had taken on the role of major worrywart since learning of her daughter's pregnancy.

"She's worried about you. I am, too, for what it's worth. Are you feeling okay?"

"I'm fine. I'm perfectly capable of taking care of myself."

"And as I told you, you don't have to. I don't run away from my responsibilities."

"This baby is not your responsibility. I think—"

"I don't care what you think. It's still my child. Nothing you can say will change that fact."

Noting how upset Jack was becoming, Samantha heaved a sigh. "Let's not argue. You've had a difficult few days."

Jack nodded. "How are things with your dad? Any change there? He seemed very quiet at the funeral."

Biting the inside of her cheek so she wouldn't cry, Samantha shook her head. "He barely spoke two words to me while I was home. I guess it's going to take more time for Dad to get used to the idea that I'm not perfect."

Jack's smile was sad. "I guess it takes all of us a long time to figure that out. My dad had a lot of flaws, and in the end I wasn't able to forgive him for them. Guess I'm not as good a man as I'd hoped to be."

"Listen, Jack, I know you feel bad about your father's death, but you can't rewrite history at this late date. Your dad might have turned over a new leaf these past few months, but the years he was a drunken, neglectful parent can't be changed. You had every right to feel the way you did about him, so don't let guilt overrule your good sense. You were the best son you could be, under the circumstances. Like you said, none of us are perfect, and that goes for parents, too."

"I've made a lot of mistakes that I've come to regret. I wish—"

She raised her hand, unable to listen to what he had to say. "You're sad, lonely and vulnerable right now. And I'm not ready to hear anything pertaining to our situation, if that's where this conversation is heading. I've finally gotten my head on straight, and I'd like to keep it there a while longer." She had spent weeks crying her eyes out over Jack, mourning the life they would never have together, but that was in the past and she intended to keep those feelings at bay.

He looked over at her. "How did you get so strong all of a sudden?"

Smiling softly, she continued staring out the front window at the gently falling snow. "I've never been a weak person, just an unfocused one. Being pregnant has given me a purpose in life, direction that was lacking before. I had goals, just like I do now, but I never had the impetus to reach them. That's all changed now." Becoming pregnant was quite possibly the best thing that had ever happened to Samantha, in spite of the resulting turmoil, but not for the reasons she'd originally thought. She'd become a different person, a better person—someone responsible, self-confident and driven to succeed.

"That's great. Sometimes it takes a slap upside the head to make a person realize just what it is they want out of life."

She recalled her father saying something similar once, but didn't respond. Instead, she asked, "How's your mom dealing with all of this? Do you think she'll be okay, now that you've left?"

Jack nodded. "My mother's strong in her own way. She'll survive this because she has to. That's how she got through life with my father and that's how she'll go through life without him. Lilly's been a godsend. My mom opens up to her and reveals things about herself that she would never confess to me. And, of course, she knows about the baby. I think the fact that she's going to be a grandmother has lessened some of the hurt."

"Jack, we've already discussed the baby and your role in its life. You have none. You shouldn't allow your mother to think that she's going to be grand-parenting this child, because she isn't. That's just not the reality of how things are going to be." It was a harsh statement, but one that had to be made.

His fingers tightened on the steering wheel, his knuckles turning white. "I have parental rights, and I'm not giving them up. I intend to be a father to this child, and my mother will be one of the baby's grandmothers, whether you like that or not. It's im-portant to me now more than ever. If my dad's death taught me anything, it's that life is too short to waste on regrets. I intend to be the kind of father to *our* child that I never had while growing up."

Though Samantha was touched by Jack's sincerity and understood where he was coming from, she couldn't allow herself to weaken or change her mind. She and Jack had no future together, despite the biological fact that they were going to be parents. She intended to remain strong. She wouldn't let him hurt her again, no matter what.

"I think it's clear that we will always be there for each other, Jack. That's the kind of relationship we've always had and it's not likely to change, despite our present circumstances. But don't kid yourself into thinking that we'll ever be more than friends. And even that is going to take time and a lot more effort on both our parts. I hope you can understand that. I'm not trying to be mean, but that's just the way it has to be."

"You must think I'm a fool, that I'll allow you to make all of the decisions and go along with them, no matter what. Well, I've got news for you, Samantha. That's not going to happen. I'm not going to take this lying down."

"I could say the same about you. I chose to stand on my own two feet rather than become dependent on anyone, and that's exactly what I intend to keep doing."

"We'd be good together, Samantha. Why can't you see that? Our child needs both of us."

"Nothing's changed. You and I will go on leading separate lives. Sometimes our lives will cross, but most often they will not."

"I'm telling you, it doesn't have to be that way."

"Yes," she said emphatically, "it does."

WHEN SAMANTHA returned to her apartment later that evening she was exhausted, and wanted nothing more than a hot bath and a good night's sleep.

Her neighbor, much to her relief, had redeposited Jake in his portable kennel after boarding him at her apartment these past few days, and she hurried to let him out before the anxious pup clawed his way to freedom. "Hey, sweetie, Mommy's home. See, I told you I wouldn't be gone too long. Have you been a good boy?"

Jake barked excitedly, and when she picked him up to hug him, promptly peed all over the front of her raincoat. "I'm happy to see you, too. I think." Removing the offending garment, quite relieved it was waterproof, she tossed the coat on the floor and noticed her message machine light was blinking.

Smothering the exuberant puppy with kisses, that were returned tenfold, she punched the button and listened. "Hello, Samantha. It's Ellen. I just wanted you to know that Ross has officially broken up with me. I haven't decided what I'm going to do yet, but I may take your advice about coming to New York. I'll let you know what my plans are when, and if, I decide to come. Please don't mention this call to Ross. Thanks. Bye."

Samantha's eyes widened. Ellen was considering taking her advice? Well, that was interesting, to say the least.

Deciding that she couldn't take any more drama for one evening, Samantha made her way into the bedroom to shed her worries and her clothes. Taking a page from Scarlett O'Hara's book, she decided to think about everything tomorrow.

THE SELF-CONFIDENCE Samantha had felt only two short weeks ago when she'd proclaimed her independence to Jack had evaporated like an early morning mist rising from the Hudson. At the time she thought she had her life under control. Now, nothing seemed to be going right.

Ross had moved out of her apartment and into a hotel. He'd returned from Rhinebeck with the news that he had broken things off with Ellen and intended to pursue Patty in earnest. Nothing Samantha had said could dissuade him, so she'd finally had to wish him well in his decision, and in his search for an apartment closer to Patty's.

Jack hadn't called or visited since their last meeting, and Samantha missed him terribly, despite all her false bravado. Being alone definitely sucked! Most of the time she felt isolated, tired, depressed and overworked. The manuscripts she'd been hired to edit kept coming, as did the rejection letters on her book. She was no closer to selling her novel than she'd been months ago. At least now she was making rent.

There'd been no word from her father, though her mother had called several times to check up on her, as had Lucas, who'd actually told her he loved her and was looking forward to being an uncle. That conversation had made her cry. Of course, most things made her cry these days.

Her tummy was finally starting to expand. At five months she looked slightly overweight, but not terribly pregnant. Dr. Phillips had said during her last appointment that she was as healthy as a horse and the baby was doing just fine.

Glancing at the phone, then at the clock on the mantel, Samantha knew her father would be working on his accounts this time of day. She had the greatest need to hear the sound of his voice, to talk to him about the most mundane things and tell him how much she missed him.

So just do it. What are you afraid of? He's your father. He can't stay mad at you forever.

Picking up the phone, she dialed; her father answered on the third ring. "Fred Brady," came the familiar voice over the line, the sound of it making her heart ache.

"Hi, Dad! It's me, Samantha."

There was a long silence on the other end, and then, "Your mother isn't here right now. You'll need to call back later. I'll tell her you called."

"I didn't call to talk to Mom. I called to talk to you, Dad." She prayed he wouldn't hang up on her. It was clear he didn't want to talk.

"Don't have time for idle chitchat. I'm busy. And I'm sure you must have a million things to do, too."

"I love you, Dad. Why won't you talk to me? I'm sorry I disappointed you, but—"

"I can't talk right now, Samantha," her father said, then abruptly hung up the phone. She thought she heard tears in his voice, but couldn't be sure.

She was sure, however, of the tears running down her own cheeks.

Her pregnancy had seemed like the answer to a dream. But now she wondered. It had cost her the man she loved, the father who respected and adored her and—

"I wish I'd never gotten pregnant! I've ruined my life. I've ruined all the relationships that were important to me. How could I have been so stupid and selfish to think that this baby would be the answer to my prayers?"

The phone rang again and she answered it quickly, hoping it was her dad calling back to apologize and tell her he loved her, too. But it was Patty on the other end, not her father.

"Hello, Samantha! How are you?"

She couldn't keep the disappointment out of her voice. "Fine, I guess."

"You don't sound fine. Anything I can do?"

It was on the tip of her tongue to tell the woman that she'd done quite enough already, by taking her brother for a joyride and ruining his relationship with Ellen, but she thought better of it. Patty was one of her closest friends, and she didn't have many of those at the moment. "I tried to call my dad. He wouldn't talk to me," she told her.

"I'm sorry, Samantha. Give him more time. He'll come around eventually. You'll see."

"I guess," Samantha said, then asked, "Was there something you wanted, Patty? I'm surprised to hear from you. It's been weeks since you've called." And Samantha had been too angry to call her.

"I know, and I apologize for that. I've just been preoccupied with…work and things." *With Ross,* Samantha thought. "Would you like to have lunch today? I've missed you. It would be like old times."

"I guess we could. I'm sick of staying inside this apartment all the time." And she was lonely, so very lonely. "What time do you want to meet?"

"Let's say noon at that little Italian place around the corner from you. How does that sound?"

Samantha wondered what Patty wanted to discuss. She sure as hell hoped it didn't have anything to do with marrying Ross, because that subject was likely to send her right over the edge, and she was teetering there already.

PATTY WAS already seated, with a glass of Merlot in hand, when Samantha entered the nearly empty restaurant. Her friend's eyes widened when they caught sight of her. "You're finally starting to look a bit pregnant, Samantha. How much weight have you gained, if you don't mind my asking?"

"I don't think I look very pregnant at all. And I haven't gained that much weight. Why? Do you think I look fat?" She patted her abdomen.

"Not fat exactly, just bigger than you were. You always had such an adorable figure, and now...well, now you're a bit pudgy, that's all."

"I've only gained about twelve pounds so far."

"Well, the extra weight looks very good on you. Though I must say they still haven't designed very fashionable maternity clothes."

"Oh, they have them. I just can't afford to buy any. I've been doing my shopping online to find the best bargains. Motherhood Maternity has become my new favorite store." Her dark green wool slacks and matching sweater didn't have quite the same pizzazz as Patty's Ralph Lauren dress.

"Really? How interesting. I ordered you a caffeine-free Diet Coke, since I figured you can't drink wine or alcohol now that you're pregnant."

"Thanks!" Samantha took a sip. "I don't miss alcohol that much. As long as I don't have to give up ice cream or chocolate, I can survive just about anything."

"Well, be careful you don't gain too much weight. Men are so picky these days about overweight women, and with a baby in tow, you'll have a tougher time meeting them when the time comes."

Knowing Patty's heart was in the right place, even if her mouth wasn't, Samantha counted to ten, and then replied, "I have no interest in meeting men, and I'm being careful with what I eat." She limited herself to only one gallon of ice cream and two Snickers bars a day. One had to remain in control, after all. "I thought you wanted to meet for lunch because you had something to talk to me about. And I doubt it's the size of my waistline."

Patty's cheeks filled with color, which was quite unusual. There wasn't much that embarrassed the woman. "I wanted to talk to you about Ross."

Samantha sighed. "I figured as much. So are you two running away together or something? You might as well tell me, so I can throw up now and get it over with."

Her friend laughed. "I've missed you, Samantha. And no, I've no intention of running off with your brother. Quite the opposite, in fact. I intend to break things off with Ross, but I wanted to talk to you about my decision first, so you wouldn't hate me too much."

"You didn't seem to mind my anger when you took up with him against my wishes," Samantha reminded her.

"I know. And I'm sorry for that. Sometimes my libido gets in the way of my better judgment. I realize now that dating Ross was a big mistake, for all the reasons you tried to warn me about."

"He's in love with you, isn't he?" Poor stupid Ross!

"Ross asked me to marry him. I told him I had no intention of ever marrying, but he seems to think he can change my mind. He's been looking for an apartment close to mine, though he hasn't found one yet, thank God. I—" She shook her head and reached for her wine. "I like my space, you know that. I don't want Ross breathing down my neck, and I don't want him believing that we're a couple. Unfortunately, he's convinced himself of that."

"And you did nothing to give him that impression?"

She shook her head. "No, I swear! For me, it was only about the sex, which was great. But I made it clear I wasn't interested in more than that."

"Ross broke up with his girlfriend for you. I have a feeling you're stuck with him, Patty, unless Ellen can convince him to come back to her."

Patty heaved a sigh. "He thinks she's boring."

"Ellen's quiet and not at all flashy. I suggested she do a makeover and try to compete with you for him, but she doesn't think she can."

Suddenly, Patty's face lit. "But that's perfect! Don't you see? If we can convince Ellen to come to New York, and I suddenly turn into the biggest bitch on the face of the planet, I'd have to lose by comparison, no?"

Samantha mulled over her friend's idea. It had a wee bit of merit. "I don't know. Ellen's got self-esteem issues. I'm not sure she would want to go toe-to-toe with you. What if she lost? It would devastate her."

"You've got to convince her to come. Ellen doesn't have to know that we spoke. I'll make an appointment for her at the Red Door and pay in advance for her to have a complete makeover. You can take her to Barney's and help her pick out some dynamite clothes and shoes. Just put it all on my account. Then we'll arrange for her to accidentally run into Ross when he's with me. Trust me, I'll pale by comparison."

Samantha smiled. "You must really be anxious to get rid of my brother, if you want to go to so much trouble and expense. Why don't you just ditch him, like you've done with all the others?"

"I like Ross. I don't want to hurt him. And besides, he is your brother, so if there's a way to let him down easy, I—"

Samantha's eyes widened. "I think you care about him more than you're letting on."

"Don't be ridiculous. I want my life back. Plus, from what you've told me, Ross will be much happier in the long run with Ellen. And if he sees that she's gone to so much trouble to win him back… Well, he can't help but be impressed, right? Maybe I should call her?"

She shook her head. "No, that wouldn't be a good idea. Let me do it. I'll try to convince her to come."

"That would be great. The sooner the better."

"I—" Suddenly, a shooting pain seared Samantha's stomach and she clutched it, her eyes filling with tears.

"What is it? What's wrong?"

"I'm… I'm not sure. I'm cramping. There's something wrong with the baby, I just know it." Another cramp hit and she let loose a bloodcurdling scream that had several of the waiters rushing over.

Patty moved to her side and helped the ailing woman to her feet. When she did, she noticed Samantha was bleeding and had paled considerably. "You're bleeding! I'll call for help. We've got to get you to the hospital right away."

One of the waiters had already called for an ambulance, and a short time later, Samantha and Patty were in the back of the vehicle, sirens blaring, on the way to the hospital.

"This is all my fault, Patty. If I hadn't said that I didn't want to be pregnant, this wouldn't have happened. I've brought down God's wrath on my head. Oh God! I'm going to lose my baby."

"Don't be silly. You didn't cause this. Sometimes things like this just happen for no reason. Do you want me to call your doctor?" Patty took her cell phone out of her purse.

"No. I want you to call Jack. Tell him what happened and ask him to meet us at the hospital. I have to see him. I don't want to go through this without Jack."

"Do you think that's wise? I mean, you told him you didn't want him to be involved with this pregnancy."

Samantha started to cry. "I don't care what I told him! I need him with me. Please, Patty, just call him and quit giving me the third degree!" The last word was pronounced *degreeeee* as another cramp hit her. "He'll come. You'll see."

CHAPTER TWENTY

JACK WAS LIKE a man possessed as he made his way to the hospital, yelling at the cabdriver to go faster.

She'd asked him to come, and there was no way in hell he wouldn't be there for her.

Please God! Don't let Samantha lose the baby. I love her, and she wants this child so much. He continued to pray silently as the cab pulled up in front of the medical facility.

Obstetrics was on the eighth floor of the building, and he paused briefly at the nurses' station to find out where Samantha was being treated. "Samantha Brady's room, please!"

"Are you a relative, sir?" the gray-haired nurse asked.

"No, but I'm the father of the baby."

Recognition lighting her eyes, the older woman rose to her feet, rounded the desk and grabbed Jack's arm. "Right this way, Mr. Turner. We've been expecting you. Ms. Brady's been asking for you. Carried on something awful, until the doctor threatened to sedate her if she didn't calm down." As she led him down the long hallway, he spotted Patty standing in front of a closed door, looking worried. He'd never seen Patty look worried before.

"Thank God you're here!" she said when she finally looked up. "I've never seen Samantha so hysterical. She's been calling for you, insisting that God is punishing her and is going to take the baby from her. It's just awful, Jack. I wasn't sure what to do. I hope you can calm her down, talk some sense to her. I haven't been able to."

"Can I see her?"

Patty shook her head. "There are two doctors in there right now doing an examination. They said we could go in after they were done."

"Do you know what happened?"

"Samantha started bleeding. That's all I know. We were having lunch, and then all of a sudden she started cramping up. It gave me quite a scare, I can tell you that."

He brushed agitated fingers through his hair. "I don't know what'll happen if Samantha loses this baby. She wants it so badly." And the damnedest thing was, he wanted the baby, too. It was their child, a part of them, a symbol of their night of passion and the love they'd shared.

"But you don't?"

The question took Jack aback. "That's none of your damn business, Patty!"

The attorney's shocked look grew apologetic. "I'm sorry. I didn't mean—"

"I wasn't prepared for the news about the baby at first," he interrupted. "But now that I've had time to think things over, I know I'd make a good father. I told Samantha I wanted to be part of the baby's life, but she has other ideas."

"At least you showed up. I admit I was surprised to see you here. Most men wouldn't give a shit."

"I'm not most men, and I care a lot about Samantha. We have a long history between us. And I—"

"Love her?"

"I care about her." Of course he loved Samantha; he'd always loved her. He'd just been too stupid to realize it when they were living together. And he'd never forgive himself for being so blind and bullheaded.

The door to Samantha's room opened and the doctors walked out. They looked calm, not overly concerned, and that served to ease Jack's fears a bit. "You can go in now, Ms. Bradshaw. Ms. Brady's condition has stabilized, but we want her to rest."

"I'll make it brief, Doctor Phillips." Patty glanced at Jack, her expression softening. "I'll let Samantha know you're here."

He nodded, and then said to the physicians, "I'm

Jack Turner, the baby's father. Can you tell me what's going on with Samantha?"

"Not without Ms. Brady's permission, I'm afraid. But you're free to see her, as long as you don't upset her."

"Of course. I have no intention of upsetting Samantha," he replied before entering the room and walking straight to her bedside.

Her face lit with relief and happiness when she saw him, and the sight of her radiant smile went straight to his heart. He loved her, truly loved her. "Oh, Jack, I knew you'd come! See, Patty?" she told her friend. "I told you he'd come."

He seated himself in the metal chair next to her bed, and when he did, Patty rose to her feet.

"I've got to get back to work, kiddo. I'll call you later," she told Samantha before disappearing out the door, leaving Jack alone with her and grateful for the privacy.

"Of course I came. I dropped everything and hurried over here as fast as I could. It was the worst taxi ride of my life. I've been so worried about you."

"I'm sorry you had to leave work."

"There's nothing to be sorry about. Tom's taking over my appointments, so I'm yours for as long as you want me." Jack realized at the moment that he meant it. He wanted Samantha in his life permanently. He wanted to make a life with her and the baby. He wanted to marry Samantha and never be apart from her again.

"Did you talk to the doctor?" she asked.

"I tried, but he wouldn't tell me anything because we're not related, said if I wanted to know I'd have to ask you. So tell me everything."

"There's not a whole lot to tell. I had some bleeding while having lunch with Patty, but everything seems to be fine now. I'm being kept here for observation. If I don't exhibit any more symptoms for the next twenty-four hours, I can go home. But I have to remain in a reclining position, in bed or on the sofa, for at least ten days. And that is going to drive me absolutely bonkers."

Jack breathed a deep sigh of relief that didn't go unnoticed. "Are you sure? I mean, has the bleeding stopped for good?"

She nodded. "They did a sonogram—the baby seems to be fine." She had thanked God many times for that. "Dr. Phillips still isn't sure what caused the bleeding, but he said that it happens from time to time. He also said that stress could be a contributing factor. I've been upset lately—about my dad, about Ross and Ellen, about…other things."

"I'd never forgive myself if you lost this baby because of me." He reached out to clasp her hand. "I never meant to hurt you. Please believe me."

"You're not to blame for any of this, Jack. I stress

over everything—you know that. I just need to learn to relax more. This incident has taught me a good lesson. From now on, I'm not going to let things I have no control over bother me."

"I don't want you worrying about a thing. I'll take care of everything, just like before."

She heaved a sigh. "Jack, we've talked about this. I like my independence." It was a lie, pure and simple, but one that needed to be told.

"I…I love you, Samantha. I want to marry you. I want to be a husband to you and a father to our child. I've thought long and hard about this, and I realize how stupid I've been, how selfish. I'd be honored if you would marry me, Samantha Brady."

The proposal was unexpected and very sweet, as was Jack's concern over her and the baby's well being. Samantha wanted nothing more than to confess her love, tell him how she wanted to be with him forever, but she knew she couldn't. She had no intention of trapping him into a relationship he didn't really want, or take advantage of his vulnerability at such an emotional time. That wouldn't be fair to either of them.

"I'm honored by your proposal, Jack, but I can't accept it." When he opened his mouth to object, she held up her hand to forestall his argument. "I do want us to be friends, however. And if you choose, I'd like you to be part of the baby's life. As you pointed out, a baby needs both parents. And I know you would be a good father." *A great father, she amended silently.*

"Thank you. But I'm not willing to accept your decision as final. I'm going to prove to you that I can make you happy, that I'm the only man you should marry. And I'm going to do my damnedest to make you see that what I'm telling you is the God's honest truth."

Smiling softly, she patted his cheek. "Careful, Jack, you're starting to sound smitten."

She'd meant it as a joke, but his reply wasn't the least bit funny. In fact, it was shocking and quite unexpected. "That's exactly what I am. And I intend to court you like any good suitor."

Her mouth gaped open, and then, when she'd regained her composure, she said, "It's not going to work, Jack. *We're* not going to work."

"We'll see about that. Now just sit back and relax while I read to you." He picked up the book on the nightstand that Patty had purchased at the gift shop for her and frowned as he looked at the cover art.

"It's a romance," she warned. "I doubt you'll like it."

"Ha! A lot you know. I'm a very romantic guy."

THE FOLLOWING DAY, after Jack had carted her home in a taxi, he set out to prove, once and for all, that he could sweep Ms. Samantha Brady off her feet—even if she was in a reclining position on the sofa at the moment.

"I can't believe they actually use the word 'member' to refer to a guy's dick. What's with that?" He looked down at his crotch. "It sounds like it should be part of a club or something."

Samantha giggled. "It is. The good old boys' club. Actually, it's called a euphemism. You're reading a historical romance and they always use terms like that."

"And I thought the rosy nipples and thrusting loins were bad," he said with a bemused smile and shake of his head.

"Don't you need to go to work? I feel guilty that you've taken so much time away from your business to stay home and read to me."

"I have a partner who's capable of taking care of things, and you're more important. My business is taking care of you right now. This is where I want to be, Samantha. I want to be with you, now and forever."

Her eyes misted. "But—" His words touched her deeply, and she shook her head to dispel the moment. "My mother's offered to come and stay with me, Jack. You needn't feel obligated to do this."

"She called me, too. I told Lilly it wasn't necessary for her to come, that I'd be here for you.

And she seemed perfectly willing to let me do it. In fact, Lilly seemed quite thrilled by the prospect."

"Only because Mom likes to meddle in my business."

"Good. I can use all the help I can get," he said with a grin, then kept on reading. A few moments later, his eyes widened, and there was a shocked look on his face. "This stuff's pornographic! Are you putting sex like this in your book?"

She heaved a sigh. "Of course. Sex is a normal part of any relationship. But a romance novel isn't just about sex—it's about two people coming together and forming a committed relationship."

"Sort of like us, huh?" He grinned, giving her a rakish wink worthy of any romance novel hero.

She shook her head. "For a man who always feared any commitment beyond going to work in the morning, you sure are singing a different tune." And she had to admit it was becoming music to her ears. If only she could trust what he said.

"Listen to this." He began reading: "The masked stranger known only as The Phantom crept to the young woman's bed, and while she was still asleep, untied the strings of her chemise and parted the material. Her nipples, all rosy and hard, were too tempting to resist and he licked them until they puckered, then pinched them until she groaned."

"Ouch! I've never pinched a woman's nipples in my life," Jack admitted, his face a mask of disbelief.

Samantha grinned. "Maybe that's why you're still single."

"Very funny. Do women really like this sort of treatment? Wouldn't it be construed in the same way as, say a spanking?"

"It's fiction, Jack."

"Well, I find this absolutely fascinating. I guess I figured that the kind of books you're writing—the funny dating stuff—were what all romances were like. I had no idea there were so many different kinds."

"If men read more romance they might actually figure out what women want."

He scoffed. "I don't believe modern women want to be treated like the women in these books."

"You're right. But they want the romance of it, the passion, the 'If I can't have you I'll die' kind of feeling. There's something to be said for knights in shining armor, rugged cowboys and Regency dukes. I don't know of any woman who wouldn't want to be swept off her feet, carried into the bedroom and have a man make mad passionate love to her."

"Is that what you want, Samantha? Do you want to be swept off your feet and made love to?"

The question hung in the air for several moments, and the heated look he gave her could have scorched the socks right off her feet. Samantha's cheeks turned a becoming shade of pink. Pulling the afghan up around her neck, even though she felt very warm from the heated conversation, she replied, "Since that's not likely to happen any time soon I don't sit around and think about it. There are no more modern day heroes, anyway. All the good ones are in books."

"Not even ones who rescue aspiring writers from living on the street?" He winked, and she blushed again.

"That book hasn't been finished yet," Samantha hedged, "so I'm not sure if the hero remains heroic. Most men don't." But somewhere in her heart she knew that Jack would always be a hero.

"But not all men, right?"

"No, not all men." Feeling very uncomfortable by how intimate the conversation had become, Samantha assumed an indignant posture.

"I thought you were taking care of me. I'm starving. Are you going to make us some dinner?"

"Due to the fact that I'm a terrible cook, I've ordered Chinese." He checked his watch. "It should be here in about fifteen minutes."

Samantha's stomach grumbled. "And what's for dessert?"

"Fortune cookies?" he asked hopefully.

"No way. I need chocolate if I'm going to make a speedy recovery. Can't you bake us some brownies? I'm dying for chocolate frosted brownies. You can use my recipe."

He looked horrified by the suggestion. "You know I can't bake. I'd end up burning the damn things."

She crossed her arms over her chest and smiled wickedly. "A real hero would know how to bake brownies, and he wouldn't make excuses or flinch from a challenge. A real hero always rescues a damsel in distress, especially if said damsel is pregnant and addicted to chocolate brownies. Are you telling me that you're not a real hero?"

He arched a brow. "You're throwing down the gauntlet, aren't you?"

"Exactly. If you want to be considered Sir Galahad then you must bake brownies."

"And if I do, will you promise to take a nap after dinner? You've hardly slept all day, and the doctor said you need plenty of rest."

"I promise. But don't forget, you promised to watch *Pride and Prejudice* with me. You haven't forgotten, have you?"

Jack, who had once sworn he would never watch six hours of men cavorting around in tight pants and wearing frills, groaned loudly. "All right," he agreed, but his expression looked tortured, which made Samantha smile even wider.

Jack was definitely hero material. And he was all hers, for the time being.

CHAPTER TWENTY-ONE

JACK ENTERED Samantha's apartment early the next morning to find her asleep on the sofa, the snoring puppy lying atop her slightly swollen abdomen. The sunlight streaming in through the window illuminated the contented expression on her face, as if she was having the most wonderful dream.

Smiling softly, his heart warmed at the sight of the woman he loved, her body swollen with his child, her hand resting lightly on the puppy's head.

At night when he lay in his lonely bed, he thought about Samantha, about making love to her again, and he would dream of how their life together would be—wonderful, complete, fulfilling—if only she would agree to marry him.

And that was a big, fat *IF!*

Samantha was without a doubt the most stubborn woman he knew. Once she made up her mind about something she rarely changed it.

But he had to convince her. Somehow, someway he had to show her just how important she was to him, how his life meant nothing without her in it; and not just because of the baby, but because he loved her.

The brownies he'd baked the previous evening had been a step in the right direction. They'd tasted awful—the tops had been burned, the bottoms uncooked—but the pleased expression on Samantha's face when she declared them to be "the best brownies she'd ever tasted" had made the effort and the embarrassment of their failure worthwhile.

Glancing down at the warm metal pan in his hands, he smiled proudly. He'd gotten up at five this morning to bake cinnamon rolls for Samantha's breakfast, but not without a great deal of cursing and anguish first.

They weren't the prettiest rolls he'd ever seen, but they were edible, had been baked with love, and he was pleased that he could do something nice for her, after all the years she had cooked and cleaned up after him.

It was nice to finally commit to another person. Now if he could just convince Samantha....

Approaching the sofa, he held the pan up to her nose and waited. Jake awoke instantly and growled, but then recognizing who had intruded into his space, resumed a disinterested state and went back to sleep.

Samantha sniffed the air several times, wrinkling

her nose, and then her stomach growled loudly, making Jack grin. Slowly her eyes opened.

"You'd better have a good reason for—" Her eyes landed on the rolls and widened. "You made cinnamon buns? I don't believe it. When did you do it? How?"

"Believe it, sweetheart. I borrowed one of your cookbooks last night. They're not half-bad, if I say so myself. In fact, I'm rather proud of the way they turned out."

Her eyes filled with tears. "But that's so sweet. I can't believe you did that. What ever possessed you?"

"Well, if I thought they were going to make you cry I wouldn't have."

She smiled. "I cry over everything these days, you know that. The other morning Jake farted, and the sound scared him so much that he jumped. It was so funny and touching that I cried."

"Good lord!" He rolled his eyes. "Your hormones must be totally out of whack, if you're crying over a farting dog."

She pushed herself to a sitting position and rubbed the small of her back. "I dozed off on the couch last night after you left. Guess I never did make it to my bed. My back's killing me now."

Jack frowned. "That's not good, Samantha. Dr. Phillips said you need as much rest as possible and sleeping on the couch isn't going to cut it. I guess I'm just going to have to tuck you in at night to be sure you're following the doctor's instructions. Now roll over and I'll rub your back for you."

Samantha knew she should refuse. Having Jack's hands on her body was just too great of a temptation. But her back and neck muscles were knotted, so she finally gave in. "All right. But only for a minute."

He began to massage her neck, kneading the tight muscles and then moving his clever fingers up and down her spine. "*Ooooh!* That feels *soooo* good."

"Why don't you take off your top, so I can do a more thorough job? I promise you'll like it."

She knew she would like it, too much, and that was the problem. "I will not!" Samantha flipped over and bolted upright. "Come on. Let's go into the kitchen. I can't wait to try one of these rolls." She made to get up, but he pushed her back down gently.

"Not so fast. You're not supposed to be moving around, remember? The doctor said short trips to the bathroom, and that's it. I'll bring the rolls and coffee to you."

She sighed, looking quite indignant. "I'm not an invalid, you know. And I'm feeling much better."

"You are for the next week and a half," he argued, "so try to cooperate, okay? This nursing business is new to me; don't make it any harder than it is."

"Boy, you sure are a grump in the morning. I never noticed that before. You're obviously caffeine-deprived."

"You never noticed because you always slept late."

She smiled at the truth of his words and her tone softened. "I appreciate your taking care of me, Jack. You've been great company, and I want to thank you for everything. You're a good friend, and—" She stopped, paused to take a breath, as if reconsidering what she was about to admit, and then said, "The baking is a big surprise." She smiled widely. "Thank you so much!"

Jack pushed the dog out of the way and sat down next to her on the sofa, taking her hand in his. "I love you, Samantha. I always have, I guess. And I'm going to keep on saying that until you believe me. You've got to believe me."

Her eyes filled with tears, and she looked as if she wanted to say something similar in return. "I know you love me, Jack."

His eyes widened. "You do?"

She nodded. "But only as a dear friend. Anything else you might be feeling right now is motivated by the baby. You're just emotional and caught up in the moment. I think that's perfectly natural."

"Dammit, Samantha, that's not true! I do mean it. I love you more than I ever thought I could love anyone. And it's not just because of the baby. I'd love you even if there was no baby."

Samantha digested his words, studying his face for any sign of deception; she found none. "But you didn't love me before. How do you explain that? You never said a word about your feelings toward me. How do you expect me to believe you now?" She shook her head. "None of this makes any sense, which leaves me to conclude the obvious. I'm not as naive as you think."

He rubbed the back of his neck. "Hell, I don't know. I'm stupid when it comes to women. That shouldn't come as a surprise to you. I've never had any successful past relationships, you know that."

Crossing her arms over her chest, defiance lit her eyes. "As I said before, I want you to be part of this baby's life, but marriage is out of the question. I'm very firm on that, so don't try to talk me into something we'll both regret."

"What if we just lived together in sin?" he teased, unwilling to upset her further.

"That is not going to happen, so change the subject."

"How's your mom doing?" he asked to make her happy.

"She's driving me nuts. You'd think I was the first woman on earth to be having a baby. She's been calling here five times a day. The last time, she asked me if my bowels were working properly. I mean, really!"

He smiled. "It's her first grandchild. You've got to give Lilly some space and let her revel in it for a while. Becoming a grandparent is a big deal, especially when it's your only daughter's."

Samantha heaved a deep sigh. "If only my dad were as excited, but I can't even get him to talk to me. I don't know what to do about it. I'm so upset and heartbroken over his unwillingness to accept the way things are—to accept me."

"That's my fault. I should have spoken to Fred at the funeral, explained things." It was something he needed to rectify, for both his and Samantha's sake.

"I tried talking to him, but it didn't do any good. I've fallen off the pedestal Dad had me on, and he's not willing or able to accept that his baby is having a baby and raising it on her own."

Jack's frown deepened, his eyes filling with regret and determination. "Fred will come around, you'll see."

"But how can you be so sure? Dad is so stubborn. He comes from the old school."

"I just am. Now quit worrying about it and eat your cinnamon rolls. I want to be appreciated, after slaving over a hot stove all morning."

Samantha giggled. "Yes, dear."

"I'M SORRY it's taken me so long to come over and visit, Samantha," her brother said two days later, seating himself on the sofa next to her. "I wasn't sure I could handle being around Jack. I'm still pissed at him for what he did."

What we did, Samantha thought, but didn't voice it aloud. Ross was a lot more stubborn than she. In fact, stubbornness ran in the family, in a straight line from Fred Brady.

Her brother looked genuinely contrite about his previous neglect, so Samantha restrained from telling him how stupid she thought he was being with regard to Patty and Ellen. Instead, she took his callused hand and pulled herself up to a sitting position.

"You've got to get over your hard feelings toward Jack. If you could see how kind and generous he's been since my release from the hospital, you wouldn't harbor any ill will. You two have been best friends for a long time, Ross. Please, please, don't ruin your friendship over me. You'll regret it if you do. And so will I."

He sighed. "I know. And I miss Jack. But you're my sister, Samantha, and I've got to protect you."

"You need to look out for yourself. I'll be perfectly fine once I get done with this stupid confinement and am able to resume all of my usual activities. This lying about doing nothing is driving me nuts."

Glancing down at the stack of manuscripts on the floor next to the couch, he shook his head. "Looks like your work hasn't stopped. Do you have to read all this stuff? Must be boring as hell. I don't envy you, but then, I was never much of a reader."

"I enjoy reading most of it, though sometimes I come across a real clunker. At any rate, reading takes my mind off things." Like Jack's startling declaration of love.

If only she could believe him. Her life would be so much simpler, not to mention happier. But his admission went against good old common sense.

"Well, you mustn't work too hard. If you're short of cash, I can give you some. I don't want you jeopardizing your health. I know for a fact it's not worth it."

It was the first time he'd offered to help her, monetarily or otherwise, and she was touched by the gesture. "I'm fine, really. So how are things with Patty? Are you still dating her?" She already knew the answer, but wanted to get Ross's take on things, to see how they matched up with the attorney's, who sometimes exaggerated to make a point.

His smile was boyishly charming and enthusiastic, which didn't bode well for her commitment-phobic friend. "Great! Couldn't be better. I'm in love with her, Samantha."

"In love or in lust? You haven't been dating her very long. Are you sure it isn't just infatuation that you're feeling? Love takes time to grow—it doesn't just happen overnight."

"Oh no? What about love at first sight? Are you saying that doesn't exist?"

"Most sensible people don't believe in it."

"I'd marry Patty in a heartbeat, if she'd have me. I've asked her, but she said no. I'm not giving up, though."

So Patty had been telling the truth. Her brother, it seemed, would soon be getting a taste of his own medicine—the same medicine he'd spooned out to Ellen. "I think that would be a big mistake, if you want my opinion." Not that he ever did but, as his sister, it was her duty to give it anyway.

"Why not? I thought she was your friend."

"Patty's a great friend. But she'd make you a terrible wife. You two have so little in common. Think about it. You hate crowds, fancy parties and confined spaces, and New York City is pretty damn confined. Patty is caviar and champagne, while you're beer and KFC."

"I can adapt. She's the hottest woman I've ever met."

"It takes more than sex to make a relationship. What about shared interests, values, that sort of thing? Why, even your personalities are different. I doubt you could even understand what makes her tick. Patty is a very complicated woman."

"Patty's not as hard and tough as everyone thinks. She has a vulnerable side. I've seen it, from time to time, when she's let her guard down."

And it was that vulnerable side that made Patty want to run away from commitment. "I know all about Patty's vulnerability. But I also know that the woman is married to her career and the lifestyle she's chosen for herself. I don't think there's room there for anything else, including you."

He shook his head. "Why do you always have to be so negative, Samantha? Nothing you or anyone else can say is going to change my mind. I intend to marry Patty Bradshaw. I'm in love with her."

Noting the determined glint in his eye, and knowing there was no use in arguing further, Samantha squeezed her brother's hand. "Good luck, Ross. I hope you find what you're looking for."

He smiled back. "I'm crazy about Patty, Samantha. Crazy in love with her."

"YOUR BROTHER is driving me crazy!" Patty said on the telephone, later that same afternoon. "When are you going to call Ellen and put our plan into motion? I'm desperate to get this situation resolved."

"Why don't you call her, if you're in such a hurry?"

"I've thought about it. But I think you'll agree that it would be better coming from you."

"What aren't you telling me?"

"Ross is insisting that we go to Tiffany's this weekend and look at engagement rings, even though I've told him no a thousand times. I'd rather have my pubic hairs plucked out one by one than get engaged to your brother, or anyone else for that matter."

"Well, your take on this relationship is quite different from my brother's. He couldn't be happier. And he's determined to marry you. He told me so, quite emphatically, I might add."

"Oh, shit!"

"I tried to warn you, remember?"

"But you said you'd help me. You said you'd call Ellen and see about having her come to New York, so she could get a makeover. We have to make the woman into a femme fatale so Ross will go gaga over her."

"I haven't had a lot of opportunity for scheming, Patty, what with being on my back twenty-four/seven for the past several days."

"I know. I know. And I'm sorry to be so pushy."

"Since when have you ever been any other way?"

"I'm at my wit's end, Samantha. I'm getting to the point of filing a restraining order to keep Ross away from me."

Patty's threat filled Samantha with dismay, and it

also made her wonder if the woman was in danger of losing her heart and determined to fight against it. Patty's voice always softened when she spoke of Ross; she'd never said an unkind thing about him, up till now.

Her friend had been hurt badly in the past, had vowed to remain single, but perhaps Ross had touched a part of her that no other man had been able to reach.

"Oh, Patty, don't do that. You'll hurt him too much. Please promise me you won't."

A deep sigh, then, "Of course I won't. But I need help, and Ellen is the only one who can provide it. Are you feeling well enough to call her? Of course, she mustn't know what we've cooked up. She has to believe that she won Ross back on her own merits."

"Yes, I'm feeling fine—quite good, in fact. And I guess if Ellen agrees to come and holds off visiting for another week or so, the timing should be about right for me to be up and about."

"Don't let Jack know, okay? He might tip off Ross and then all our efforts will be in vain."

"Jack's not here. Tom had a problem with one of their real estate closings, so Jack went down to the office for a few hours. He'll be back later." And she missed him. Samantha had gotten used to having Jack around again. They watched movies together, played cards and board games and did many of the same things they'd done while growing up. It had been fun, familiar, and she didn't want it to end.

And it wouldn't, if she agreed to marry Jack.

But, of course, she couldn't do that. He might be foolish enough to think he was in love with her, but she knew deep down that he wasn't, and she couldn't bring herself to trap him into an unwanted marriage. They'd end up hating each other, and she couldn't stand the thought of that happening. She loved Jack too much and wanted him to be happy.

"Great! So if you call her right now Jack won't know anything about it."

"All right, I'll call. But I can't make any promises, so don't get your hopes up. Ellen might be over Ross completely by now. She doesn't strike me as the type of woman who would sit around and wallow in self-pity." *Someone like me, for instance.* "I haven't heard a peep out of her, and my mother hasn't seen her lately, either. I asked Mom the last time we spoke."

"Well call her anyway. If Ellen wants her boyfriend back she can have him, all tied up in a big red bow. Give me a call on my cell after you've talked to her and let me know if she's coming, so I can set up her salon appointment at Elizabeth Arden and authorize you to charge on my Barney's account."

"I will. But like I said—"

"I know. Don't get my hopes up. Well, I am getting them up because if this doesn't work, Ross is going to be scheduling an appointment with his therapist."

Surprise filled Samantha's voice. "Ross has a therapist?"

"Yes. He's been seeing some woman in Rhinebeck for the past six months, trying to get his head on straight and figure out what to do with the rest of his life."

"So what did she advise him?"

"That bitch told him to do what felt good. Not what was right or responsible, but what felt good. Can you imagine? She should have her license yanked."

Samantha swallowed hard. "Houston, we have a problem."

"No shit! And I'm about to crash and burn."

CHAPTER TWENTY-TWO

ELLEN'S ARRIVAL the following week couldn't have come at a better time. Samantha was feeling like her old self again and had resumed her regular routine.

Jack had gone out of town to settle a business matter and wasn't expected to return for a few days. She hadn't told him about the matchmaking scheme that she and Patty had cooked up for Ellen and Ross, because she knew without a doubt that he would hate the idea and would most likely tell her brother.

When it came to interfering females, men usually stuck together.

"It was so nice of you to ask me to stay with you, Samantha," Ellen said, hurrying to keep pace with her new roommate. "To be honest, I've been a bit concerned about finances, and I wasn't sure if I could afford New York or not. The city is so expensive, and I feared the hotel costs would be prohibitive. I don't make that much money as a teacher."

"Trust me. I can relate."

"Are you sure you can afford this makeover? I'm

grateful, of course, but I don't want you spending money you don't have."

They were walking down Fifth Avenue on their way to Elizabeth Arden's Red Door salon, and Samantha smiled at her experiment in the making. Ellen was more than willing to have a makeover in an effort to win back Ross and had enthusiastically agreed to allow Samantha to treat her to the salon, which, in reality, Patty was paying for, but, of course, Ellen didn't know that.

Samantha considered her reply carefully, then said, "I have a friend who works at the salon. He got me a free gift certificate, so it's not costing me a thing. And having lived here for as long as I have, I know how expensive this city is. I've got plenty of room, so there's no problem about you staying with me. Besides, it's fun having another woman around. Although Jack was a wonderful nurse, he has totally different tastes in movies and TV shows than I do. Like Ross, he's a big sports nut."

A woman could only take so much football, wrestling and ice hockey before she went bonkers.

"I'm worried that Ross might come over unannounced and ruin our surprise before we're ready for him to see me," Ellen said. "I don't want him to think I'm desperate, even if I am. Marital prospects in Rhinebeck are slim to none, as you know."

"He won't. I told him I'd be out of town for a few

days. Ross thinks I'm traveling with Jack, so he has no reason to come over."

"Do you really think this makeover idea will work? I'm not a very glamorous person, and I wonder if Ross is really worth all this trouble. I mean, I love him, but why can't he like me for who I am? Am I really so ugly and unappealing that I have to change completely?"

"Don't be silly. Of course Ross likes you, Ellen. He has for years, don't forget. But like most men, he's become infatuated with a pretty face and a flashy lifestyle. You and I both know that kind of life isn't going to make him happy."

"I'm not so sure. I—"

"My brother is a homebody at heart. You've got to trust me on this. I know Ross as well as I know myself." Which, admittedly, wasn't well at all, and it was scary to be giving advice to others when it could very well blow up in your face. But she knew she had to try. After all, not everyone had as bad luck as she did when it came to love and relationships.

"Well, I've seen your friend, Patty," Ellen said, drawing Samantha's attention back and not looking at all convinced, "and like I said before I can't compete with her. There's no amount of makeup that can change that fact. Plus, she has a sense of style that I will never have. Something like that takes years to develop, not days."

The corduroy jumpers that Ellen was fond of wearing were a bit of a concern. Had they *ever* been in style, or was it a plot by designers to homogenize the world?

Smiling as confidently as she could—corduroy was a lot to overcome—Samantha linked her arm through Ellen's. "Don't be too sure about that. Patty might be attractive, but she has flaws like the rest of us. At some point, the makeup has to come off to reveal what's beneath the surface. Don't get me wrong, I like Patty…we're good friends. But she's not perfect, by any means."

"I hope you're right."

"You need to quit worrying and believe in yourself, see what I see. You're a very attractive woman."

Ellen sighed. "I'm a very practical woman, and what we're about to do goes against most of my principles. I don't like pretending to be something I'm not."

"You're doing nothing of the kind. God made you into a lovely woman with a great figure. You just have to flaunt what you've got.

"Most men need to be hit over the head a few times before they can see the big picture and appreciate what they have. Sometimes it's sitting right in front of them and they don't even know it."

Am I talking about Ellen and Ross or me and Jack?

"I must say I'm flattered and somewhat surprised

that you want Ross and me to end up together. We've never really had all that much to say to each other in the past, Samantha, so why is this so important to you?"

"Because I want my brother to be happy, and I think he will be with you. Ross wants kids and a normal life. Oh, I know all about his football dreams and worldly aspirations, but deep down he's still Ross Brady from Rhinebeck, and the things that are most important to him—marriage, family, values—haven't changed. They've just been pushed to the back burner." Ellen was far more suitable for Ross than Patty could ever hope to be. In time she hoped he would see that.

They paused in front of the tall red doors of the salon and the skeptical woman took a deep breath. "Well, here goes nothing," Ellen remarked with a sick smile. "Last chance to back out and save your hard-earned money."

"Trust me, sweetie. This is going to be the best investment I've ever made. You wait and see."

JACK STOOD at the threshold of the Bradys' living room, trying to decide the best way to approach Samantha's father. He was determined to repair the damage he'd done, however inadvertently, to the father/daughter relationship.

"Thanks for agreeing to see me, Fred. I know I'm

not your favorite person at the moment, and I can certainly understand why you're upset." He walked into the room and seated himself on the sofa.

Fred said nothing. He just continued rocking back and forth in his favorite recliner that rested by the big stone fireplace. A blazing fire roared within, heating the cozy room against the inclement weather, though it couldn't take away the chill that emanated from the older man, making Jack wonder if his coming here had been a big mistake.

He didn't want to make matters worse than they already were. Samantha would never forgive him for that.

"I want you to understand," Jack continued despite the lack of response, "that what happened between Samantha and me was an accident, pure and simple. Neither of us intended to… um, for *that* to happen. And though that's not an excuse, I'm taking full responsibility. As you know, we were drunk at the time or this episode would never have occurred."

The rocker stopped, and Fred turned, eyes cold and jaw set, to look Jack squarely in the eye. "My daughter's pregnant. I can't believe Samantha behaved so foolishly, so out of character. She's always been such a perfect child. You expect boys to mess up, but not a daughter, not Samantha."

"Samantha is still the same, sweet girl you've always known, Fred. And your total disregard of her has made her miserable and upset, which isn't good, especially now that she's pregnant. She loves you. She wants your love and respect, as do I."

The older man's eyes widened at Jack's admission, then his features softened a bit and he said, "I never told you how sorry I was about your dad's passing. I know it was hard on you."

Jack shrugged. "There was no need. I knew you cared when you showed up at the funeral service. And you know damn well that you were always more of a father to me than Martin ever was. I spent most of my childhood in this house with you and Lilly."

"Your mother did the best she could. Martin was a troubled soul."

"Yes, he was. And I hope he's resting in peace now. But for years he took the coward's way out, unlike your daughter, who is facing the consequences of her actions head on. You should be proud of her for that."

Rubbing at his arthritic knees, which plagued him whenever it rained, the older man took a moment to consider Jack's words before replying. "Samantha's always been my perfect princess. I took the news real hard. Maybe I overreacted. Lilly says I did. I don't know. I just know it hurts. I've always expected so much from her—she's never disappointed me before."

"Kids eventually have to grow up, Fred. And I think you're forgetting something very important— you're going to have a grandchild soon, maybe another girl to spoil rotten, though I'm secretly hoping for a boy." He hadn't told anyone that yet, including Samantha. But he wanted the opportunity to raise a boy and give his son the love and attention that had been missing from his own childhood. He wanted to be a hands-on, play-with-your-kid kind of dad.

"How's Samantha doing? I'm ashamed I didn't visit her in the hospital. Lilly gave me hell for that."

"She wasn't there for very long, just a day or two. And she's doing fine now. No more bleeding, and she's eating like a horse." He'd become a real expert at baking brownies. Samantha devoured them by the handful.

Fred's smile was filled with happy memories. "That girl always could put the food away. She gave her brothers a run for their money at the dinner table, I'll tell you that."

Taking a deep breath, Jack decided to go for broke. "I know Samantha would love to see you. I'm planning on giving her a surprise baby shower soon, and I hope you'll think about coming. Seeing you would be the best medicine in the world for her. And I think it would be good for you, too."

Samantha's father stared intently into Jack's eyes. "You love her, don't you, son?"

"With all my heart and soul. I'm just sorry it took me so long to realize it. Of course, Samantha doesn't believe me when I tell her that. She thinks my change of heart is because of the baby. But it's not. I want to marry her, spend my life with her."

Knowing a thing or two about stubborn women, the older man shook his head and cursed beneath his breath. "Damn stubborn girl! She's just like her mother. You keep after my daughter to marry you, you hear? That baby needs both a mother and father. And I'm talking full-time, not this visitation on the weekends crap that's so in fashion. It's no wonder kids are so screwed up these days."

Jack's eyes widened. "Then you would approve of having me for a son-in-law, if Samantha said yes?"

"Oh, for chrissake, Jack! We've had you lined up for that role since you were six."

Jack grinned, as did Fred, then the two men hugged, both of them vowing silently to bring Samantha to her senses one way or another.

"MY GOD, you look gorgeous! I can't believe it's really you." Samantha stared in openmouthed amazement at the woman, unable to believe it was actually Ellen.

The pretty woman's cheeks filled with color, and she tugged at the skirt of her dress, clearly uncomfortable in it. "Are you sure this dress isn't too tight? I've never worn a knit like this before. And black isn't really my color. I prefer pastels."

Spending five hundred dollars of Patty's money on a new dress, hairstyle and makeup application had resulted in a modern miracle. If Samantha hadn't seen the transformation with her own two eyes, she wouldn't have believed it.

Money definitely talked. And sometimes it even shouted!

"You look ravishing and quite sexy. Trust me. When Ross sees you tonight he's going to—"

"Tonight!" The horrified woman gasped and palmed her burning cheeks. "Ross is going to see me tonight? How? Where? I'm not ready. It's too soon. I need time to get used to how I look. When I look in the mirror I see a stranger."

Once they were safely seated inside the taxi that Samantha had just hailed she smiled, patting Ellen's hand reassuringly. "I know for a fact that Patty and Ross are having dinner at Le Cirque tonight. It's a very posh restaurant, which means it's right up Patty's alley." Patty never used Zagat to rate a restaurant. Instead, she preferred to look at the menu and base her decision on how much everything cost. And in New York City, where most restaurant prices were through the roof, that could be risky. But Le Cirque definitely lived up to its sterling reputation and expensive offerings.

"We're going to drop by, quite by accident, you see, and—"

"So they don't know I'm here?"

Samantha crossed her fingers in her lap. "No. It'll be a total surprise for Ross."

"But I can't afford to have dinner at a place like Le Cirque! Ross will know immediately that it's a setup."

"Not if I tell him it was my idea—that I sold a magazine article and we've come out to celebrate."

"But how will I explain what I'm doing here? He knows you and I have never been the best of friends. He'll be suspicious."

"I've thought of that. If he asks, I've decided to tell him that it was my mother's idea—that she asked you to come check up on me and see if I needed anything while Jack is out of town. Ross knows how overprotective our mother is. He'll believe that excuse in a heartbeat."

Ellen still remained skeptical. "Are you sure this is going to work? I feel so sneaky and dishonest. I hate playing relationship games."

"Why dishonest? Because you look hot and you're trying to interest the man you love? There's nothing wrong with that. Every woman in America would be accused of dishonesty if that were the case."

"Lady, listen to your friend," the cabbie, who'd apparently been listening to the entire conversation, interjected from the front seat. "If your boyfriend doesn't want you, come and see me. I think you're a knockout."

Ellen's cheeks turned fire engine-red, and she stammered a thank-you.

"See, even our cabdriver thinks this will work. And he's unbiased." Samantha smiled gratefully at the handsome man reflected in the rearview mirror, and he winked back.

The plan had to work, or else Ellen would be miserable, Patty suicidal and Samantha would become an even bigger failure in the romance department that she already was.

As SAMANTHA and the scheming attorney had previously arranged, Ross and Patty were waiting by the maître d's desk at precisely eight o'clock that evening when she and Ellen walked into Le Cirque.

"Is my makeup melting?" the nervous woman wanted to know. "I'm so frazzled I'm sweating more than Lucas's hogs." She removed a tissue from her purse and began dabbing at her nose.

"You look lovely. Try and relax. And your makeup is perfect." Samantha, on the other hand, felt like Shamu the Whale's younger sister. The black maternity dress she wore, though stylish—or as stylish as a maternity dress could be—hugged her protruding belly, making it look like an extra large bowling ball.

Samantha caught Patty's eye and smiled. The woman winked back, then declared in a loud voice, "Oh look, Ross! It's Samantha and that little teacher you know from home. What's her name? Eileen?"

Ross spun on his heel, eyes widening. "Ellen! Ellen?" He peered at the woman standing beside his sister and his forehead crinkled in confusion. "Ellen Drury, is that you?"

Samantha unobtrusively elbowed a terrified Ellen in the side, urging her to reply. "Yes…yes, it's me," she managed to get out.

"Don't be such a dolt, Ross. Of course it's your schoolteacher friend. She's just cleaned herself up finally." Patty smiled thinly at Ellen. "Nice dress. Did you run out of corduroy?"

Samantha winced and felt Ellen's pain and embarrassment. Apparently Ross did, too, because his lips thinned and his eyes darkened. "Be quiet, Patty! You're embarrassing me."

Before Ross and Patty could come to blows, Samantha blurted, "Ellen's come to stay with me for a few days." She then related the story they'd concocted about her mother's interference. "I canceled my trip with Jack so I could show Ellen around the city. We've been having a great time, though I'm not able to do as much as I'd like."

"How long have you been here?" Ross wanted to know, unable to take his eyes off the pretty woman.

"I must say you look amazing. I like your hair that way. It really brings out your eyes."

The salon had put highlights in Ellen's hair and it shimmered in the glow of the overhead lights. "Thank you! I've made a few changes, and—"

"Quit gushing over her like an ass, Ross darling. I thought you told me provincial wasn't your cup of tea anymore."

He glared at Patty, as if seeing her for the very first time, and then latched on to Ellen's arm. "Can I buy you a drink?" Not waiting for her response, he dragged her off in the direction of the bar.

When the couple was out of earshot, Patty asked with a satisfied smile, "How am I doing? Am I bitchy enough? Do you think Ellen knows I'm in on this?"

"No, she doesn't suspect a thing. And trust me when I say that superbitch has nothing on you. But don't you think you were a bit harsh? I mean, Ellen looked devastated."

"But happy as a lark when your brother dragged her off. I knew he wouldn't allow her to be insulted much longer. Ross might not be perfect, but he is a gentleman. Your mom and dad raised him right."

"Yes, they were very strict about manners and the like. Not to change the subject, but do we actually have dinner reservations here? If so, I'm praying either you or Ross is paying because neither Ellen or I can afford to."

"I made the reservation for four, then tipped off the maître d' when Ross was in the men's room. Everything's taken care of. Don't worry. If we're lucky, Ross will pick up the tab to impress Ellen."

"Don't worry?" Samantha looked at Patty as if she was deranged. "Are you serious? I have that woman's happiness in my hands, not to mention my brother's. If this gets messed up——"

"It won't. Now come on. Let's go find your soon-to-be engaged brother and his fiancée. Our table should be ready."

As USUAL, the attorney was right. Ross hadn't been able to take his eyes off Ellen all evening and had clung to her every word, even the ones about the children in her class, which he usually found totally boring.

As dessert was being devoured, Ross turned to Ellen and said, "Why don't I show you around the city tomorrow? I'm sure my sister could use a rest, and Patty will be in court all day. We can have the whole day to ourselves."

"Well, that sounds exciting as hell," Patty said, motioning the waiter over.

"Please bring me a vodka martini. I'm in need of revival from this boring conversation."

Ross opened his mouth to say something—nasty, no doubt—but Samantha clasped his hand and cut him off. "I appreciate your doing this for me, Ross. I was going to suggest it. I fear I'm still not back to normal quite yet. And Jack will give me hell if I overdo while he's gone. He's really quite a bossy man."

"But a handsome one," Patty said, rolling her tongue around the olive from her drink. "I really think it's a waste that you're not sleeping with him, Samantha. If I were you—"

"Well, you're not, Patty, so just drop it. My sister's relationship with Jack Turner is none of your business."

"It's none of yours either, Ross," Samantha reminded him with a gentle smile. "Though I appreciate everyone's advice, I'll make my own decisions about my life."

"You're very wise to do that, Samantha. I think all women should make their own decisions. Which is why," Ellen said, surprising everyone, including Ross, "I won't be staying in New York after this evening. I've decided to go back to Rhinebeck where I belong."

"But what about me showing you around?" he wanted to know, clearly disappointed.

"Maybe some other time. I've got commitments at home and I need to take care of them. This was a lovely jaunt but now I must go home before my carriage turns into a pumpkin." Ellen looked at Samantha and smiled.

"I'll miss you, Ellen," she said. "But I totally understand. Your students are important and must come first."

Ross looked as if he'd been poleaxed. "But—"

Patty's smile was nasty. "Oh, Ross, you'll get over the disappointment. We'll have our own fun here, darling."

But as Ross stared between the two women—his newfound love and the woman who'd held his heart for the last two years—the look of indecisiveness on his face was touching, and Samantha knew it wouldn't be long before her brother realized what he'd been missing upstate.

CHAPTER TWENTY-THREE

ELLEN DEPARTED early the following morning, but not before thanking Samantha profusely for all she had done, and not before explaining that she didn't want to win Ross's affections by pretending to be someone she wasn't.

It was Ellen's opinion that if Ross wanted a woman like Patty Bradshaw, then he wasn't the man she thought he was, and Samantha couldn't argue with that.

The object of their discussion dropped by unannounced two hours later.

As soon as he entered Samantha's apartment, Ross glanced around, hoping to find Ellen still in residence and ignoring Jake, who didn't take kindly to such treatment and kept yapping and tugging at the man's pant leg to gain his attention.

"Is she gone? Am I too late?" he asked, shaking his right leg in an effort to dislodge the persistent animal, but to no avail. Jake the Wonder Dog was not about to be ignored, by anyone.

Brows lifting, Samantha crossed her arms over her chest, though it was difficult to look intimidating in flannel pj's and fuzzy pink slippers. "Too late for what?" she asked, pretending not to know what he was talking about.

"Ellen, of course. Is she gone? I was hoping to catch her, to try and convince her to stay in the city a while longer."

The fuzzy-covered foot began to tap. "Why? I thought she bored you."

Tap. Tap. Tap.

Ross's cheeks filled with color. "I think I've made a huge mistake."

Tap. Tap. Tap.

"In what way?"

"Ellen seemed very different last night. Didn't you think so?"

"You mean she looked different?"

Tap. Tap. Tap.

He shook his head. "No. Well, yes. She looked amazing, but that wasn't it. She seemed more self-possessed, more assertive, and— Hell, I don't know. Just different."

"Well, Ellen's a whole lot different from Patty, that's for sure."

"Yeah, so I noticed." Ross pulled a face. "Patty was very rude to Ellen last night and for no apparent reason. I couldn't believe she was acting like such a bitch."

Samantha felt like rolling her eyes. Was this the pot calling the kettle black, or what? Sure sounded like it to her.

"What do you care? You're with Patty now," she said, biting the inside of her cheek to keep from smiling.

Tap. Tap. Tap.

"I've made a mess of everything, Samantha. I'm so confused. I thought I loved Patty, but after seeing Ellen I realized that I still have feelings for her, too."

"Listen, Ross, I don't want to be rude or judgmental, but you really need to work this out for yourself. You already know how I feel about your situation with Patty. It's pointless for us to discuss it further. We obviously don't see eye to eye on the matter."

"I know. And I've given what you've said a lot of thought."

Her eyes widened. "You have? That's a first."

"I think I'm going to go home for a while, see if I can set things right with Ellen. I realized after seeing her again that I miss her, that feelings I thought dead and buried are still deep inside me and need to be dealt with. You were right when you said I was running away. I was scared. Still am scared, if you want to know the truth. I'm worried that I'm never going to amount to anything but a broken-down old has-been of a football player. But I'm even more scared of losing Ellen. I've been such a fool. But you already know that."

Though she was saddened by her brother's insecurities, Samantha's heart lightened and she felt like shouting with joy and relief. She asked, "But what about Patty and your plans to marry her? I thought you told me—"

"Patty doesn't want to get married, and I've decided I do. Besides, you were right. Good sex doesn't make a relationship, it only enhances it. And Ellen and I don't have any problems in that area."

"Sounds to me like you've done a lot of soul-searching these past twelve hours."

"I have. And it hasn't been easy. I care for Patty a great deal, but I see now that it would never have worked between us. Patty doesn't want children. She said if she'd gotten pregnant, like you, she'd have had an abortion. Once she said that, I couldn't get it out of my mind. I want kids, and I want to be with someone who wants them, too. I guess when push came to shove, I realized just how different she and I are."

"And Ellen?"

"My feelings for her are too strong to deny. I think I'm still in love with her. In fact, I know I am. I only hope she'll take me back after the lousy way I've treated her. I intend to do everything in my power to win her back."

Samantha clutched her brother's arm and squeezed affectionately. "I'm glad you finally figured things out, Ross. I hope it works out for you and Ellen. For what it's worth, I think you made the right choice."

"So, what are you going to do about Jack?" he asked, effectively turning the tables on her. "It's no secret the guy's in love with you."

Samantha's mouth dropped open, then she snapped it shut. "How do you know that? I mean, Jack's told me as much, but—"

Ross shook his head. "Jesus, Samantha! I thought you were the smart one when it came to relationships. You only have to look at Jack to see he's a goner. The way he stares at you… I felt like punching him out a few times."

Samantha tried to ignore the kernels of excitement starting to pop in her belly. "Don't be ridiculous! We're back to being just friends."

Grinning, he patted his sister's tummy. "And where did that get you? I think you might be better off just marrying the poor bastard and putting him out of his misery."

Samantha felt as if she'd slipped into an episode of the *X-Files*. "Who are you? Certainly not my cynical brother Ross."

"When's Jack coming home? It might be nice if you fixed dinner for him or something, to thank him for taking such good care of you."

"For your information, I've already thought of that. He's coming home today, as a matter of fact, and I've left a note on his front door inviting him to dinner this evening. So you can just butt out, Ross. I don't need your advice. And you're hardly the one to be giving it anyway."

Smiling ruefully, Ross kissed his sister's cheek. "I'll call and let you know how things go with Ellen. Thanks for caring, and for trying to talk sense into my thick skull. I know I've been an ass, and I'm sorry."

"Just remember you said that the next time I want to butt into your business. And give my love to everyone at home. Tell them I miss them." Not that it would do any good where her dad was concerned. He was still ticked off at her, for being human, she supposed.

"Will do. And remember what I said about Jack. You two belong together." He grinned at her shocked expression, saying, "Bye," then slammed the door behind him before Samantha could utter another word.

But then, what was there left to say?

CLUTCHING A LARGE spring bouquet of yellow daffodils, purple hyacinth and baby's breath, Jack paused before the door of her apartment and took a deep breath.

He was nervous—nervous and excited. His meeting with Fred had hardened his resolve to marry Samantha. And now that he had the Bradys' blessing, he intended to do just that. The only obstacle in his way was Samantha.

He was determined.

She was stubborn.

They had been fated for each other since childhood.

She was stubborn!

Jack had decided not to tell Samantha about his recent visit to Rhinebeck. If Fred came to New York—and there was every indication that he would attend the baby shower—Samantha needed to believe that it was her father's idea to make amends, not Jack's.

Knocking twice on the door, he waited but a moment for Samantha to answer it. Her radiant smile when she pulled open the door took his breath away.

"You look beautiful," he said, noting the rosy glow to her cheeks and the swelling of her belly that was charmingly encased in a bright blue velour pants outfit that matched her eyes.

"Well, hello, stranger. Welcome back."

"Have I been missed?" he asked, drawing the bouquet from behind his back and handing it to her. "These are for you." Her eyes lit with pleasure.

"Thank you," she said almost shyly.

With an excited yap and several tall Michael Jordan style leaps, Jake suddenly declared quite emphatically that he had indeed missed Jack very much.

"Hey, buddy! Have you been a good boy?" Removing a doggie treat from his jacket pocket, he fed it to the grateful animal, who devoured it in about ten seconds.

"The flowers are just beautiful, Jack." Samantha crushed them to her chest. "Thank you again for thinking of me. And Jake thanks you, too. It was sweet of you to remember him."

The dog barked in apparent agreement, then promptly went in search of his favorite chew toy.

"I've missed you, Samantha. I thought about you every minute I was away." He followed her into the kitchen, watching while she placed the bouquet in a tall glass vase and arranged them.

"Well," she said, turning to look at him over her shoulder, "to be perfectly honest, I've missed you, too. Though it hasn't been boring around here, I can tell you that."

His brow shot up. "How's that?"

"Ellen Drury came to visit for a few days."

"At your invitation?" He could tell by the way she was shifting from foot to foot that she was mentally debating whether or not to confide in him. "If this is about Ross, you have my word I won't tell him what you've been up to. And by that innocent expression on your face, I'd say it can't be very good."

Samantha, who'd never been able to keep a secret for any length of time, looked ready to burst. "You have to promise you won't tell anyone, especially Ross. Scout's honor?"

Heaving a sigh and rolling his eyes, Jack made the Boy Scout sign. "I promise. Now what is it?"

"I think Ellen and Ross are getting back together. Ross said as much the last time we spoke."

"But I thought he had the hots for Patty. What made him change his mind?"

"He was infatuated with Patty, but then Ellen had a makeover, and—"

He arched a brow. "Uh-oh. I smell a conspiracy."

"Just a small one. Patty paid for the makeover and wardrobe." She went on to explain about the lawyer's feelings toward Ross and their subsequent plan to help Ellen win him back.

Jack dropped into the kitchen chair and shook his head. "I thought you didn't approve of matchmaking."

"Normally I don't. But sometimes it's necessary."

"I'll say," he replied, and she looked at him strangely.

"What's that supposed to mean?"

"The table looks nice," he said, skirting the question. "Are those new dishes? I don't think I've seen them before."

She nodded. "Mom sent them. She said the rooster pattern would remind me of home and encourage me to visit more often."

Jack grinned. "Lilly never misses a trick."

"No, she doesn't. How's Charlotte doing?"

"Fine. I—" He was about to admit that he'd just seen her but caught himself in time. "I spoke to her on the phone earlier. She said she's doing great. Mom's working at the church office and volunteering at the nursing home, so she's keeping pretty busy. Your mom's been helping to find things to occupy her time."

Samantha opened the oven door and peered in. "The leg of lamb is about done. Are you hungry? I certainly am. But that's nothing new. I'm always hungry these days. I have a feeling this kid is going to be a giant."

"Are you kidding? I'm starved. Did you make dessert, too?" he asked, though he had something a bit more decadent in mind to finish off the evening.

She smiled proudly. "Carrot cake with cream cheese frosting."

"Sounds good, but I'd rather have you."

Startled by the frank admission, Samantha nearly dropped the roasting pan she held in her hands. "Now, Jack, you mustn't say things like that." She placed it on top of the stove, wiping her hands on a towel.

"Why not?" He came up behind Samantha, turning her to face him. "I've thought of nothing else but you for days and nights. I want you, Samantha. I want you more than I've ever wanted anyone." He kissed her with all the pent-up longing of a starving man and was surprised to discover that she was kissing him back.

The fact that Samantha wasn't immune to his charms gave him hope.

But would she welcome him back to her bed?

FOR THE FIRST TIME in a very long time, Samantha was nervous. She loved Jack. She loved the way he made her feel when he kissed her. She loved his kisses, period. And she wasn't sure she had the strength to resist him.

More importantly, she wasn't certain she wanted to.

Pulling out of his embrace, Samantha took a deep breath and finally said, "I think we'd better eat before everything gets cold, don't you?"

"Are you sure?" he asked, caressing her cheek with his fingertip. "I want you, Samantha. I want to make love to you."

She could feel heat rise to her cheeks and needed to dispel the seductive web he was weaving around her. So she laughed, and the sound that resulted was borderline hysteria. "Don't be ridiculous, Jack. I invited you here for dinner, nothing more. I thought I'd made it clear—"

"Your kisses tell me differently. I know you want me. Why do you fight it?"

She shook her head. "I don't. Your ego is just unable to accept that a woman isn't interested in you in that way. You've had too many successful conquests."

"I could toss your lovely dinner dishes to the floor and take you here and now on this kitchen table, like the heroes in those romance novels you read, and I doubt you would resist. But I won't. I want you to come to me willingly, and because you want me as much as I want you."

Her heart was beating so fast at the mental image he'd created she wasn't sure she could breathe, let alone talk. "That's not going to happen, so we may as well eat the dinner I've worked so hard to prepare."

"We'll see," was all he said, but the passion in his eyes told her she was in deep, deep trouble. And the responding flutter of desire she felt only confirmed that fact.

They ate dinner in relative silence, though the sound of their hearts beating seemed to reverberate around the room. Once they had adjourned to the living room for dessert and coffee, Samantha knew something had to be done to alleviate the tension between them.

"How are things at work?" she asked, choosing a safe topic. "Is everything going okay?"

Jack looked up from the cake he was eating. "I can't concentrate on work right now. You've been occupying all my thoughts," he admitted, licking the frosting from the fork in such a suggestive manner that Samantha's mouth went dry.

Good Lord! She never realized a tongue could be so fascinating.

She swallowed the large lump in her throat. "So I guess Tom is running things for the time being?"

He nodded absently, continuing to stare at her. "Do you know how beautiful you are? Pregnancy seems to agree with you."

"Ha! You say that because you've never had to puke your guts out on a regular and annoying basis. Trust me. Nothing about being pregnant agrees with me, especially the clothes. For all the advances women have made over the years, you'd think maternity fashion would have caught up with them. Not that anything can make you look good when you're six months pregnant."

"I think you grow more beautiful every day. Do you know what it's like for a man to watch the woman he loves blossom with his child? I'm in awe."

Her cheeks filled with color. "Thank you."

"I was thinking that if we got married, we might

consider moving back to Rhinebeck. That way our child would be able to have grandparents and other family members around him."

"Or her." Samantha shook her head. "You certainly don't listen very well, do you?"

"I'm determined to marry you, Samantha, and I'll do whatever it takes to make that happen. We can stay in Manhattan or move upstate. It's up to you. I just want to be part of your life. And it's not because of the baby—it's because I'm in love with you, have probably been in love with you my entire life and was just too stupid to realize it."

"I—" She wanted to tell Jack she loved him, that she would marry him, but she was afraid. She'd thought long and hard about what their life would be like together, and she knew without a doubt that Jack would make a terrific father and caring husband.

But was she ready to accept his change of heart?

And was she ready to make a life with a man whose love had only surfaced after finding out she was pregnant?

She had doubts. And until those doubts were gone, she felt paralyzed and couldn't make a decision about her future.

"It's too soon to be talking about things like this, Jack. I'm not sure how I feel about you, about getting married, about moving back home." She shrugged. "I just don't know.

"You talk of *we,* but I'm not thinking that way. I'm still thinking of *me.* I haven't given up my dream of getting published." Though it was fading fast, unfortunately.

"I'm not asking you to. You can write your novels wherever we decide to live."

"Would you like more cake?" she asked when he set down his plate, eager to change the subject and not feed his fantasy of happily ever after—even if it was a very pretty picture.

Jack scooted closer to her, and then taking the dessert plate out of her hands, set it down and pulled her toward him. "Kiss me, Samantha. Let me feel how much you want me."

She shook her head, terrified at the prospect of feeling his lips upon hers again. "I can't. I—"

He took the decision out of her hands and pressed his lips over hers in masterful persuasion. The kiss was gentle, yet insistent, and Samantha felt a fluttering of excitement low in her belly that had nothing to do with the baby. And when he caressed her tongue with his, she lost her ability to resist any longer.

"I love you, Samantha. I want you. Here. Now. Tonight." He kissed away any bit of resistance she might have offered and she melted under the onslaught of his desire.

Sensing this, and without lifting his mouth from

hers, Jack lifted her into his arms and carried her into the bedroom, laying her gently on the bed.

I should marry him just based on his ability to lift me!

Slowly he began to undress her, first removing her shoes, then pulling at the elastic waistband of her pants and drawing them down.

She grabbed his hand. "Jack, don't!"

"Is it because of the bleeding? I thought the doctor said—"

"No, it's not that. I look horrid without my clothes on. Like an overripe watermelon."

He smiled gently and began to unbutton her maternity top. "You're beautiful. You're the mother of my child, so how could you be anything but beautiful? Don't be embarrassed. I want to see your swollen belly and feel our child moving within you."

His words moved her to tears and weakened whatever resolve she had left. "Oh, Jack. All right. But don't say I didn't warn you."

He finished undressing her, and then himself, until they were both lying naked on the bed. Samantha drew the sheet up in an attempt to cover herself, but Jack would have none of it and pushed it back down.

"Your breasts are lush and ripe." He flicked her nipples with his tongue and Samantha thought she would explode from the sheer joy of it. With his finger, he followed the prominent vein there, circling her nipple with his thumb and forefinger, while continuing to kiss her deeply and thoroughly.

When his hand moved down to caress between her legs, she stiffened. "Relax. I'm going to be very gentle. Trust me. I would never hurt you. I swear on the life of our child."

She nodded. "Don't ask me why, but I trust you."

"Thank you. That means a lot to me."

She drew his head down and kissed him, as he continued his gentle exploration. Samantha thought at first she would be mortified. The last time she'd had sex with Jack both of them had been too drunk to notice much of anything. Now, stone sober, and with the light blazing, she was exposed to his scrutiny. But she felt beautiful when she looked into his eyes.

The ardor she saw blazing there almost frightened her. There was something else there, too, but she wouldn't allow herself to believe it.

He entered her then and all doubts fled as she concentrated on the intense pleasure. Jack was careful not to crush her; she could tell he was very mindful of the baby and was trying to hold himself back. And she found that very endearing.

"The baby's fine," she whispered in his ear. "You're not going to hurt either one of us."

"Are you sure you're okay?"

I'll be a whole lot better once I have an orgasm, she wanted to say, but instead replied, "I'm fine. More than fine. I feel—"

Suddenly he increased the movement, stroking harder and deeper, until she couldn't catch her breath. Jack was taking her to a place she had never been before.

"Oh!" she screeched. "Oh my!"

Higher and higher they climbed, like determined explorers eager to reach their destination. The intense expression on Jack's face told her he was holding back, trying to make it good for both of them.

Samantha decided that if it got any better, she would die from the sheer ecstasy of it.

The pace increased, her breathing grew shallow and beads of perspiration dotted her upper lip and his forehead. And then it happened. Millions of stars exploded before her eyes, and then so did she, with the best orgasm of her life.

She felt complete, deliriously happy and content. And so much in love it was scary. And from the sated and euphoric expression on Jack's face, she could tell the experience had been good for him, too.

"I love you, Samantha. You're wonderful."

"I—" She bit her lip to keep from admitting what she felt. "That was pretty amazing, Jack." Samantha could tell he was disappointed that she hadn't confessed her love. But she had to be sure of his feelings before she made a commitment that would change her and the baby's life forever.

She had to be sure.

CHAPTER TWENTY-FOUR

"WELL, IT LOOKS LIKE our mission was accomplished," Patty said over lunch at The Palm the following day. "And if I do say so myself, we did a great job. Ross is gone, I'm relieved and hopefully Ellen is happy."

Picking the mushrooms out of her salad, Samantha nodded absently, unable to get the previous night's lovemaking out of her mind. An apt term, because she must have been *out of her mind* to make love with Jack, delicious though it had been.

In the light of day, with her pulse back to normal and her mind clear of passion, she could admit that making love with Jack had been a huge mistake. Matters had been complicated enough between them without tossing sex back into the equation, and she feared now she had created even more of a whopping mess.

Jack professed to love her, and she could almost believe him, except for the fact that she was pregnant with his baby, and knew that a man—especially a man like Jack, who'd had a miserable childhood—would go to any lengths to remain close to his unborn child in order to compensate for what had been missing from his own life.

If only I could be sure…

"Earth to Samantha. Are you all right? I don't think you've heard a word I've said. And most of my friends don't find me that boring."

Samantha smiled apologetically, trying to mollify her friend. "I'm sorry, Patty. I'm just preoccupied. Something happened last night, and I'm not sure what to do about it."

Heaving an impatient sigh, she asked, "Shall I guess, or are you going to tell me what it is that's got you frowning so deeply? If you don't quit that, you're going to get wrinkles."

"I slept with Jack last night. Well, actually, we didn't do much sleeping. We made love for most of the night and part of this morning, too." He'd left her bed early this morning, while she pretended to sleep, fearing he would want to discuss what had transpired and knowing she couldn't face any kind of confrontation right now. Her emotions were still too raw.

"Can you do that? I mean, you're pregnant and all."

"I did it quite well and enjoyed every minute of it, thank you very much. And now I'm having sec-

ond thoughts. I've made a gigantic mess of everything, not to mention a huge mistake."

"But why? Jack's a great guy. You could do a lot
worse. And it's convenient that he's the father of
your child. I mean, there was a time when you were
willing to let a total stranger impregnate you."

"I know all that. But what I don't know is Jack's
motivation for wanting to marry me."

Patty's eyes widened. "Jack's asked you to
marry him?"

Samantha nodded. "Several times. But I don't have
an answer. I'm so confused. I don't know what to do."

"Has Jack told you he loves you?"

"Yes. And I love him. But I'm scared—afraid that
his love is really for the child I'm carrying, and not
for me. I don't want a marriage based on pity or self-
sacrifice. I want to be loved for me, warts and all."
And she had plenty of the latter, but then, nobody
was perfect, despite what her father thought.

Reaching out across the white cloth-covered
table, and ignoring the waiter who'd come to refill
the water glasses, Patty clasped Samantha's hand.
"I'm hardly one to be giving advice when it comes
to relationships, but I think you should marry Jack.
It'll be easier for you and the baby, if you do. And
Jack doesn't strike me as the kind of man who would
lie about his feelings. He's always been upfront with
you in the past. Why should you doubt him now?"

Samantha didn't bother to hide her disappointment. "I was expecting more of a feminist argument from you. Whatever happened to women not needing men to be complete and all that? I never expected you, of all people, Patty, to be telling me to get married. Quite frankly, I expected you to tell me to cut and run."

"I never make excuses for who I am, or how I live my life. That would be pointless. But it can be very lonely living on your own with no one to share things with."

"But if you feel that way, why didn't you—"

"Let Ross into my life? Have a relationship with him?"

Samantha nodded. "Ross adored you."

"Because I don't do relationships, and I knew Ross and I would never work. Your brother's a sweet guy, but we want different things out of life. You were so right about that. In the end, we would have made each other miserable. And though I was attracted to him sexually, I didn't love him, not the way Ellen loves him.

"Living alone might not always be perfect or completely satisfying, but it keeps my heart in one piece and my sanity intact. I'm through with relationships and all they entail. That's just not who I am anymore."

"But—"

"But it *is* who you are, Samantha. You were meant to be half of a whole. If I were you, I'd marry Jack

Turner and live happily ever after, if there is such a thing. And I hope for your sake there is. True love doesn't happen very often, so when it comes along, you should grab hold of it."

Samantha digested everything Patty had to say, then finally shook her head, saying, "You amaze me. I never expected to hear this from you."

Patty smiled. "Sometimes I amaze myself," she said, and then her tone grew serious. "Listen, not to change the subject, but there's something I need to ask you—a favor, if you will."

"Of course. Ask away. I owe you a lot, and I'm happy to help."

"I was hoping you'd say that." Patty grinned, and then released the breath she'd been holding. "I'm having a small gathering at my apartment on Saturday night, and I'd like you to come. My brother and his dragon-lady wife are coming to town for a short visit, and I can't bear to face her alone. She's an absolutely horrible woman."

The last thing Samantha wanted to do was visit with someone else's relatives, especially nasty ones, but Patty rarely asked for a favor, and her calendar certainly wasn't full, to provide her with a decent excuse.

"Of course I'll come. What time? And what should I wear? My choices are rather limited these days, so I hope it's not a fancy event."

"Around seven. And wear something pretty but comfortable. I'll be serving drinks and plenty of hors d'oeuvres, so you won't need to eat dinner beforehand. There'll be lots of food on hand. And I'll be sure to have lots of milk for the mother-to-be."

"Okay, but I should warn you I eat a lot these days."

Patty's smile was enigmatic. "I'll be very prepared, you can count on that. Just be sure you show up on time. I want you to be at my place before my brother and the witch arrive, okay? The idea of spending time alone with them gives me hives."

Though Samantha nodded, she couldn't help but wonder why Patty seemed so nervous about her brother and sister-in-law's visit. After all, it wasn't as if it was their first time to come to New York City. But Patty's moods were changeable, her feelings for her family lamentable, so Samantha thought it best not to question her further.

FRIDAY STARTED OUT like most other days. Jack had stopped by for an early breakfast before heading off to work. There still had been no mention of their lovemaking, for which Samantha was grateful, so she assumed that Jack realized, as she did, that what had happened between them had been a huge mistake. After breakfast, Samantha had dug into a pile of manuscripts awaiting her attention, and then right before noon she had taken Jake out for a short stroll to get some exercise—as much as she'd been eating lately, she needed it far more than the dog—and had just returned home when the phone rang.

Hoping it wasn't Jack canceling his promise to pick up sandwiches for their prearranged lunch, she answered on the third ring.

"May I speak to Samantha Brady, please?"

"This is Samantha," she answered warily, hoping it wasn't another obnoxious sales call. She had yet to place her phone number on the government's Do Not Call list and was still plagued by annoying phone solicitations.

"Hello, Samantha. This is Joyce Stetson from Apex Publishing."

Samantha's eyes widened in surprise and her jaw nearly hit the floor. "Hello." Her heart was beating so fast she thought she might faint and plopped down on the sofa, nearly squishing Jake in the process.

"I'm calling to make an offer on your book. I'd like to buy it, if it's still available."

"It's still available," Samantha said quickly.

"Do you have an agent, or will you be handling this negotiation on your own?"

An offer on her book?

Ohmigod! Ohmigod!

Negotiation?

Having never negotiated anything in her entire life, Samantha wished Jack were here to help her.

"I don't know. I mean I never expected to get this call. I guess I can handle this myself."

"I'm prepared to offer you a two-book contract. Of course, I'll be requiring some revisions on the first book you submitted, but we can go over those at a later time." Joyce Stetson went on to offer a generous amount of money for a first book and a decent royalty rate, and she was willing to give Samantha the weekend to think about it.

"As I said, feel free to take your time to consider the offer. You can get back to me on Monday, and—"

Was the woman kidding? There was no way Samantha was going to take the chance that this editor would change her mind.

"I don't need the weekend!" Samantha blurted. "I accept your offer, and I'm thrilled that you liked the book."

The editor laughed. "I liked it very much. Your story is fun and fresh. It will make an excellent addition to our line."

"Thank you!"

"Call me if you have any questions, Samantha." She gave Samantha her direct office number. "You can expect a contract to follow in a few weeks. Once that's signed and ratified we'll cut your advance check." Her new editor went on to provide more details, but all Samantha could think about was the fact that she had sold her book and was actually going to be published. Finally she was going to earn money for doing something she loved.

How cool was that?

After hanging up the phone, Samantha picked Jake up and hugged him to her breast. "Did you hear that, sweetie? I'm a published author! I sold my book." Seeming to understand the import of her words, the dog licked her face enthusiastically.

Suddenly, there was a knock on the door and Samantha, hoping it was Jack, flew to open it.

"Guess what?" she told a startled Jack, who had just arrived with lunch, throwing herself into his arms and hugging his waist.

"You've decided to marry me?" he asked hopefully.

She shook her head. "No, not that. I just got off the phone with an editor from Apex. They're buying my book!" She went on to relate the details of the offer.

Grinning, Jack picked Samantha up off the floor and swung her around, while Jake barked furiously in protest. "Congratulations! I knew you could do it."

"Thanks! But if you don't put me down I'm going to puke all over you."

"Do you know what this means, Samantha?

You're a published author. You're right up there with Charles Dickens and Shakespeare. And more importantly, you met the goal you set for yourself. I'm so proud of you."

Samantha was touched by Jack's praise and happy that she could share this moment with him. He knew better than anyone how long and hard she had struggled to finish her book and sell it. "I can't begin to tell you how grateful I am to you for nagging me into finishing my book and sending it out. I couldn't have done this without you, Jack."

"You're wrong. I had nothing to do with it. It was your talent and your dream that got you where you are, Samantha."

"I feel like celebrating. Let's go out tonight and do something fun."

Jack's face fell. "Gee, I'm sorry, Samantha, but I can't tonight. I've got a late appointment. Tom's been holding down the fort a lot lately, so when he asked me to take one of his clients tonight, I couldn't refuse. It seems he has a hot date."

"That's okay. We can do it tomorrow." And then she remembered her promise to Patty and heaved a deep sigh. "Never mind," she added. "I can't do it tomorrow, either. I promised Patty I'd attend some family thing at her house." She went on to explain about Patty's uneasy relationship with her brother and sister-in-law.

"Would Sunday work? I'm free all day. We can start with brunch and just keep going until dinner. How does that sound?"

Disappointment filled her voice. "Fine, I guess. But it seems rather anticlimactic." This wasn't the way it was supposed to happen. Where was the champagne, fireworks and brass marching band? Didn't anyone realize what a big deal this was?

"We'll have a great time on Sunday, you'll see. Besides, some things are worth waiting for." He kissed her cheek and she blushed, recalling their passionate encounter.

"I've got an Italian sub with your name on it." He held up the bag enticingly.

"Did you get cookies, too?"

"Chocolate chip and oatmeal raisin. And I had them throw in a couple of sugar cookies for good measure."

She grinned. "Then you're forgiven."

"Just like that? You're not even going to torture me? Not even a little?"

"I'm too fat to torture anybody." She patted her belly. "I feel like I swallowed a whole bottle of yeast. This kid just keeps on rising."

Jack laughed, and then his expression grew earnest. "I think you're beautiful. In fact, I've never seen you look lovelier, Samantha, and I mean that."

"That's because you haven't seen me naked."

His brow arched. "Oh yes I have, and I'm not changing my opinion. You're the most beautiful woman I have ever laid eyes on."

Samantha blushed to the tips of her toes. "I forgot."

"I haven't. I can't wait to see you naked again."

"You shouldn't say things like that. It's not…not proper to talk to a pregnant woman like that." Especially a *horny* pregnant woman.

"You're so sexy I forget all about you being pregnant."

"Ha! Ha! Ha! And you're so full of shit that I haven't forgotten you're in sales."

Jack grinned. "If all my customers were as tough as you, I'd be broke."

She patted his cheek, seating herself at the kitchen table. "Poor Jack. Finally met his match."

"Oh I wouldn't say that, sweetheart. You might be tough, but I still intend to come out on top, in more ways than one."

Samantha blushed again. "You're incorrigible."

"No, just in love with my best friend."

"Jack Turner, you'd better stop talking like that."

"Like what?" he asked innocently.

Biting into her sandwich, Samantha didn't bother to respond, though they both knew that their hunger wasn't going to be sated by a couple of deli delights.

AT PRECISELY FIVE MINUTES before seven on Saturday evening, Samantha arrived at Patty's apartment, wearing a rose and green floral jersey knit dress that made her look only slightly larger than a baby elephant.

So much for pretty and casual.

She knocked several times, but Patty was slow to answer. When she finally did, her smile was radiant and relieved, as if she couldn't quite believe that Samantha had actually showed up as promised.

"You're here. Thanks for rescuing me."

"Are your relatives here yet?" Samantha was anxious to meet the nefarious sister-in-law that she'd heard so much about.

Patty shook her head. "No, not yet. But I'm expecting them at any moment. Come on in. You look very nice."

Scrutinizing Patty's black lace dress and four-inch heels, Samantha replied, "I feel like the dumpy country cousin—the turkey next to the swan. I'm not going to stand next to you all evening."

"Don't be silly. You look wonderful."

"I'm starving. Where's the food?" She looked about the large apartment, but didn't see food trays of any kind and wondered why. Patty's apartment was huge by New York standards, and she had a kitchen that most chefs would kill for. The irony was that the successful attorney didn't cook, so it was a complete waste of a fantasy kitchen, in Samantha's opinion.

"Everything's still in the kitchen," Patty said, as if she could read her mind. "Go ahead and help yourself to something to eat, while I check on the bar supplies. I'll only be a minute."

In the mood for something salty, Samantha headed toward the kitchen, hoping Patty had something common to munch on, like nuts or potato chips. She was not about to eat caviar or any other kind of fish eggs, no matter how expensive they were.

Pushing open the swinging door that separated the kitchen from the living area, she paused momentarily, wondering why the lights weren't on.

Suddenly, a loud roar of *"Surprise!"* came up, and the room was lit to reveal some very familiar faces. Samantha's mouth fell open.

Jack was standing next to her mother, grinning like a fox in a henhouse. Her brother Ross was there with Ellen, who looked happier than Samantha had ever seen her.

"What's going on? What are you all doing here? And where is that sneaky Patty?"

"Right behind you," her friend said, smiling widely when Samantha turned around. "Sorry about the deception, but Jack thought it would be best to have the baby shower at my place."

"Baby shower?" Her eyes widened. "We're having a baby shower? With men?" Suddenly her eyes fell on her father, and she couldn't quite believe he was here in New York. Fred Brady never left the farm.

"Dad! I didn't see you standing there. I guess I wasn't expecting to see you."

"Hello, Princess," Fred said, coming forward to lock his daughter in a tight embrace. "Can you ever forgive a foolish old man?" he whispered for her ears alone, before kissing her cheek.

Tears welled in Samantha's eyes. "There's nothing to forgive," she replied, kissing him back. Then she was hugging her mother, Jack and everyone else in the room she could get her arms around.

"I can't believe you're all here."

"Jack's been a nervous wreck these past two weeks planning this shower," her mother informed her. "He was so afraid you were going to catch on and spoil the surprise."

Samantha arched a brow at Jack. "Jack's full of surprises, isn't he?"

He came to stand next to her, wrapping his arm about her thick waist. "Forgive me?" he asked, and then said to the group, "I think Samantha has something she wants to share with everyone."

"If it's about the baby," Ross quipped, "we already know."

Jack laughed good-naturedly, and Samantha

shook her head. "It's not about the baby. Well, not about this baby anyway. I've finally sold my book. I got the call yesterday."

Everyone cheered, and then began clapping.

Patty asked, "Who negotiated the deal for you? I thought you were going to call me when the time came."

"I know, I know. But I didn't want to take the chance that the editor would change her mind. I was at the point of paying someone to publish the damn thing." Samantha grinned. "You can read the contract before I sign it, okay?" The offer seemed to appease the lady lawyer.

Lilly and Fred came forward to hug their daughter. "We're so proud of you," her mother said. "This really makes everything perfect, doesn't it?"

Samantha looked up at Jack and smiled. "Not quite. But it's pretty darn close."

Later, after the presents had been opened and cooed over, Samantha found herself seated next to her dad on the sofa. He was staring suspiciously at the canapé he held.

"I understand it's chicken liver mousse," she told him. "I think it's safe to eat."

Fred didn't look very convinced. "I had something earlier that tasted like raw fish." He made a face of disgust. "Doesn't your friend own a stove?"

Samantha laughed. "Yes, but Patty doesn't cook.

At any rate, I think what you ate was sushi. It's meant to be eaten raw."

"Disgusting stuff. I can buy bait, if I want to eat raw fish."

"I agree. I don't eat it, either."

"So tell me, Samantha, when are you going to quit playing hard to get and marry Jack? Your mother's been driving me nuts about it."

Lilly called Samantha regularly to see if she had gotten engaged, so she knew exactly what her father was talking about. "I'm not playing hard to get, Dad. I just want to be sure. At this point, with the baby and all, I can't afford to make any mistakes."

Fred took his daughter's hand and patted it. "Jack loves you, princess. He told me so."

Samantha searched the room until she found the object of their conversation standing by the window talking to Ross, and her heart flip-flopped in her chest. "He did?"

"Jack came to see me a few weeks back. He made me see how badly I'd treated you. He also wanted to ask for my blessing, so he could marry you."

Her eyes widened in surprise. "He did?"

"You need to marry that boy, Samantha. No sense fighting what's been ordained from the get-go. You and Jack belong together, every bit as much as Lilly and me. Your marriage may never be perfect, but it'll be happy. On that you have my word."

It was thirty minutes later when Samantha finally found herself alone with Jack.

"So I guess you think you're pretty smart to have pulled this off, huh?"

Grinning, he kissed her cheek. "It's not easy keeping things from you, as nosy as you are."

"Thank you, Jack, for giving me this baby shower. I received some wonderful gifts for the baby, and… Well, it was very thoughtful of you."

"I loved doing it. Mom helped me with some of the arrangements, like what kind of cake to order."

"Where is Charlotte? Why didn't she come?"

"Home in bed with the flu. She sends her best and says she'll mail her present as soon as she's up and around."

"Tell her to get well. I know what barfing is all about, and I don't envy her being sick."

Jack smiled. "You still have one more present to open, sweetheart, but it's not here. I had it delivered to your apartment."

"You shouldn't have bought me anything, not after giving me this wonderful shower. It's too much."

"Well, it's not really for you—it's for the baby. I have something for you, but I won't give it to you until tomorrow."

"So we're still going out to celebrate?"

"Of course. You didn't think I'd let something as

important as your book sale slip by unnoticed, did you?"

Samantha felt like throwing herself at Jack and smothering him with kisses, but she held back, mostly because everyone in the room kept staring at them.

"Are you ready to go and open your last shower gift?"

She glanced at the clock on the mantel to see that it was nearly midnight. "Yes, even though I won't turn into a pumpkin at the stroke of midnight, seeing as how I've already become one."

"Pumpkin is one of my favorite things to eat."

At Jack's words, Samantha's blood heated to boiling and she didn't need to wear a coat, despite the bone-numbing temperatures. As the song said, she had her love to keep her warm.

CHAPTER TWENTY-FIVE

ON SUNDAY NIGHT Samantha and Jack were back at their favorite restaurant, and she couldn't help but recall the conversation she'd had with Jack so many months ago at El Toula's about her desire to get pregnant and his adamant opposition to it.

How things had changed. In just three short months, Samantha was due to have the baby she'd always wanted; Jack, the man she loved with all her heart and soul, was the baby's father, and he was over the moon at the prospect of impending fatherhood.

Last night when they'd arrived back at the apartment after the surprise baby shower, a small wooden cradle had been waiting for her in the center of the living room. To her surprise, the cradle had been occupied, not by a baby, but by a sleepy-eyed Boston terrier, who'd thought nothing of jumping in and making himself right at home.

Samantha had burst out laughing at the sight of Jake snuggled in the baby's bed. Jack had not been quite as amused that the dog had chosen to sleep in one of the new receiving blankets he'd just purchased for the baby, but eventually even he found the humor in the situation.

"What are you smiling about?" Jack asked, handing her the breadbasket, which was a dangerous move at best. Samantha hadn't met a carb she didn't like, especially lately.

"I was just thinking about Jake and the baby cradle. He's going to be really put out when we actually put a baby in there. Jake's had us all to himself these past months, and I'm not sure he's going to like sharing us with another tiny creature. He thinks he's the baby of the family."

"I like the way you say *us*. It makes me feel like we really are a couple, in all the ways that count."

"Well, we have been together a long time, that's for certain, and we certainly have gone through a lot of stuff together."

"Yeah, like all those losers you dated."

"And all those bimbos you brought home, week after week after—"

"Okay, I get the picture. I guess neither one of us was very good at making the right choices when it came to the opposite sex."

"Sometimes I think we put unreasonable demands and expectations on those relationships, so they'd fail and we'd have a reason to break it off."

"You know, I've often thought the same thing. And I think I've figured out why."

Her brows rose. "Really? Why?"

"Because you can't make a successful relationship with someone else when you're already in love with someone you care deeply about."

"Are you saying that we were in love with each all those years and didn't know it?"

He nodded. "I was in love with you then, Samantha, and I'm in love with you now. And there are no strings attached to my love. I'd love you with or without a baby, and I hope you've finally come to realize that."

Samantha heaved a deep sigh, knowing what she was about to admit would change her life forever. But she couldn't hide her feelings any longer. "I love you, too, Jack. I guess I always have."

He looked as if she'd just handed him the world on a silver platter. "We must be a pretty dense pair to have spent all these years together and not realized what our true feelings are."

"Love is blind, as they say, and we weren't in any hurry to find someone else because we had each other. I guess the strings to my heart have always been attached to you, Jack Turner. You're the best man I know. And I love you."

Pushing his chair back, Jack stood and walked around to Samantha's side of the table, kneeling down beside her. When he reached into his pocket and pulled out a small velvet case, her heart started pounding loud in her ears.

Opening it, he said, "Will you marry me, Samantha Brady, for better or for worse? I love you like crazy. Always have and always will, till death do us part."

Samantha gasped when she saw the size of the engagement ring, and there was a long, drawn-out moment of silence while she stared at it in disbelief. Then someone from the next table shouted, "Say, yes, honey. He's getting his pants dirty."

With tears streaming down her face, Samantha smiled. "Yes, I'll marry you, Jack Turner, and I'll love you all of my life. This is the happiest moment of my life."

He winked at her. "Well, I'm hoping the happiest moment will come a little later this evening."

She grinned. "I hope so, too, because I love you so much I'm about to burst."

They both stared down at her belly and then laughed, with joy, love and the promise of things to come.

* * * * *

Turn the page for a look at
Millie Criswell's rollicking new romantic comedy

ASKING FOR TROUBLE

coming from HQN Books
in 2006

BETH CONTINUED TO GAPE AT THE bones, and what she was thinking was…well, unthinkable.

Iris and Ivy had been acting stranger than usual of late, if that was possible. The old ladies had a reputation for bizarre, eccentric behavior, and for being a bit off their rockers. She couldn't deny that they were both somewhat addled.

How many old ladies were into witchcraft and porn? And worse, how many old ladies had been engaged to someone who'd been murdered?

Shivers of foreboding tripped down her spine as she tried to decide what to do about the bones. After a few moments, Beth came to a decision: they had to be reburied. If anyone else found them, it would reflect very badly on her aunts.

But what if they were guilty?

What if Iris had done away with Lyle McMurtry and then had enlisted the aid of her sister to bury the poor guy in the cellar, as everyone suspected? As hideous as that thought was, it had to be considered.

If she reburied the bones, she'd be an accessory after the fact. Hiding evidence was a crime, not to mention immoral. But what choice did she have? She was responsible for the two old ladies. They'd always been there for her; she couldn't just abandon them now.

Picking up the camp shovel, she set to her task, vowing to get to the bottom of the mystery, and knowing that until she did, the bones would have to remain hidden. It might not be the wisest decision, but it was the best one she could come up with at the moment.

She paused, remembering the frantic phone messages she'd received on her answering machine from a Dr. Bradley Donovan about his missing father, who'd been a guest at the inn some weeks back.

Were two gentlemen who'd been in contact with her aunts now missing?

She didn't like the odds.

OPENING THE DOOR, Beth stared at the dark-haired man on her porch. He was tall, handsome and looked to be in his mid-to-late thirties, judging by the crow's feet appearing at the corner of his eyes. And he was definitely not her type. Anyone classified as male was not her type.

The stranger smiled, and she caught a glimpse of perfect white teeth. The man's parents had obviously spent a fortune on orthodontics when he was a kid. "Mrs. Randall?"

She smiled in greeting. "It's *Ms.* Randall. Can I help you?" she asked.

"I hope so. I'm Brad Donovan."

She held out her hand. "Welcome to the Two Sisters, Mr. Donovan." When he clasped her hand, she looked up to find that hundred-watt, hundred-thousand-dollar smile shining down on her and felt its warmth.

"Actually, it's *Dr.* Donovan. I've left several messages on your answering machine about my father. When I didn't get a response I decided to come in person to see if you have any information as to his whereabouts."

Oh great! It was that Dr. Donovan. The missing man's son had arrived. Who would appear next—the grim reaper?

"Come in," Beth said, remembering her manners and leading him into the front parlor.

Her gaze lifted, and Beth had the strangest sense of coming home as she stared into Bradley Donovan's warm, comforting eyes. She shook her head to dispel the notion. "I'm very sorry about not returning your phone calls, Dr. Donovan. I'm not usually so inconsiderate, but I had several pressing business matters to attend to and forgot all about it." *Not to mention, there's a pile of buried bones in my base-*

*ment, which may or may not belong to Lyle Mc-
Murtry. And...oh yes, your father might be down
there, too.*

Momentarily appeased, he nodded, and then went
on to talk about the attractiveness of the inn, the
traffic he'd encountered on the interstate, and the
weather. Though she did her best to listen intently,
nodding at the appropriate times, she found herself
mesmerized by the color of his blue eyes, which she
thought was odd. Beth had met many men since her
divorce and had never given a hoot about the color
of their eyes, or any other part of their anatomy. Her
relationships hadn't lasted long enough to find out
if size really mattered.

Assuming a businesslike posture, she folded her
hands primly in her lap. "Your last message indicated you'd be staying at the inn for an indetermi-
nate length of time, Dr. Donovan. I've booked you
into a room with two twin beds on the second floor.
I hope that'll be satisfactory."

"That'll be just fine. And call me Brad."

Their gazes locked and held for a brief moment,
then the front door opened, breaking the spell, which
relieved Beth to no end. She was already up to her
armpits in complications; she didn't need another
one.

Despite her best efforts not to, Beth found
Bradley Donovan quite likeable. He seemed kind

and caring, and she couldn't help but notice how handsome he was, how blue his eyes were.

"Handsome is as handsome does," her aunts were fond of saying, and she wasn't about to forget that lesson.

Besides, she needed a man in her life right now, like she needed another dead body in her cellar.

A BARKING DOG CAUGHT Brad's attention and he gazed in the direction of the barn to find Beth tossing a ball for her dog. She was laughing at the animal's antics and Brad felt his throat constrict at the sight of her.

There was no doubt he was attracted to the pretty innkeeper, but he had to keep things in perspective. She might know more about his father's disappearance than she admitted, and they really had very little in common.

Beth was his total opposite in every way imaginable. She seemed to live for the moment, while he planned everything out to the last detail. He'd already purchased the funeral plot next to Carol's.

His position in the community dictated that he find a competent, emotionally well-balanced woman, who could perform the duties of a doctor's wife, if he ever decided to marry again.

Beth seemed well organized, in her own fashion. But she wasn't as well grounded as he'd originally thought. There were times she came across as nutty as her aunts. Yet, he knew from their conversations that she was intelligent and kind. Caring for elderly family members took patience and love; the inn-keeper had exhibited both toward her aunts.

Why the hell am I thinking about this? I hardly know the woman, Stacy dislikes her intensely and my father is still missing.

Brad shook his head and walked toward the barn, as if pulled by a force he had no control over.

When Beth spotted Brad her first instinct was to run into the barn and hide. But he called out to her and waved, and she knew it was too late to escape.

Pasting on a smile, she asked, "Did you enjoy your trip into town?"

"Yes, it was very enlightening. I learned a great deal about Mediocrity's history and some of the town's inhabitants."

"Really? That's nice." Feeling uncomfortable at his nearness, she took a step back, but he stepped forward. "I've…I've got to fetch some hay bales, so—"

"I think we need to talk, Beth. I ran into Sheriff Murdock in town."

Her stomach churned acid. "I'm busy right now. Perhaps we can discuss this—"

"Now, Beth! I want to talk now. I need to know about Lyle McMurtry. I understand he was engaged to your aunt, before he disappeared. Why didn't you tell me?"

"I don't know much about him. My aunt's very reluctant to talk about him or the reasons for their breakup. And it's really none of my business, anyway."

"Why didn't you tell me there was another missing person in this town besides my father?"

"I didn't think a fifty-year-old matter had anything to do with your father. And I'm not in the habit of discussing my aunt's personal business. She's suffered enough over the years."

"Why does everyone in town, including the sheriff, think your aunts are involved in McMurtry's disappearance?"

"I have no idea. But I will tell you this—there are many people in this town who like to gossip and spread malicious rumors. They speculate when they have no basis for their unkind suspicions."

"Do you know what happened to McMurtry?"

Beth thought of the bones buried in her basement and her cheeks grew hot, but she shook her head. "No, of course not. Why would I? I wasn't even born when that happened."

"And my father? Do you know what happened to him?"

"I told you—I have no idea what happened to Mr. Donovan."

"I think you're hiding something."

Her eyes flashed fire. "How dare you accuse me of such a thing? You don't even know me."

"You're not a very good liar, Beth. I know that much."

"And you're no gentleman. Now, if you'll excuse me." She tried to walk past him, but he clasped her arm.

"Not so fast. I have more questions."

She gasped at his audacity. "Let me go."

"Or what?"

"I'll scream down this barn, if I have to. Now let me go." She tried to yank her arm free, but he merely tightened his hold, so she opened her mouth to make good on her threat, and he pulled her to him and crushed her lips beneath his own.